A Proper Family Christmas

JANE GORDON-CUMMING

ACCENT

First published in Great Britain in 2019 by
HEADLINE ACCENT
An imprint of HEADLINE PUBLISHING GROUP

2

Cataloguing in Publication Data is available from the British Library

ISBN 978 1 7861 5 7232

Typeset in Times New Roman

Printed and bound in Great Britain by Clays Ltd, Elcograf S.p.A.

Headline's policy is to use papers that are natural, renewable and recyclable
products and made from wood grown in well-managed forests and other
controlled sources. The logging and manufacturing processes are expected
to conform to the environmental regulations of the country of origin.

HEADLINE PUBLISHING GROUP
An Hachette UK Company
Carmelite House
50 Victoria Embankment
London EC4Y 0DZ

www.tinderpress.co.uk
www.headline.co.uk
www.hachette.co.uk

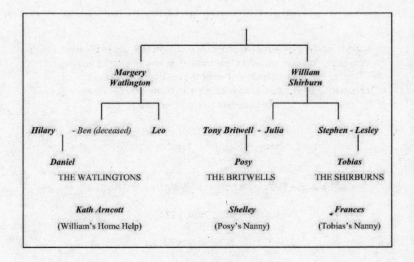

FAMILY TREE

Prologue

Haseley House is pretty ghastly really – one of those mansions where the architect seems to have been terrified of omitting any style of any period, and so bunged it all in somewhere. Coming upon it suddenly, as one does, after the discreet little cottages of Haseley village, it represents a major onslaught on the sensibilities.

And yet, it's a house to stir the imagination. One can picture archers crouching behind the battlements, knights errant scaling the rusticated walls to rescue fair ladies from that ridiculous turret at the corner. And who knows what Agatha Christie murders have been committed behind those stained-glass windows, or Wodehousian romances played out to the sound of nightingales on the ivy-draped terrace?

The place has remained largely undiscovered by those who take an interest in such things. You won't find Haseley written up in the chronicles of the Victorian Society, or see glossy pictures of its beautiful and charismatic owners in *Cotswold Life*. William Shirburn, the present owner, is neither beautiful nor charismatic. He lives alone with his cat, a plump tabby as self-centred as himself, and neither of them are the least interested in inviting a load of journalists to tramp through their house.

William has rather let the place go since his children grew up and left home –not that he couldn't afford repairs. Due to an inherent laziness about spending money, his family has accumulated considerable wealth over the years. If William bothered to investigate his various bank accounts or sell some of his numerous shares, he could probably afford to convert Haseley into a luxury mansion, complete with a swimming pool where the overgrown tennis court now stands and a sauna in the cellar. The pantry would make a good gym.

But William isn't a swimming-pool-and-sauna sort of person. His daughter Julia never liked the house anyway, and his son Stephen is busy with a demanding wife and young child. The tourists bypass Haseley with a shudder on their way to Bourton-on-the-Water, and it will probably end up as flatlets or a home for the elderly.

Chapter One

'Are you sure you've got everything?' Hilary Watlington looked doubtfully at the tiny rucksack her son was in the process of slinging on his back.

'Of course I'm not sure, Mum! Now, if I knew what I'd forgotten, that would be good. Then I could go and pack it now, instead of finding I needed it half way up a mountain.'

'Knickers, socks, hankies...' persisted Hilary.

'They are *pants*, Mum, that men wear! How often do I have to tell you?' The fact that Daniel had risen to her standing tease showed that she wasn't the only one feeling tense.

He glared at her, hating her for being left behind, just as she was hating him for going.

She fought the querulousness that welled up inside her. Rational, liberal-minded parenthood battled with her demon – the over-protective widowed mother – and lost.

'I still don't see why you want to drive up in the dark.'

'I did explain,' said Daniel, setting the rucksack down again on the hall floor with exaggerated patience. 'If we can get to Glencoe tonight, we'll be able to start climbing first thing tomorrow morning.'

'But there are so many drunks about in the evening at Christmas...'

'Rolling out of the numerous pubs on the M1? I don't think many firms choose Leicester Forest East for the office party!' He knit his thick eyebrows together in heavy sarcasm, reminding her of a ruffled owl. Ben had looked just the same when he was cross. It was funny to think that Daniel was approaching the age Ben had been when she'd first met him – almost as if she could replay her life… Oh, how could he do this to her? Subject her to the terrible possibility of it happening to her again?

'I suppose your friends will be sensible,' she heard herself saying. 'They won't play amusing medical student-type pranks like pushing each other off mountains, will they?'

'We might push Ellison off. He's become seriously boring since he met that nurse in ENT. She's religious, so it's not as if he's even getting a shag out of it. She tried to stop him coming with us, you know.'

'Perhaps' ventured Hilary ruefully, 'she was worried about someone she cared for climbing mountains in the middle of winter.'

'Bollocks! She's just afraid we'll knock his brains back into his head.'

He relented suddenly. 'Are you really going to be OK? I hate leaving you all alone in London for Christmas!'

'Who says I'll be alone?' Hilary made a face at him. 'I might have planned to have men in, for all you know.'

'Men?' Daniel raised one of the bushy eyebrows in a gesture of intense scepticism.

'There's that nice gang of builders over the road. I'm sure they wouldn't like me to be lonely.'

'They'll be at home with their wives and girlfriends – and kids,' said Daniel cuttingly.

'Well I'm looking forward to having the house to myself, as a matter of fact. I'm going to play *my* music, and watch girls' programmes on TV, and live on Chinese takeaways and tiramisu.'

'They say old people should eat chocolate,' said Daniel, dodging out of her reach. 'Keeps up the iron intake.'

'Go on, if you're going, go!' Hilary picked up his rucksack and thrust it into his hands. 'You'll be late picking up the others.'

But he hesitated, a confession to make. 'Er … I've told Gran you'll be on your own.'

'Oh no, Daniel! She'll involve me in something – you know what Margery's like.'

'Well, actually, she said something about going down to Haseley. She's got this architect friend she thinks ought to look at the house.'

'But I thought William always went over to Stephen and Ratso's …'

'Poor old sod! I suppose they think Christmas dinner once a year will persuade him to leave all his money to that awful child.' Daniel grimaced. 'Well, Gran's quite capable of inviting someone to stay with her brother without telling him. You'd better go too – make it a house party.'

'Haseley, in the middle of winter? No thanks!' Hilary shuddered. 'I shall be perfectly all right here – I like to have all my *things* round me. Quite honestly, at my age one prefers the comfort of one's own home.'

'At your age? Honestly, Mum! What are you – forty-five?' Daniel scowled. 'Perhaps I'd better book you on a Saga trip to Eastbourne!'

'That would be nice! Come on,' she opened the door, 'let's see if that old rust-bucket of yours will start.'

'Melanie is a Classic Car! The man at the garage couldn't believe I still had one of these old Rileys on the road.'

'Just so long as it stays there!' She watched him stow his bag in the boot, suppressing the feeling that surely this child of hers wasn't old enough to drive, never mind own a car. And then suddenly, in the shadow of the boot lid cast by the street light, it was Ben leaning over their old Morris.

He shut the lid, Daniel again – yet now she saw the twenty-year-old man, not the boy.

He turned to hug her. 'Take care, Mum. I'm only going for a week. I'll be back before you know it.'

'Take care of yourself.' She squeezed him crossly. 'I don't suppose they teach you any First Aid at medical school?'

'Of course not! But if any of us develops a rare genetic disorder, we'll be well away! I'm going. Don't stand out here in the cold.'

'I'm not,' said Hilary, and went back into the house and turned all the lights on.

♣ ♣ ♣

Scratch the Cat was a little bored. He had been asleep all day in an excellent new place he'd found, on an old coat of William's that had long ago dropped from its peg into a dark corner near the back stairs. The hot-water pipes from the kitchen boiler emerged to dispose most of their heat here, before beginning their long and largely fruitless journey to the upper regions of Haseley House. It was the sort of hidden place a cat could suddenly leap out from, just as people like Mrs Arncott, William's daily help, were walking down the passage with a heavy tray. Scratch had done that this morning with gratifying results, and he was waiting till she had forgotten about it before taking the opportunity to try it again.

The dark December evening didn't tempt Scratch to take more than a sniff through his catflap in the back door. He was past the age of seeking entertainment down in the village, and anyway, since a rather undignified operation insisted on by Mrs Arncott soon after he had chosen to come and live at Haseley, he didn't really feel the urge. He wandered into the drawing room to see what William was doing. Scratch didn't hold to the theory of the cat who walked by himself. He liked company – human company – and as they lived alone in this huge house, William was the one to provide it.

William, however, had not yet woken from his own nap. He sat there with head slumped and mouth open, assaulting sensitive ears with unpleasantly penetrating snores. Scratch was not immune from snoring himself on occasion, but there is something very irritating about a person being blatantly dead to the world when you are awake and ready for action. He sat on his haunches and wondered how to remedy the situation. Direct measures seemed the best. Scratch drew back, and sprang into his master's lap.

'Bugger you!' William shot into the air. Scratch tried and failed to cling on, wounding William in the process, and ending up paws akimbo on the floor. The two of them glowered at one another, mutually aggrieved.

William had been having a pleasant dream. He couldn't remember much about it, but it certainly hadn't been Christmas there, and he resented being so painfully jolted back to grim reality.

'What the hell's wrong with you, you flea-ridden mangy old monster?' he said to the cat, who was attempting to recover his dignity by pretending to wash. 'If you think I'm going to feed you now that you've shredded my bloody leg to pieces…'

On the whole, William was pretty content with life. He and his house suited each other – both a little creaky in the joints, more than a little eccentric, with the air of self-assurance that goes with having been around a long time and intending to be around a good bit longer. He didn't in the least mind living alone. Mrs Arncott came in every morning, making sure he hadn't fallen down dead, and keeping him supplied with anchovy paste and tinned stew and gossip from the village. They had a satisfactory relationship based on mutual nagging, which kept their minds lively and added interest and amusement to the day.

Often in the holidays he was treated to the additional enlivening company of her two boys, Grime and Brine, since Kath, as she never failed to point out, was a Single Parent. The exploits of Mr Arncott, who had flown the coop as soon as he realised his sons were turning out in his own image, were relayed in daily episodes of ever-increasing luridness. Only that morning William had been entertained by the full details of his latest bimbo, a babe of the first order according to the boys, but a bottle-blonde slut with a skirt up to her knickers according to their mother.

There was only one cloud on William's horizon – the awful prospect of the Festive Season. William really wasn't into Christmas. All that jingly tinselly presenty stuff that his daughter Julia was so good at made him feel queasy. He had no interest in watching the bright eyes of little children as they opened their gifts from Santa. In William's experience, if children were enjoying themselves it meant that he wasn't.

Not that, left to himself, he couldn't have had a good time. He would have drunk a bit, and shared turkey with the cat, watched *Die Hard* and James Bond, and fried up plum pudding for breakfast. But, unfortunately for William, someone, probably in Brussels, has decreed that elderly people are not allowed to rest in peace at Yuletide, but have to be dragged from their own homes and forced to pretend to enjoy themselves in somebody else's. Poor William was condemned to his son and daughter-in-law's uncomfortable house in Oxford.

Stephen was a Classics Fellow, who'd lived for years a bachelor, donnish life in his College, bothering no one at Christmas, since he preferred to work through the holiday. But then the College librarian turned thirty and decided it was time she acquired a husband and child before it was too late. To his family's horror, her eye fell on Stephen, and before anyone knew it, she was walking up the aisle in cement-coloured satin with a bunch of wilting lilies and a smug smile. She then set her mind to conception, and the baby followed within a year.

None of this would have mattered to William, who would have ignored his son married as happily as he had done when single, but Lesley had chosen to take on the role of Dutiful Daughter-in-law. She could not seem to be persuaded of William's total lack of interest in his grandson, and inflicted them on each other at all too frequent intervals. Christmas was compulsory. Three horrendous days loomed before him, to be spent in the company of Stephen and Ratso and the unspeakable Tobias, before he was to be allowed to return to Haseley House.

However, they weren't coming to collect him till Saturday, and sufficient unto Saturday was the evil thereof. Today was only Thursday, and William settled down to make the most of his last days of freedom.

He flicked on the telly. It was the easiest way of finding out what time it was, since no one remembered to wind the clock on the mantelpiece. Somewhere about Countdown, he estimated. He enjoyed that, though he was secretly even more enthralled by the wonderful programme that followed, in which the lower orders of America aired their personal problems with such a spellbinding lack of inhibition.

He waited patiently through an advert break, only to recoil in horror. What was this? Carol-singing? Some pop singer and a bunch of tone-deaf primary-school children dressed in Santa Claus outfits, instead of his proper programmes!

'Pah!' said William, who thought Scrooge had been much maligned. 'Bloody Christmas!'

♣ ♣ ♣

'I am *not* going to mind being alone!' said Hilary to the mirror on the hallstand. She said it out loud, and her voice echoed in a strange way, as if Daniel's absence had caused an unusual space in the house. 'It's only for a week. Lots of people spend Christmas on their own.' It was the first sign, wasn't it – talking to oneself? She was beginning to get eccentric already, and Daniel had only been out of the house five minutes.

Never mind, no one could hear her. There was no one to care what she did. She could sing, or take all her clothes off and dance on the table if she wanted to, or break down. She never had broken down when Ben died. It had always seemed best to postpone the moment until a more convenient time: after the funeral, or when she hadn't to discuss mortgage arrears with the building-society manager, or look sane and capable enough to be given a job. Somehow she had never got round to giving way, and after three years it seemed a bit late.

The woman in the mirror looked perfectly capable of spending Christmas alone. She stared resolutely back at Hilary, calm, efficient, neat dark curls just hinting at grey. She had the air of a prep-school mistress perhaps, kindly but detached.

'Christ! When did I become matronly?' Hilary glared at the figure, who frowned as if about to give her a hundred lines.

She went down into the kitchen, craving the comforting warmth of the Rayburn. Ben's cousin Julia had been horrified when they first showed her this room, shortly after they had moved in. 'Oh dear, a basement kitchen! Never mind, you'll just have to make everything as light as possible. White paint everywhere, with perhaps a hint of blue in the curtains, and you should get away with it...' Instead Hilary had installed dark wooden furniture, with thick plum-coloured curtains and cushions and deep William Morris wallpaper. It was a room to shut the world out of, an underground burrow. Ben had teased her about its womb-like atmosphere, saying she must be compensating for having lost her mother at an early age.

Tonight it suddenly seemed oppressive. She was aware of the weight of the whole house heavy on top of her – layers and layers of empty rooms above her head. She hurried back upstairs, needing at least one floor beneath her to regain some control of the house.

But up here she felt too exposed. She and Ben had deliberately made the living room as large and light as possible by knocking the two ground floor rooms into one, with big windows at each end. Now the space looked ridiculously vast, and the dark panels of uncovered glass dangerously expansive.

People had tried to persuade her to move after Ben died. There had been an awful family meeting, when Ben's cousins had decided to 'rally round' and arrived *en masse* one morning, bearing alcohol and goodwill. Still in the coma of bereavement, she had let them in, hoping for some sort of comfort. Instead they rearranged her life as if she had no part in it.

'Darling, you simply must get out of this house!' Julia had looked about her with a shudder. 'Every single thing must remind you… Oh, it's ghastly! Tony'll find you somewhere cheap near us in Wimbledon … not that I mean…' catching her husband's eye, '…but what a pity about the life assurance! If only you'd come to us, Tony would have got you a really good deal.'

Tony winked at Hilary, whether in confirmation or reparation for Julia's tactlessness, she wasn't sure.

'Mind you, I suppose there *isn't* anything cheap in Wimbledon – not our end, anyway,' Julia abandoned her scheme regretfully. 'What you must do, Hilary, is sell up here – this would fetch a bit, wouldn't it, Tony? You are just about in Fulham, after all. You can pay off the loan on the printing business, and buy a lovely little house in the country! It would be wonderful for Daniel. You could grow things, and make your own wine, and we'd all come and visit you.'

'A lot of this stuff could go,' said Lesley, then new to the family and revelling in this opportunity to validate her position. 'Stephen and I will help you clear things out if it's too painful.'

If Hilary had had any idea of ridding herself of her last memories of Ben, the thought of Lesley going through their things would have put it to flight for ever. Daniel, with all the outraged fire of seventeen, threatened to rush down to Oxford, when he heard, and turn out Lesley's cupboards. Hilary had laughed in spite of herself and, in a way, the incident had given her the jolt she needed.

Certainly she had no intention of losing her home as well as her husband. So much of Ben was in this house – not only the things they had bought together, which would have moved with her, but their positions in each room –

little corners of familiarity. She was surprised to realise how much they mattered to her.

She drew the curtains quickly, turned on the stereo and poured herself a drink, then wondered if she should be keeping a clear head. She alone was responsible for dealing with anything that might happen now. Would she be capable of seeing off Jehovah's Witnesses, or mending a fuse, or saving the neighbours from a fire, if her faculties were numbed by alcohol? And with music on, one couldn't be sure what other sounds it was disguising. A host of burglars might be tramping through those supposedly empty rooms above her.

She really had meant it when she'd told Daniel that she didn't mind spending Christmas alone, that evening, weeks ago it seemed, when he'd first mentioned the climbing scheme. Since Ben's death they had always gone to friends or a small hotel, making a rather over-conscious effort not to let the season get them down, but she still found Christmas one of her worst times. The idea of ignoring it altogether had seemed infinitely appealing.

'You'll have to go to someone's for Christmas Day,' Daniel had warned her. 'It's all very well saying it's sentimental rubbish, but when there's sod all on telly and you see everyone else in the street playing happy families round the Christmas tree ... well, you'll miss Dad like buggery, for a start.'

'As if I didn't already!' Hilary had made a face.

'Phone Julia and Tony. They'd *adore* to have you!' He imitated Julia at her most gushing. 'It'll be the real thing – you know how Julia loves all that Christmas crap. You can see it through in an alcoholic haze. Good prezzies, too, I shouldn't wonder.'

'Oh yes, and have Tony taking me into corners and asking me how I *am* all the time, and Julia telling poor little Posy not to bother Auntie Hilary, as if I was an uncertain-tempered cat, and everyone avoiding the subject of husbands and feeling guilty if they laugh by mistake …'

'OK, OK!' Daniel had grinned. 'Trash the Wimbledon idea. But I still think you'll want to go somewhere, when it comes to it.'

'Nonsense. I shall just put my head down and let the whole thing pass me by. It'll be heaven.'

Well, here she was, just as she had wanted it – alone for Christmas.

'Sod it!' she admitted out loud. 'I'm lonely already.'

Chapter Two

William was getting his tea, an operation as full of ritual and longstanding custom as any ceremony in Japan. He had put the kettle on some time ago – the proper kettle, not that stupid electric thing – and now it was spluttering on the old gas stove with just the right kind of hiss that told him it was time to open the toffee tin with the bent spoon he kept for the purpose and get out a teabag.

His daughter-in-law had once spent some time explaining to William that if he didn't fill the kettle completely, it wouldn't take so long to boil. William, as always, had listened with polite interest to her discourse on freshly drawn water, energy conservation and the prevention of limescale build-up, and continued to do as he always had, quite failing to see the point of making extra trips to the sink, when a good full kettle might last him several days.

Not that he was totally behind the times. William had recently discovered round tea bags, and he paused a moment to admire the satisfying way the bag aligned so perfectly with the round base of his mug, before taking it out again. Nothing would persuade him that a decent cup of tea could ever permeate a paper wrapping, and he carefully split the bag open and shook out the contents into the mug. He tipped the kettle slowly, watching the water dance into his cup and splurge tea all the way up the sides but just stay within bounds, in a way that he always found immensely satisfying.

Scratch the Cat watched the proceedings keenly. Although he had already been fed, he had a strong suspicion that William would be dining on something more interesting than cat food, and he didn't want to risk missing out just because he wasn't really hungry.

William cut himself one and a half slices of bread, and spread the half slice with Marmite and the full slice with butter and jam, topping both bits with a layer of strong cheddar cheese. This done, he began the rather precarious journey across the hall. Mrs Arncott had suggested that if he ate his tea in the kitchen it would mean fewer crumbs for her to clear off the sitting room carpet in the mornings, and less chance of him tripping over the hall rug and breaking something – whether a cup or a leg she didn't specify. William, who knew she'd do anything to make less work for herself, had pointed out that the TV was in the sitting room, and he could hardly be expected to eat a meal with nothing to look at but his plate.

He turned on *The Bill*, wincing at the statutory Christmas decorations adorning the police station despite the suspiciously full-leaved trees in the exterior scenes. Scratch placed a paw against his leg, and when that was ignored, stressed his point with a strategic amount of claw until he was given a bit of cheese and marmite. The pair of them settled down to a peaceful evening.

Something bleeped somewhere. William ignored it. He was beginning to get hold of the plot of *The Bill*. This greasy-haired yob had stolen something from the black

15

one, and the third one, who was really a goodie, despite his earring and leather jacket …

The bleep became louder, more and more insistent. William knew what it was – that annoying machine Stephen and Ratso had bought him, 'because you don't always seem to hear the phone, Dad.' It had buttons and aerials and little red lights, and if you ignored it, it went on and on bleeping louder and louder until you pressed and pulled the right combination of things to make it stop.

But William had discovered an easier solution, and slowly, with a lingering eye on *The Bill*, he went out and picked up the receiver on the proper telephone in the hall.

'Well?'

This uncompromising greeting usually put off any caller persistent enough to get him to answer the phone in the first place. But this one knew William.

'Hello, Dad.'

'Huh.'

'How are you?'

'Having my tea.'

Stephen paused in vain for an echo to his polite enquiry, then answered it anyway. 'Bit of a panic here.'

There was always a bit of a panic where Stephen and Ratso were concerned. William waited to hear whether little Tobias had caught a snuffle, or whether their local shops had run out of Christmas pudding, and strained to pick up on *The Bill* round the corner of the sitting-room door.

'Seems our damp-proof course has broken down.'

'What a shame.'

16

As he'd thought, they'd arrested the wrong youth, leaving the greasy-haired one free to walk over to that block of flats …

'Yes, it is rather,' said Stephen acidly, knowing full well his father's mind was elsewhere. 'The house is quite untenable – you know how dank Oxford gets in winter.'

'Can't you buy a new one?'

'We can hardly move again so soon. And we'd never find such a…'

'I mean a new… What did you say had broken down?'

'The damp-proof course, Dad! Apparently they don't last for ever in these old Victorian houses. Lesley's already found mould at the bottom of one of the curtains, and of course Tobias has a tendency to weak lungs…'

William's contact with his grandson so far had given him quite the opposite impression, but he didn't argue. With a bit of luck Stephen was leading up to the news that they couldn't have him to stay after all! He prepared a speech of polite regret and reassurance that he would be perfectly all right on his own.

'So Lesley and I really don't feel we can have you to stay for Christmas.'

'Oh, what a pity! But…'

'We couldn't risk you catching pneumonia or rheumatism or something while you were here.'

'That's very thoughtful…'

'Children find invalids so distressing, don't they? And Tobias is at such a vulnerable age.'

'Yes, well – I shall be perfectly all right…'

'However, we both feel that it would be a tragedy for him to miss out on a proper family Christmas at this essential stage of his social development...'

'Quite.'

He wished Stephen would hurry up. The greasy-haired yob was about to attack an old lady. She had foolishly turned up a lonely passageway and he was creeping up behind her...

'...so it means we'll have to come to you.'

'What!' William's head swam as if he'd been mugged himself. 'You can't possibly ... I haven't got anything in. There's no room!' He snatched at excuses desperately. If Stephen and Ratso once installed themselves at Haseley House, there'd be no getting rid of them before New Year.

'There's plenty of room, Dad. You've nine bedrooms, for heaven's sake! Surely Mrs Arncott can bestir herself to make up one of them – well, two, actually. We've got a nanny now, did I tell you? And we'll bring food. Tobias only eats organic products anyway...'

William put the phone down with a shaking hand. Stephen and Ratso for Christmas! Spreading their things all over his house! Making him eat 'proper' meals and watch *their* television programmes...! He flicked the TV off angrily as a comedy came on ... telling him the gadgets he ought to buy and the repairs he ought to make, as if they owned Haseley House already!

Well, he would get Mrs Arncott to prepare the rooms at the far end of the attic, which were probably damp and certainly dust and spider-ridden, where Tobias could exercise his weak lungs well insulated from the rest of the house. If Stephen and Ratso stuck it out for more than two days, he doubted the new nanny would. Nannies were fussy creatures, as he well remembered. They bustled about in white aprons, wanting everything just so. He hoped this one would be fat and cosy – William liked fat people. Mrs Arncott was reassuringly plump.

♣ ♣ ♣

Frances, Tobias's new nanny, was actually rather thin, and she had long, delicate hands and feet, which made her appear even more so. Her hair was a wispy blonde, which she wore piled on top of her head to make her look responsible and older than her nineteen years. Being Nanny to Tobias Sebastian Shirburn was rather a responsibility, as she had soon discovered.

'Come on, the water's lovely and hot now.'

'You've made it too hot,' said Tobias suspiciously.

'No, I haven't,' said Frances, splashing her arm in the bath to prove it was neither too cold, as Tobias had first complained, nor too hot. 'Why don't you get in and see?'

Tobias put one leg over the side and grimaced, but with a look at Frances's face, gave in and clambered into the bath. 'I need my boats.'

'Here…'

'No. The other ones. *Those* two.'

'What about a wash first?'

'Not *soap*!' said Tobias witheringly. 'I have my special stuff – there.'

'You remind me of the Chinese Boy-Emperor,' said Frances.

'Who's he?'

'A little boy who had to have everything special,' sighed Frances, anointing his arm, 'and liked to have his orders obeyed. What sort of games do you play with your boats? Sailing races, or discovering desert islands – or battles?'

'Battles,' said Tobias firmly, retrieving his arm in order to stage a head-on collision with a boat in each hand. 'A-a-a-a!! These boats have got guns and they've both sunk and everyone's drowned.'

'Right,' said Frances. 'Um – what about if one boat was hiding from the other, behind your back, say, or in this cave under your knee? Then the other one might go sailing all round here trying to find him…'

Tobias giggled.

'Keep still, or you'll have him on the rocks!'

'We prefer Tobias to structure his own imaginative play.' Mrs Shirburn stood in the doorway, trying to temper her reprimand with a tight smile. She had a long thin nose and long mousy hair, and made no attempt to disguise her thin mouth and rather pink eyes with any make-up.

'Right,' sighed Frances again, not wanting to jeopardise her job so early. 'Let's wash this other arm then.'

It had seemed such a good idea at the time, coming to work for an academic family in a romantic place like Oxford. Frances had left her Warwickshire village with visions of starting a whole new life in the City of Dreaming Spires.

Living at home with her mother and three young brothers and working just round the corner meant that she never seemed to go anywhere or meet anybody new. In Oxford she saw herself mixing with exciting, lively minded people, joining in their witty, intellectual conversations, and of course meeting *the* person – her soulmate – who would love her for the rest of her life.

She had come down for an interview with the Shirburns, not really expecting to get the job. They were obviously dreadfully fussy, and a childcare course at the local college and a couple of years looking after the local doctor's family wasn't going to compete against some uniformed Norland Nanny with generations of satisfied aristocrats under her belt. Still, it was an excuse to have a day out in Oxford, and she spent the morning wandering round the colleges, soaking up the atmosphere, and trying to spot her soulmate among the students.

There was a suitable air of romantic decay about the Shirburns' rather dilapidated Victorian house. Frances longed to paint the contrast of straight architectural lines half smothered in tangled vegetation, the glimpses of vivid orange brickwork under the dull greens and browns of December foliage.

But there was nothing romantic about Dr Shirburn, with his flat pale hair, thin-rimmed glasses, selfish, turned-in mouth, or his rat-faced wife. They led her into a dingily furnished living room, sat her in an uncomfortable chair, and explained that they were looking to replace their previous nanny 'who unfortunately did *not* understand the needs of a gifted and sensitive child like Tobias.'

The 'gifted and sensitive child' sat between them, apparently sizing her up as attentively as his parents. They must have had Tobias late in life – in fact there was a bachelor-spinster quality about them which suggested a late marriage – and they had clearly devoted themselves to the subject of childrearing with the same thoroughness they would apply to academic research. They talked of books and diets and educational methods. Frances said 'yes' in what she hoped was the right places, and watched Tobias surreptitiously pulling the fringe out of a cushion and waiting to be told not to. His parents hadn't noticed, and she didn't think it was up to her to indulge him until she was being paid for it.

At the end they had said 'Thank you. We'll let you know' and Frances assumed that was that, and tried not to be disappointed.

Then the letter had come.

'Wow!' she'd screamed at the breakfast table. 'They want me after all. I've got into Oxford!'

They'd teased her of course, laughing at the self-satisfied way the Shirburns' letter gave no option for her to turn the job down, and the horrific-sounding contract enclosed with it.

'"Suitable dress at all times",' quoted Joe, pulling gleefully at the long T-shirt which was all she happened to be wearing.

'"No men in your room at *any* time",' chanted Liam. 'We can't visit you, then – and nor can little Tobias.'

'That kid sounds a pain,' said Alex, with eight-year-old superiority. 'I don't think you ought to go.'

'You did say the parents were awful and the child was a monster,' Mum reminded her. 'Are you sure you'll be happy working for them?'

'She thinks she's going to meet all these cool new people – men!' Joe explained. 'You're such a little mouse, you won't dare talk to them. And if they're Oxford students they'll think you're just a thickie nanny…'

'Frances isn't thick at all!' Mum had interrupted. 'She'd be at university now, if she wasn't so pig-headed!'

Frances grinned. Her mother had been horrified when she had insisted on leaving school and starting to earn her own living, instead of taking A-levels and going on to art college, as had always been planned. But when her father had died, she simply didn't feel she could let Mum go on supporting her as well as the boys, just so that she could indulge her childhood dream of becoming an artist. She still thought she'd made the right decision – her job didn't bring in much, but at least she paid her way at home – just sometimes she couldn't help wondering what would have happened if things had been different, and what that other Frances would be doing now. In a way she saw Oxford as a second chance that she mustn't miss out on.

The doctor's family had wept, and gave her a hugely expensive box of oil paints as a leaving present. The boys kept telling each other how much more room there'd be in the house and how nice it would be not having an older sister bossing them around, and bought her a silly great teddy 'so she'd have something to cuddle in Oxford until she found a boyfriend'. Mum obviously thought she was doing the wrong thing, but didn't feel she could say so after the row about leaving school. The whole family waved her off from Warwick Station as if she were a Pilgrim Father, setting off to discover the New World.

Well now she was coming down to earth, if not with a bump, at least with an unpleasant rush of cold air. Far from introducing her to their intellectual friends, the Shirburns seemed determined to keep her firmly in what they saw as her place. They were obviously appalling snobs, and she was beginning to think they had chosen her more for her educated accent and the fact that her parents had been teachers than for her childcare skills. Mum had been right, the job was a nightmare, but having left home with such ceremony, she could hardly go back and tell them that she couldn't hack it. Thank goodness the Christmas holiday wasn't too far away!

With Lesley present, the rest of the bathing carried on in silence. Not wanting to keep a dog and bark herself, she was nevertheless obviously itching to seize her child and take over.

'All clean now, Tobias?' she asked, as Frances prepared to lift him out of the bath. 'Who would you like to read you your bedtime story – Nanny or Mummy?'

This was a minefield, Frances knew. Tobias looked from one to the other, eyes gleaming, revelling in control.

'I'm sure Mummy reads much better.' Frances seized the reins, risking the implication she wasn't up to the job rather than leave Tobias with this golden opportunity in his hands.

Lesley muttered something about 'quality time' and bore her son away, leaving Frances to clear up the bathroom with a sigh of relief.

Dr Shirburn was putting the phone down when she went downstairs an hour or so later.

'That's all fixed up then,' he said, thinking it was his wife, and broke off with an embarrassed 'Ah!'

Frances found her position awkward outside 'office hours'. Once Tobias had gone to bed and her function was over, the Shirburns obviously didn't know what to do with her. The previous nanny had not lived in.

'We'll be spending Christmas at Haseley House,' Stephen informed her. '...my father's place in Gloucestershire.'

'We?' She felt a sudden pang of foreboding.

'You were employed on the understanding you would be available over the Christmas period...'

'What? Yes, but I thought you meant...' Surely they were going to let her home for at least Christmas Day?

'We leave on Saturday. The old man's a bit eccentric, I should warn you, but the house is a magnificent old place, though he doesn't keep it up as he should...'

'Did you tell him what we'd arranged?' asked Lesley, coming down the stairs. 'This house is quite uninhabitable at the moment, and surely Father wouldn't be so selfish as to deny his own family a roof over their heads at Christmas...?' Her voice rose, ready to counter argument.

'No, no. It's all settled. I said we'd be there about lunchtime.'

Lesley, unwilling to let a good grievance go, turned to Frances. 'It's not as if he doesn't have masses of room at Haseley. In fact it's quite ridiculous – an old man on his own. We must have another talk to him, Stephen ... and we really can't expect Tobias to stay in Oxford with water streaming down the walls. I'm sure you agree with me, Nanny.'

Frances winced. She wished the Shirburns would call her by her name. She hadn't actually noticed any damp, and she certainly didn't want to spend Christmas in some pile in Gloucestershire with this awful family and a dotty old man who obviously didn't want them. She wanted to go home!

'Yes, of course,' she said again. 'I mean, of course we can't. Would it be all right if I made a cup of coffee?'

♣ ♣ ♣

At nine, William received another phone call.

'Yes I'm *quite* well, thank you! I wish you wouldn't answer in that silly way!' said his sister Margery crossly. 'Are you going to be there for Christmas?'

'Yes, unfor…'

'Good. I'm bringing Oliver Leafield down to see the house.'

'Who?'

'The architectural historian – surely you've heard of him? He's a friend of Nigel Rofford's.'

'That old pansy!'

'I met him at dinner there the other day. He's very keen to see Haseley and he happens to be free over Christmas.'

'That's all very well…'

'It's high time it was written up in *Country Life* or something – adds thousands to the value if you sell…'

'I don't *want* to sell it…!'

'Of course you do! It'll fetch a packet, and you can live in luxury for the rest of your life. No sense in hanging on to the old ruin just so Stephen can play "lord of the manor" when you've gone!'

'And where am I supposed to live?'

'Anywhere you like … Spain, the Bahamas. There's a nice flat going here in Rutland Gate. Anyway, Oliver will need to take photos, so get that Mrs Thing of yours to move her fat backside and spruce the place up a bit. See you Saturday evening.'

'But…'

'It's all right, you don't have to feed us! I'll make Oliver take me out somewhere.'

William stumped back to his chair crossly. Only Margery would have the nerve to invite a perfect stranger to someone else's house for Christmas. As if Stephen and Ratso weren't enough to cope with, now he was supposed to spruce the place up so that some shirt-lifter could ponce about taking photographs!

He was still seething when the phone went again. This time he snatched the machine on the table and pressed all its buttons until it stopped. 'Well, what?' he shouted into the mouthpiece.

'Pull the aerial out, you silly old fool!' It was Margery again. 'Apparently poor Hilary'll be alone for Christmas. Daniel's off on an expedition with the university, climbing or caving or something equally mad.'

'Oh yes?'

'So she'll be all on her own,' repeated Margery.

'Good for her.'

'I thought it would be nice if you invited her to stay as well.'

'She's your daughter-in-law, not mine.'

'Well, of course, if you'd rather have Ratso!' said Margery scornfully.

William was at last able to drop his bombshell.

'I *am* having Ratso! You didn't give me a chance to tell you. Some damp thing's broken down in their house and they insist on coming here – even the nanny!'

'Dire!' sympathised Margery. 'Where are you putting them?'

'In the east attic.'

'Fine, well put Oliver Leafield in the west wing, as far from that wretched child as possible, and Hilary and I...'

'I didn't say I was inviting Hilary.'

'Of course you are – she'll talk to Lesley. You know how kind-hearted she is.'

'Well, as long as I don't have to have Leo.'

'Oh, Leo doesn't approve of Christmas,' Margery reassured him. 'And he certainly doesn't approve of any of his relatives.'

'More sense than I thought,' muttered Leo's uncle.

'Phone Hilary now, before she goes to bed.'

♣ ♣ ♣

Hilary jumped when the phone rang. It was too soon to be Daniel telling her that he had arrived safely, but suppose it was the police, and he hadn't...?

But the gruff old voice bore no resemblance to any suave official. William never announced himself, expressing surprise and impatience at anyone who dared enquire who was calling, but there was rarely any need. Hilary smiled with relief at his familiar, un-dulcet tones.

'I'm told I must invite you here for Christmas.'

'Oh yes? And who told you that?'

'Margery, bugger her. She's decided my Christmas isn't going to be hellish enough, so she's taken it upon herself to invite a load of strangers to stay in my house.'

28

'Oh dear, William! But aren't you going to Stephen and Lesley's?'

'That would have been bad enough, but no, they've decided to inflict themselves on me instead, *with* the child, *and* its nanny…' William vented full details of his grievances.

'It sounds ghastly, but I don't see why Margery thinks you have to invite me down there as well…'

'Apparently you'll pine away if you're left on your own at Christmas. Sounds a bloody good idea to me,' said William wistfully.

'Me too. I'm looking forward to it.'

'Well, tough!' William was only taken aback for a moment. 'I don't see why you should be the only one to escape Christmas.'

'I'm a widow. I'm allowed to do what I like,' Hilary reminded him smugly.

'Balls! You're to come down here and suffer along with the rest of us,' William decreed. 'Being a widow doesn't entitle you to get out of having a miserable time.'

Hilary sighed. William and Margery had obviously got together and decided she shouldn't spend Christmas alone. Was there any point in protesting? Probably not. Margery's decisions were final.

Hilary loved her mother-in-law dearly. Never would she forget the way Margery had concealed her own grief to take charge at that appalling moment, three years ago, of a shock-stricken widow and bemused teenage boy. It was Margery's strength and courage that had seen her through, Margery who had cooked meals and talked to undertakers and shown her that life could and must carry on. With no

29

family of her own, she had clung to her mother-in-law as the only rock in a sea of chaos, and Margery had prevented her from drowning.

So she would never be a party to the family's grumbling at Margery's despotic way of deciding exactly how other people should run their lives. After all, being certain she knew what was best for people, Margery saw no reason not to enlighten them, and make sure that they carried it out.

It seemed that Margery wasn't convinced that Hilary would really enjoy a week completely on her own while everyone else was doing Christmas. Reluctant as she was to admit it, Margery was just possibly right. Besides, Hilary recognised William's peremptory demands as a plea for her support. They were fond of each other, and if he wanted her down there, it would be churlish not to go.

'You're a manipulative old bully.' she told him.

'Good. You're coming.'

'I suppose so.'

Chapter Three

Kath Arncott made her way up to the east wing next morning with a bad grace. She'd been looking forward to a bit of peace and quiet over Christmas with the old bloke away … not that you could exactly call it 'peace and quiet' with her boys around, but she hadn't expected to do any cleaning, or much cooking if they could still get in to the White Hart's Christmas dinner, and she certainly hadn't thought to be asked to trail the Hoover up three flights of stairs to get a set of musty old attics ready because half the old man's relatives had decided to visit.

She stood in the doorway of the room Mr Shirburn had chosen for his son and daughter-in-law, and let out a breath of disapproval. From the stained mattress, to the curling carpet, to the layer of dead flies on the windowsill, the place was a tip. It would take a week to do properly, and she certainly wasn't going to that much trouble for Stephen Shirburn and his snotty wife! What was she when it came down to it? A secretary or something at his College. Lord knew how she'd trapped him into marrying her – not with sex appeal, that was for sure!

They'd all thought Stephen was a confirmed bachelor, or she might have been tempted to have a go there herself. After all, he wasn't so bad looking in a wimpish kind of way, and one assumed he'd come in for this place when the old man went – Julia obviously wasn't bothered, more's the pity.

Yes, Kath could see herself as mistress of Haseley – wearing a hat at garden parties, playing hostess at little dos for the local nobs. All that would be wasted on Lesley Shirburn, who looked like she got her make-up tips from *Nun's Monthly*.

Kath stooped to peer through the dust of the dressing table mirror and prodded her curls. Nice perm this, with the chestnut highlights …

🌲 🌲 🌲

Frances was babysitting that night. Stephen and Lesley had gone to the College Christmas dinner, Lesley in a quite dreadful dress with grey pleats that made her look like a dirty lampshade. Tobias was already in bed, but it didn't stop them leaving a host of instructions as to what he might need if he woke, and a series of telephone numbers, starting with the Porters' Lodge and ending with the Dean of the College's private line, in case she needed to get hold of them in an emergency.

They had been gone about an hour and Frances was just settling in to a TV programme, when the phone rang. She sighed. People hardly ever phoned the Shirburns – they didn't seem to have many friends, and she had no doubt it was Lesley ringing to check that she wasn't taking advantage of their absence to ill-treat Tobias.

But the rich, warm, earth-mother voice was a world away from Lesley's. 'Don't tell me they're not in!'

'No, I'm afraid not.'

'You mean, someone's *invited* them somewhere?' the voice exclaimed, with a hint of golden laughter.

Frances heard the news being relayed in muffled tones, and a male chuckle in the background.

'You must be Tobias's new nanny... It's the nanny, Tony... No, the new one!'

'Can I take a message?' asked Frances.

'Oh, it's not in the least important,' the friendly voice went on. 'We only rang to wish them "Happy Christmas", but I'll ring again on the day. They're having the old man over, aren't they?'

'Actually there's been a change of plan.' Frances explained about the damp-proof course.

'Oh, how dreadful for them! So you're all going over to Haseley for Christmas?'

This too was passed on to Tony.

'Are they, by God?' she heard him say.

There was some whispered conversation, questions, exclamations.

'We'll catch them there then. Thank you, darling, you've been most helpful.'

'Er ... who shall I say rang?' asked Frances quickly, before the mysterious caller could vanish into the ether for ever.

'It's Julia, of course.'

'Of course,' murmured Frances as she put the receiver down. 'Who the hell is Julia?'

'She's my auntie,' the reply came unexpectedly. Tobias was standing by the door. 'She wears big dresses and she smells nice, and for my birthday she gave me a toy theatre – only I have to wait for it till I'm bigger.'

'I see,' Frances digested this. 'Why aren't you in bed?'

'She's Posy's mummy,' Tobias continued to expound his family history, moving to settle down beside her.

'Right. And what about a hot drink before you go back to sleep?'

'I'm not going back. I'm waiting here for Mummy to come home.'

'I don't think so. Let's see what we can find in the kitchen.'

Tobias eyed her for a moment, then took her outstretched hand. 'Posy's got a nanny,' he informed her. 'That's why I had to.'

🎄 🎄 🎄

Hilary packed for Haseley with mixed feelings. Having been so firm about spending Christmas on her own in London, she felt rather as if she was betraying something by not seeing the thing through. On the other hand it would have been idiotic to let William down for some silly principle. He needed her, and she tried not to feel guilty at her relief at being offered such a perfect excuse not to test herself.

You're quite mad, she thought, as she packed her thickest jerseys, long johns and a hairy old skirt she hadn't worn for years. It'll be freezing down there, and you could have been warm and comfortable at home.

She was just wondering whether she ought to be trying to find Christmas presents for the Shirburns, when the phone rang. Hilary recognised her brother-in-law's voice, and groaned inwardly.

'I hear everyone's going to Haseley House for Christmas.'

Leo always spoke with a plaintive, upward inflection that seemed to imply a second half to his sentences, an unspoken sub-text.

'Oh, not *everyone*, I don't think…'

Who had told him? Certainly not William, who couldn't stand Leo. And Margery had no time for her younger son.

'They are, you know. I've just been talking to Julia. Stephen and Ratso are driving down tomorrow – she heard it from their nanny, and she and Tony are bringing Posy and *her* nanny …'

'Oh no! Are you sure? William didn't mention it.' Why had Julia taken it into her head to join them for Christmas, and what on *earth* had possessed her to let Leo know? Didn't she realise that if he thought he was missing out on some mass family gathering, they'd be lumbered with him at Haseley too?

'I suppose, if everyone's going, I'd better do my family duty.'

'Oh no…' Her brain raced for the right words. She wondered if other people had this feeling of being put on their guard whenever they were talking to Leo, and if so, whether he noticed.

'Your mother got William to invite me down because Daniel's away, but it's really only the Shirburns…'

'On the contrary. William told Julia that Mother's bringing some guy to look at the house. I think I ought to be there,' persisted Leo.

'I'm sure there's no need for you to go…' She heard herself beginning to gabble. 'You're well out of it. William

35

only talked me into coming to protect him from Ratso, but it doesn't look as if it was necessary really…'

'You shouldn't let people take advantage of you, Hilary. Being a widow doesn't mean you have to play the victim, you know,' said her loathsome brother-in-law. 'William's a real old manipulator if you let him, and Mother's worse – I seem to be the only member of the family with the nerve to stand up to her.'

Hilary, who had seen Leo reduced to a stammering wreck by his mother's withering remarks, let this pass. More important was to prevent him from inflicting himself on them all at Haseley.

'I'm afraid I'll have to go down there, now that I've said I would.' She tried to sound casual.'But there's no point in you letting yourself in for a ghastly family party – I know you hate them. You can snuggle down cosily with your writing in Gower Street and imagine us all freezing to death and listening to Stephen and Ratso wittering on about Tobias's Genius Rating.'

'Well I must say, I don't relish spending Christmas in the company of Tobias's fond parents. And Julia and Tony are not exactly stimulating intellectually…'

Hilary held her breath.

'On the other hand, if *you're* going to be there, Hilary, I'd at least have someone intelligent to talk to.'

'Me?' Was it she who was going to be held responsible for Leo's presence at Haseley? The others would never forgive her.

'Yes, I've always found you a remarkably intelligent woman.' He paused, presumably waiting for an embarrassed disclaimer, or an expression of gratification, while she exercised her remarkable intelligence in trying to hit upon one more good reason to keep him away.

She tried a last pre-emptive strike. 'Well, wish me luck at Haseley then. We must meet up after Christmas and I'll tell you all the gory details…'

'When were you planning to leave?'

'Tomorrow afternoon. I must go and finish packing.' She stood up, ready to put the phone down.

'I might as well give you a lift then.'

'What? Oh no!' Defeat snatched from the jaws of Victory.

'Well, how else are you going to get there? Hasn't Daniel got the car?'

'I've booked the train,' she fibbed desperately.

'But it's miles from a railway station! You'd have to get a taxi all the way from Cheltenham.'

'There's a bus to Cirencester…' Hilary knew she was losing this. No one could deny it was a nightmare journey to Haseley by public transport.

'I insist on driving you down. I don't mind going a little out of my way,' said Leo magnanimously.

Hilary gave up.

'Oh well – thank you, Leo.'

'I'll pick you up about three. You won't keep me waiting, will you?'

'No,' sighed Hilary. 'I'll be raring to go.'

Frances, strapped in the back of the car with a restless Tobias, found the journey to Gloucestershire tedious.

Stephen was basically a nervous driver, keeping to a steady fifty on the dual carriageway while hugging the centre line, but every now and then, when Frances peered round the headrests obstructing her view, she caught him taking the most horrendous risks. Lesley didn't seem to notice, despite her running commentary on his and other road users' shortcomings, but then she had the advantage of being a non-driver.

Frances retreated back behind the headrests and turned her attention to Tobias, who had tired of the journey almost before they had left the suburbs. Her efforts to entertain him were rather inhibited by the presence of the passengers in the front seat.

'Let's see who can spot the most yellow vans.'

'I can't see any.'

'Well, horses, then. There's one in that field.'

'There aren't any more.'

'There might be, in a minute.'

'Actually, we're coming to a town now, so it's not really fair on him.'

'Are you feeling sick, Tobias?' Lesley screwed round in her seat. 'He sometimes does feel sick in cars.'

Her son weighed up the idea, and decided in favour.

'Yes. I need a sweetie.'

'Oh – did Daddy remember to bring any sweeties?'

'Daddy thought Mummy was packing the food, actually.'

'Actually, Mummy thought things for the car were Daddy's responsibility.'

'I've got some peppermints in my bag,' said Frances.

'I'm afraid Tobias doesn't like mints.'

'Shall I read you a story?' Frances saw that Lesley was about to suggest looking for a sweetshop in the middle of the Witney bypass. 'We brought *The Little Blue Elephant*, didn't we?'

Tobias eyed the book, wondering how much fuss to make about the sweet, and Frances hastily began to read.

He interrupted after a sentence or two. 'Are we nearly there yet?', and this became his refrain every few miles for the rest of the way. Frances, trying to read in a jolting car in bad light, began to feel sick herself.

'I'd like one of those,' said Tobias, watching her unwrap a mint.

He finally fell asleep as they turned up the steep lane which led to Haseley village, and Frances was able to look around her.

She found that they were high up. A sweeping view of fields in every shade of brown and green stretched into the distance, lit softly by the low winter sun. The lane was bordered by an old wall, its patchwork of grey stone, green moss and yellow lichen echoing the fields beyond. The little hedged paddocks round her own village seemed suburban by contrast.

'It's beautiful!' she exclaimed. 'What a lovely place it must have been to grow up in.'

Lesley turned and put an angry finger to her lips, indicating the sleeping child.

'It's all right in the summer, I suppose,' said Stephen, who hadn't seen her. 'But of course there's no one to talk to – no one intellectual, I mean.' He nodded dismissively at the cottages they were now passing. 'Haseley's the only decent house for miles.'

Frances looked at the indecent houses huddled cosily under thatched roofs, glimpses of Christmas trees glittering in the windows, and felt a pang of homesickness.

'Here it is!'

The car turned between a pair of gaunt stone pillars and up a driveway shrouded by gloomy evergreens. Then suddenly the view opened out, revealing the house in all its glory.

'Ugh!' Frances gasped.

A Victorian monstrosity was the phrase that came to mind. It was like something out of a Gothic horror film. She gaped incredulously, taking in the battlements, the gargoyles, the stained-glass windows, and a huge turret at one end.

'It is rather fine, isn't it?' said Stephen. 'Better than anything in North Oxford, I always think.'

They had drawn up beside a flight of steps leading to an ornate Tudor-style porch. Lesley glared at the closed oak door.

'You'll have to ring the bell, Stephen. You'd think Father might have opened the door when he heard the car! Oh dear, how are we going to get Tobias out without waking him?'

Frances knew this was impossible, and steeled herself for the wail as Tobias was extracted from his safety harness. He was building up to full cry as she struggled up the steps with him, just as the door opened to reveal William Shirburn, 'Unwelcome' written all over his face.

'Here we are, Dad! Here at last.'

'I told you not to wake him! Let us in, Father, please!'

William's features screwed up to match his grandson's. He stepped aside, glaring at the disappointingly thin nanny and her burden of wailing child.

'He's very tired, poor little thing. Are you hungry, precious? Put him down, Nanny, he hates being carried – this is Nanny, by the way.'

'Frances,' said Frances, lowering Tobias to the floor thankfully. He clung to her legs, angry at this sudden loss of status.

'I expect you'd like a nice eggie. Has Grandpa got any nice eggies?'

'No,' lied William.

'He may be feeling sick. Are you feeling sick, Tobias?'

'The WC's over there,' said William helpfully.

'What about a hot bath?' suggested Frances.

'You'll have to put the immersion on if you want baths. I can't afford constant hot water,' William lied again.

At that moment, Kath Arncott came to the rescue. She had stayed on rather longer than usual that morning on the pretext of making sure everything was all right for the Shirburns when they arrived, but really in the hope of catching a glimpse of Lesley's face when she saw her room. However, the record playing on the kitchen radio had blended so well with Tobias's wails, she hadn't realised what was happening until it stopped and he was left to howl solo. She hurried into the hall.

'Here we are then! All safe and sound. Ooh, what's all this silly noise?'

Tobias, taken aback by the huge vision in an apron, paused to stare.

'That's better. He looks as if he could do with some shut-eye. Do you want to get your things in, Dr Shirburn, and I'll show you where your rooms are. Bit of a climb, I'm afraid.'

Lesley, bemused by the sudden quelling of her child, made to follow her unsuspectingly.

Stephen stayed where he was. 'We were hoping there might be something Tobias could eat. He's hungry after the drive.'

'Lord yes! There's all kinds of stuff in the cupboard. I got in some of that alphabet spaghetti. Sort of educational, isn't it?' She smiled knowingly at the Oxford don. 'Still, you don't want to spoil his appetite, do you? Come on up. Mr Shirburn's put you in the east wing.'

Frances took Tobias's hand.

'No, I'll take Tobias!' said Lesley, sharply anxious to regain control. 'You can fetch some of the luggage.'

Frances, turning to obey, caught a distinctly evil gleam in the old man's eye as he watched his daughter-in-law mount the stairs.

She was therefore not entirely surprised when a squeal that was not Tobias's greeted her and Stephen as they toiled up the last and dustiest flight.

'What is it?' gasped Stephen, unable to hurry with three suitcases.

'It's just too awful to believe!' shrilled Lesley from above.

Frances was beginning to think she could believe anything in this House of Horrors, and arrived on the landing with her own case and Tobias's toy-bag quite prepared for the old man downstairs to have filled all his spare rooms with headless corpses.

'Needs a bit of a clean-up,' Kath Arncott smirked, fully satisfied with her victim's reaction. 'But of course I hadn't the time, with you all coming at such short notice.'

'Oh dear, no reading lamp!' said Stephen, who had brought some work to do over the holiday.

'It's quite ghastly!' wailed Lesley. 'I've a good mind to go straight home!'

Kath's smile widened.

'I don't want this room,' said Tobias, catching the atmosphere. 'It's got a spider in it.'

'You're sleeping next door,' Kath informed him. 'You and your nanny.'

They followed her next door. Frances, who had not expected to have to share a room with Tobias, stood behind the others in the doorway, waiting to hear whether the verdict here was any better.

Apparently not.

'I don't want this room either. It smells pooey.'

'Shush, darling. Stephen, your father is quite impossible – sticking us up here in this pigsty'!

'You'll have to put us somewhere else,' said Stephen. 'There must be *something* in the house fit for human habitation!'

'Oh yes – but you're not the only guests here for Christmas – didn't Mr Shirburn mention it?' said Kath, knowing perfectly well he hadn't. 'And of course Mrs Watlington has to have a nice room, seeing as how she's elderly…'

'Aunt Margery? Oh Lord!'

'And she's bringing a gentleman friend – no, not *that* sort of friend!' She winked at Frances to annoy Lesley. 'Some bloke to look at the house and take photos for the paper.'

'A *journalist*?'

'And there's *young* Mrs Watlington. Her lad's away, so she would have been all on her own…'

'Oh really – it's too bad!' Lesley exclaimed. 'We were looking forward to a quiet Christmas alone with William – we had some business we particularly wanted to discuss with him. And now we find he's invited that dreadful old sister of his, and some complete stranger, *and* Hilary Watlington! … I don't know why she can't spend Christmas on her own – it *is* three years now, after all. If we'd realised all that tribe were coming, we'd never have … I mean, we could have put up with the damp-course,' she admitted crossly.

'I'm having the *other* room,' Tobias declared, nearly stomping into Frances on his way out.

'Oh, but I think Mummy and Daddy…'

'You go where you're put, young man,' said Kath, taking him by the shoulders and turning him round. Tobias drew a deep breath.

'All right, darling. Mummy and Daddy will have this room. You'll have to change the beds round, Stephen.'

Chapter Four

William, satisfied that he had made his guests as uncomfortable as possible, was enjoying an early lunch. He saw no reason why he should inconvenience himself by waiting to eat with his visitors. Mrs A. had got them a quiche, anyway, and he didn't like quiche, so he was tucking into a stew he'd made for himself the night before with tinned beef and carrot and onion. It was even better the second day.

Scratch agreed when given the plate to lick, and was not pleased to be interrupted by the tentative opening of the kitchen door behind him.

'Sorry!' exclaimed the new nanny, as cat and plate skidded across the floor. 'Er … they told me to try and find some lunch for Tobias.'

'Huh! I can't see what's to stop that child sitting down to a meal with everyone else,' said William, retrieving the evidence of his own recently consumed lunch from the floor.

'He's a bit moody after the drive,' said the nanny. 'You can't hear him down here…'

'No,' smiled William.

'…and they thought a meal might settle him down.'

'Well, it's no good expecting me to provide food for a child.' William scowled. He was making no concessions to this thin nanny and the unreasonable demands of her obnoxious charge. 'I haven't got any of that American stuff.'

'I beg your pardon?'

'Pizzas and burgers and peanut butter. That's what they eat nowadays.' William watched a great deal of children's television.

'Not Tobias! He only has natural, unprocessed food,' the nanny sighed. 'I think there's a box of his stuff somewhere.'

William did remember Stephen bringing a large box in from the car. He hadn't seen why Tobias should be indulged in silly fads, however, and had hidden it on top of the cupboard as soon as Stephen had gone.

'On the other hand, Mrs Arncott seemed to think you had some tinned spaghetti. I don't suppose that would kill him, just for once.'

William caught her eye and relented a little. She looked tired, this thin nanny. Wisps of blonde hair were escaping from her bun, and what should have been an English rose complexion was pale. He found her the spaghetti, a saucepan, and even a slice of bread.

'White,' he pointed out with a challenge. 'I'm sure Tobias has brown bread at home.'

'You bet – with little bits in!'

William watched her stir the pan. She couldn't be very old – not nearly old enough to be anyone's nanny – but she worked with an air of graceful efficiency he couldn't help admiring.

'If he wants toast, you'll have to use the grill – I haven't got a toaster.'

46

'That's OK.'

'It needs a match.'

'I see.'

She passed even this test, finding the awkward position of the jet, and managing to light it without burning her fingers. What on earth was she doing in such a diabolical job?

'I suppose you like bossing people about,' he suggested.

That made her turn round in surprise.

'I can't imagine why else anyone would want to be a nanny.'

'I've been taking care of three younger brothers all my life – that might have had something to do with it.'

'Well I hope that they were spoiled brats.'

'Not at all!' She rose to his fly. 'They're very nice kids.'

'What a pity! You've obviously no experience in dealing with children like my grandson then!'

Her lips twitched, but all she said was: 'Would you have a plate somewhere?'

He moved to fetch one from the cupboard, and a knife and fork from the drawer.

She glanced at the doorway as she spooned the spaghetti onto some toast. 'I suppose they'll bring him down in a minute. It's a bit far away to go and call.'

William felt a little pang of conscience as he remembered just how far away he had ensured it was.

'Have some stew while you're waiting,' he said. 'It's really quite good.'

'I'd better not.'

She sat down near the place she'd laid for Tobias and thoughtfully helped herself to an E from his plate. Mr Shirburn raised an eyebrow.

'I'm acting as Royal Taster,' she explained.

'What's it like?' He leaned over and took an O.

'Delicious. Tobias'll probably keel over after all these additives.'

'If he does, they'll be sure to accuse me of poisoning him. I shall tell them you're entirely responsible.'

'Your food, your cooking utensils!' retorted the nanny. 'I'm only the minion who put them together.'

An increasing wail warned them of the approach of Tobias. He made his entrance with a parent at each hand, and glared at his grandfather and his nanny with impartial animosity.

'Let's see what Nanny's found for your lunch. Oh!'

'Tinned spaghetti!' cooed William helpfully. 'On delicious toast.'

Tobias looked at him in surprise, and then at the alphabet spaghetti. 'It's got letters,' he observed.

'Perhaps you could make "Tobias",' said his nanny. 'Sit down here and we'll try and find a "T".'

'He's been able to spell his name since he was three,' said Stephen proudly.

The phone went. William pretended not to have heard.

'I wonder who that can be,' said Lesley, ostensibly to Tobias, but looking firmly at William, who gazed airily into the middle distance.

'I suppose Mrs Arncott'll get it,' said Stephen uncertainly, after a glance at Frances, who was also keeping her head down.

William watched them, amused by the battle of wills to see who was going to give in and go.

'What's she doing? They'll ring off in a minute!' said Lesley. It was going to be her. She scraped her chair back with an impatient snort and hurried out into the hall.

She returned a few moments later, her face a thundercloud. 'That was Julia. She says they'll be here at about three-thirty,' she announced in a voice of ice.

'Oh good,' said William, not meeting her eye.

'Did you *know* they were coming for Christmas?'

'Julia did mention something about it last night.'

'Well why on *earth* didn't you say so?' Lesley was beside herself. 'They're bringing Posy, and the nanny. I can't think where *they're* all supposed to sleep! Have you told Mrs Arncott?'

'No.'

'Why ever not?'

'I couldn't face any more of you' William explained simply.

Lesley gave a small shriek of frustration and stalked out of the room again.

'Oh dear, she's upset,' said William happily.

🎄 🎄 🎄

Julia's imminent arrival precipitated a family conference in the dining room, to which Frances was not invited. She was beginning to feel hungry, but she wasn't sure whether she was expected to eat with Tobias, or Stephen and Lesley, or perhaps with Mrs Arncott in some equivalent of a servants' hall. She finished feeding Tobias, who was actually quite taken with the alphabet spaghetti, and tried to avoid listening to the raised voices.

Unlike her employers, Frances had been greatly relieved to hear that another family was coming – with a nanny. It would be wonderful to have someone normal to talk to, to have a giggle about the Shirburns and exchange moans with. Posy's nanny was apparently being made to work over Christmas as well, and was probably as fed up about it as Frances was. 'What's Posy like?' she wondered aloud. 'Is she prosy?'

'What's that?' Tobias asked, amused at the sound of the word.

'Sort of good, I suppose.'

'No, she's bad. She's a *bad* influence,' he informed her carefully. 'I hope she comes soon.'

Eventually the dining-room door opened, and William could be heard announcing that it was all a plot to kill him off so his relatives could inherit his money. Kath, who had attended the meeting in her role as chatelaine, bounced into the kitchen looking smug.

'Well, we've had to change everything round, of course, now his daughter's decided to join the party. You'll be sharing with the other nanny now – dare say you won't weep over that.' She made a face at Tobias's back. 'He'll have to go in with his cousin Posy.'

'I'm not having that pooey room,' Tobias stipulated.

'No, Mummy and Daddy are staying there,' said Kath, having taken care to ensure this. 'And Posy's Mummy and Daddy will have to go on the floor below … lovely couple, Julia and Tony!' Kath's face took on a rapt expression. 'Not a bit snooty. You'd never think she was his sister.' She nodded towards the dining room to indicate Stephen. 'Older, too, but you wouldn't know it – dresses beautiful!'

She lowered her voice to a hiss designed to bypass Tobias. 'Young Posy's a bit of a madam, but I dare say their nanny will keep her in order. He's OK – Tony. Very good-looking!' She winked at Frances. 'We always have a bit of a laugh and joke, me and Tony. Think he fancies me, to be honest. Come on, young man! Better get your nanny to help you move your things.'

Frances obediently carried Tobias's belongings across to the little box room Kath had decreed to be 'nice and snug' for two children, wondering vaguely why he wasn't staying in the one originally assigned to Stephen and Lesley. Tobias, however, seemed quite happy with the arrangement.

'Which is my bed?' He bounced on both.

'Well, I expect you can choose, as you were here first.'

'I'll have this one. No ... this one.' He lay down and pretended to be asleep, with huge artificial snores.

'Here you are!' Lesley came in looking anxious. 'Mrs Arncott couldn't seem to remember ... oh, what a pokey little room! – I'm really not sure this is a good idea, you know. Posy's quite a bit older than Tobias and ... well... *Such* a pity they decided to come and disrupt everyone's plans!'

Frances remained silent. She didn't think Lesley would quite have the nerve to move things round again.

'I'm sleeping in this bed,' Tobias informed his mother, shutting his eyes again to illustrate the point.

'That's right. Why don't you snuggle down and have a little nap.'

'What are *you* going to do?'

'Daddy and I are going to have our lunch, and a little chat with Grandpa.'

'I might be lonely on my own,' Tobias ventured.

'Nanny will stay here until you're asleep.'

Frances's jaw dropped. She would have forgone the chat with Grandpa, but she could have done with some lunch herself. Tobias didn't seem in the least sleepy to her, and he certainly wouldn't drop off while he still had an audience.

'I don't like Grandpa,' he told them. 'He *looks* at me.'

'Oh, darling! Of *course* you like Grandpa!'

Frances was surprised at her tone. She hadn't thought Lesley was all that keen on Grandpa herself.

'Wouldn't you like to live in this nice house when you're big?' Lesley bent down to kiss him.

'No,' said Tobias.

His mother tittered and raised her eyebrows at Frances. 'Settle down then, precious. Do you want a drink?'

Tobias decided that perhaps he did. Frances could feel Lesley's eyes on her, and busied herself unpacking some things into a drawer.

'Oh well… Mummy will fetch you one, then.'

Frances grinned to herself. This talk with Grandpa must be pretty important if Lesley was prepared to go down three flights of stairs to the kitchen and back to keep Tobias out of the way. She and Stephen obviously wanted to get William on his own before the other relatives turned up. She would have felt sorry for the old man, being bullied by his son and daughter-in-law, if it hadn't been obvious that he was quite capable of giving as good as he got. William Shirburn was a tease, and Stephen and Lesley played up to it beautifully. She suspected that most of the time he did exactly as he liked, and moreover that he wasn't above stirring things up a bit occasionally for his own amusement.

She wondered what they were so keen to talk to him about. Money, probably. For some reason people always seemed to feel the need for secrecy where money was concerned, even when the facts were really boring. Perhaps Stephen was tired of university life, and they wanted a loan to start some exciting new venture – an escort agency or something.

'Why are you smiling?' asked Tobias.

'I'm not. My lips made a funny face by mistake. Hurry up and go to sleep, then I can go and get my lunch.'

'What are you going to have?'

'Beef burgers and custard.'

'No, you're not.' Tobias had as much sense of humour as the rest of his family. 'What *are* you going to have?'

'I don't know. Whatever your Mummy and Daddy leave me, I suppose.' She indulged in a pathetic picture of herself condemned to starve in a garret, but actually she wasn't sorry to have been let off eating with the Shirburns. With a bit of luck when Posy and her nanny came, they wouldn't be expected to sit down to formal meals with the other relatives. They sounded distinctly intimidating.

'What's the elderly lady who's coming like?' she asked, wondering how ethical it was to pump Tobias. 'Grandpa's sister. She must be your great-aunt.'

'She's Great-Aunt Margery.' Tobias confirmed. 'I don't like her.'

'You don't like many people, do you?'

Tobias considered this. 'I like Grime and Brine,' he said after a moment. 'We had a good game last time, with them and Posy, only Mummy and Daddy stopped us doing it.'

'Who on earth are Grime and Brine?'

'Their mummy's Mrs Arncott. I don't like her.'

'And what about the lady who can't spend Christmas on her own – Hilary?' Frances decided she might as well get the full score.

'Auntie Hilary's nice.'

Her opinion of Tobias's judgement was such that Frances immediately pictured an over-fond maiden aunt, cooing over Tobias and showering him with unsuitable presents, and so over-sensitised by whatever traumatic event had happened to her three years ago that she dissolved into tears at the least excuse.

'Christmas is going to be a laugh a minute, isn't it?' she sighed.

'I thought you said you weren't laughing.' said Tobias.

Lesley bustled back with some orange juice, which Tobias ignored. 'All ready for sleep now, darling?' she asked optimistically. 'Where's your special blanket? There we are! And you haven't got Cuddly Rabbit, have you? Where's Cuddly Rabbit, Nanny?'

Tobias sat up surrounded by toys, his eyes bright and eager for action.

'Night-night then, precious.'

'It's not night.'

'You have a nice little nap, anyway. Can I speak to you for a moment, Nanny?'

Frances obediently followed her onto the landing.

'Er … I do hope you find your room comfortable.'

'Yes, thank you.' Frances had been surprised when Kath had shown her to a much nicer room than the others they had seen, with two good beds and a large window overlooking the garden. Lesley seemed uneasy. Frances wondered if she was trying to engineer a swap.

'I must say, I would have expected Mrs Arncott to have put the nannies a little nearer the children!' Lesley laughed nervously. She was obviously having difficulty in reaching the point. She cleared her throat and looked down at her sensible shoes, and then out of the landing window.

'Er ... I hope you won't mind, Nanny, if we ask you to use the back stairs.'

Frances gasped.

'You did see them, didn't you? I'm sure you'll find them much more convenient – for the kitchen, *et cetera*. Perhaps you could mention it to the Britwells' nanny when she arrives.' She turned away without meeting Frances's eye, and hurried towards the front staircase.

🎄 🎄 🎄

'So many people on the road are not really fit to drive,' said Leo, coming close up behind a man doing seventy in the fast lane, and flashing his lights.

'No.' Hilary's leg tensed as she felt for an imaginary brake.

'About time!' grunted Leo, when the man was finally terrorised into cutting in between two lorries and he could get past. 'So what do you think's behind all this Christmas business?'

'What do you mean?' said Hilary, startled. Was Leo embarking on a theological debate in the middle of the motorway? It would be typical.

'Oh come on! Uncle William isn't exactly one for big family Christmases. What's the old sod up to?'

'Nothing! I mean, I think it was just accidental. Stephen and Ratso had something wrong with their house, and your mother wanted a chance to show this man round …'

'There's nothing wrong with Julia and Tony's house, as far as I know!' Leo's mouth curled into the self-satisfied expression he adopted when affecting irony.

'I expect, when they heard the others were going …' Hilary wished she'd stuck to the train. She'd forgotten how exhausting it was to be on the defensive all the time.

'A gathering of the clan,' mused Leo, overtaking a Jaguar on the inside lane. 'Uncle William sees Father Time beckoning, and is considering the disposition of his estate. Will it be to Gentle Julia, or does he favour male ascendency? Stephen has taken the precaution of getting himself a wife and a male heir to carry on the Shirburn name. That was lucky. It means he doesn't have to mate with the ghastly Lesley more than once…'

'I'm sure you've got it wrong. It was Lesley who was so keen on getting married and having a baby…'

'That's what I like about you, Hilary.' He took his eye off the road to smile kindly at her. 'You always think the best of people.'

Hilary drew a breath to defend herself against this unwarranted slur, but caught herself in time.

Leo braked to avoid the car he had nearly ploughed into. 'I'm interested in what makes people tick – you have to be, as a writer,' he said, as if it were a chore.

Hilary didn't break the family rule of never asking Leo how his book was going in case he told you, desperate though she was for a change of subject.

He raked a hand through his rather over-long hairstyle, a relic of the teenage-rebel image he had never dropped. 'No, you don't want to under-estimate William,' he went on. 'Just because he's old and eccentric, you mustn't make the mistake of thinking he's stupid.'

'No,' said Hilary, who never had. 'Don't you think he might divide the estate equally between them?'

'That would mean selling off Haseley. He'd never agree to that. And it would be a white elephant without the funds to maintain it, so the house and William's money must go as a package deal.'

Hilary turned to admire the view of motorway embankment beside her, and tried to quench the curl of embarrassment she felt at being invited to discuss somebody else's money.

'Yes, this way Father William gets them both dancing to his tune until they see which way the wind blows.'

Being a writer didn't seem to inhibit Leo from mixing his metaphors, Hilary noticed.

'I'm sure they've got more sense…' she ventured.

'Stephen's a don, so that precludes him from having any sense, by definition.'

Hilary smiled politely.

'Ratso's only a college secretary or something…'

'Librarian.'

'Julia's far too soft-hearted to know when someone's stringing her along. And you can forget Tony – charming, but a total airhead. Oh, they'll dance all right! It should be rather amusing.' Leo celebrated his forthcoming pleasure by putting his foot down.

Hilary shut her eyes against the bridges flashing past and pretended to doze.

'Of course you mustn't forget your interest in all this, Hilary.'

She jumped in spite of herself. 'I beg your pardon?'

Leo shot her a satisfied glance, his hooded eyes over that large nose making him look even more like a smug eagle.

'Haseley should have gone to Mother, as the eldest child, not William, merely because he was a boy. It would then have passed to Ben – and, of course, to his widow and son.'

He eyed her again, but this time she had herself under control.

'But it didn't go to Margery.'

'No, but if William were to pre-decease her, there would be a good case for arguing that she was his natural heir.'

'Oh come on, Leo! Margery's very comfortably off. She doesn't need William's money.'

'No, she doesn't. So I'm sure she would resign her claim in favour of you and Daniel.'

'What?'

'Ben was her eldest and, let's face it, her favourite son… No – I admit it – I've always been a bit too much of a rebel to fit in with family conventions. I wouldn't expect to benefit from anything Margery has to offer – though,

God knows, I can't think how I survive on the pittance a writer can expect to earn – one with any pretensions to literature, I should say. I'm not talking Dan Brown here...'

Hilary knew that Leo's father had left both of his sons a reasonable legacy. If Ben's had disappeared into their mortgage, Leo chose to live on the income from his share while he aspired to be a writer.

'And it's not as if you couldn't do with the money. I don't know what you make at that copy-editing, but it can't be enough to keep Daniel at medical school. You were still paying off what Ben had borrowed to set up the business when he died, according to what I heard... I beg your pardon?'

Hilary had made a growling noise in her throat, the remnants of a suppressed scream. If she feigned a heart attack, would he let her off at the next service station? Probably not.

She sighed. There was only one thing for it.

'How's your book going, Leo?'

Chapter Five

Scratch had been excluded from lunch in the dining room, and was miffed about it. He waited patiently outside the door, hoping to be noticed. But when Stephen and Lesley finally emerged with William, they were busy talking, and went straight across to the sitting room without sparing Scratch a second glance. In fact they were so engrossed in what appeared to be a heated discussion that they forgot to take the elementary precaution of either putting the food away safely or shutting the door.

Scratch couldn't believe his luck. There on the table was a totally unprotected quiche, a bowl of potato salad, and other feline delights such as butter! He leapt onto the table, prepared to sample each one.

Suddenly he was gripped round the waist. He gave a squawk of disappointment as he was lowered unceremoniously to the floor.

'Sorry, mate, but my need's greater than yours.'

Frances was even more delighted than he was to find a quiche deprived of only two small slices, the potatoes, and, despised by Scratch, a bowl of salad and some tinned fruit. Tobias had taken an age to drop off, and she was starving. There was no sign of the others. They must have adjourned without bothering to fetch her or check that she was fed.

Conscience wouldn't let her leave the debris as she'd found it, so she cleared the table when she'd finished, put the remains of the food in the fridge, watched balefully by the cat, and washed up Stephen and Lesley's plates as well as her own. After that, she craved a cup of tea.

There was an old kettle on the stove and mugs on a hook nearby – but teabags? Frances opened some cupboards. Nice china, obviously never used. Food? William apparently lived on tinned stew and packets of curry powder. But here, if she wasn't mistaken, was a brand new electric kettle, its lead still neatly coiled. She lifted it out from the back of the cupboard, and rinsed it out before filling it and plugging it in to a socket near the cooker. Further investigations led to the toffee tin of teabags, and there were several bottles of milk in the fridge.

'Indulging in a cup of tea, Nanny?'

She jumped guiltily. Stephen Shirburn had come through the open door unheard.

'Yes, I … er … would you like one?'

'We'd all like some, thank you very much. If you could bring it into the sitting room.'

He went out again. Frances made a face at the cat. 'Where's my frilly apron and cap?'

She found an old brown teapot and some of the nicer cups and saucers in the cupboard. A tray to put them on was more of a problem, until she discovered one hidden in the gap between the cooker and the fridge.

When it was all ready, she realised that she wasn't entirely sure where the sitting room was. She took the tray into the hall and listened for voices behind one of the closed doors.

It wasn't difficult. Some kind of argument was going on. '…but Father, you know it would be the sensible thing to do.'

Frances hesitated, then rested the tray on the hall table and opened the door.

'Ah!' said Lesley irritably. 'I thought you were upstairs with Tobias.'

Her face was flushed. William looked sulky, Stephen embarrassed. 'Put it down there, Nanny. Oh – no sugar?'

'You've used the brown teapot,' said William.

'It was all I could find. Sorry – I'll go and get the sugar,' said Frances, trying to make room for the tray among the brochures on the coffee table … coloured brochures with pictures of houses and the rooms inside them: 'Woodfield Court', 'Greenbanks'. Was this what they had been discussing?

Back in the kitchen, her own tea was getting cold. She gulped it, found a bowl of sugar and some teaspoons and took them to the sitting room.

'Next time, Nanny, would you use the china teapot that matches this service?' said Lesley. 'You'll find it with the rest of the set if you look carefully.'

Frances bit her lip, unable to think of a reply which would keep her her job.

Outside in the hall she took a few deep breaths. The raised voices had begun again.

'Think of Tobias, Dad!'

'I'd rather not, thank you!'

Frances turned to go. The cat, however, deciding this was where the action was, began to scratch loudly at the sitting-room door, glaring at Frances when she didn't open it.

'Shush!' she hissed, but this merely provoked him to reinforce his demand with a series of yowls that Tobias would have envied. She hovered, uncertain whether to run for it before someone else opened the door and accused her of eavesdropping, or try to let the cat in discreetly herself to stop him making that awful noise.

Then, suddenly, he did stop. Her momentary relief turned to alarm as she realised he was listening to something outside the front door … footsteps in the porch. The bell rang.

She heard exclamations from the sitting room. Any moment they would come into the hall and ask her why she hadn't opened the front door. So she opened it.

A gust of scent. A tall lady in a voluminous Indian cotton dress, with voluminous red-gold hair bound in a scarf to match.

'Hello, I'm Julia! You must be Tobias's nanny – we spoke on the phone.' She stepped forward almost as if to embrace Frances, but held out a warm hand instead. 'How lovely to meet you at last! This is our little horror – Posy.' Frances found herself facing the appraising grey eyes of a girl of about eight. 'Say hello to…?'

'Frances.'

'Lovely name!'

'Oh, there's Scratch!' said Posy, and ran to grab the cat, who dived for cover under the hall table.

'…and here's *our* nanny.' Julia indicated a bottom in a tight skirt bending to extract something from the back of the car. '…Oh, hello, Daddy! Isn't this fun? We haven't had a real family Christmas for ages. Stephen – Lesley … how super! And where's darling little Tobias?' She wafted in to where the others had gathered in an uncomfortable group in the hall.

Frances, continuing in her role as parlour maid, stayed holding the door open for the only person Julia hadn't introduced: a good-looking older man – the sort they use to advertise life-assurance – with neatly waved hair, greying an acceptable amount at the sides, and an improbably smart suit.

'So you're Tobias's new nanny. What was the name? Frances. Splendid.' He gripped her hand in a brief, professional handshake.

'Hello, Tony.'

Frances gaped. Surely that soft-voiced greeting didn't emanate from Lesley Shirburn? Good God, the pale eyelashes were almost fluttering! She watched Tony leave two bright patches of flame as he kissed his sister-in-law on both cheeks, and found it hard to suppress a grin.

Her speculations were interrupted by the return of Posy, who, having discovered that Scratch lived up to his name, was seeking more reliable sport.

'Where's Tobias?'

'I'm afraid he's asleep.'

'I'll go and wake him.' She started up the stairs.

'No, don't do that!'

'Where's his room?'

'Don't be a naughty girl, Pose,' said the owner of the tight skirt wearily. Her top was tight too, but she wore a severe jacket over it, giving the overall impression of a business-like tart. 'Hi, I'm Shelley.'

She looked round her with a shudder. 'This is a bit creepy, isn't it? Sort of Frankenstein's castle ... with Posy's Granddad as Frankenstein!' she added in a whisper. 'Oo-er! I don't think he's very pleased about us coming!'

Frances felt a sudden irrational desire to defend Haseley and William. 'He's a bit old for so many visitors – and the house is really interesting when you get used to it.'

Posy had gone to badger her aunt. 'Where's Tobias sleeping, Lesley?'

'Hello, dear. How you've grown!'

'They do at this age. Isn't it awful? The little monster eats us out of house and home.'

'Do *you* know where Tobias is, Uncle Stephen?'

'You could get lost in a place like this, couldn't you?' Shelley went on. 'Go along to the lav in the middle of the night and never find your way back ... there's that pussy again! Oi – Pose! There's the pussy!'

Curiosity had got the better of Scratch, who had incautiously poked his head out from under the table, thinking the heat was off. William startled everyone by seizing his cat and disappearing unceremoniously into the sitting room.

'Oh – I say!' said Stephen who, now that politenesses had been exchanged, didn't really want to be trapped in the hall with his sister's family.

Lesley too looked rather embarrassed. 'Well ... er ... I hope you won't be too uncomfortable,' she said. 'Unfortunately William forgot to tell Mrs Arncott you were going to be here... Well, he forgot to tell anybody, in fact. Until we arrived this morning, we were fully expecting to have Haseley to ourselves, weren't we, Stephen?' She gave her tight smile. 'I suppose you did know that Aunt Margery and Hilary are coming, and some man…?'

'Oh yes. Daddy told me all that on the phone last night.' said Julia blithely. 'Poor darling! He was really fed up about it. I thought we'd better come to cheer him up.'

'Well, we'll leave you to settle in, then.' said Lesley, obviously feeling she had done her duty. 'No, Posy, don't disturb Grandpa. Come on, Stephen.'

They disappeared into the sitting room to disturb Grandpa themselves.

Frances suddenly found everyone looking at her, and realised with alarm that, as the only menial on the premises, she was expected to show the others to their rooms. As it happened, she did know where Kath had put Tony and Julia, in a cramped little room not far from the one she was sharing with Shelley, but she resented being the one to break the news.

'Come on, Nanny!' said Tony briskly. 'Lead and we'll follow. No one's to go empty-handed, though. If I know William, he'll have put us all the way up in the attics!'

🌲 🌲 🌲

William dropped the cat and slumped down on the sofa, glaring at the glossy rubbish still littering the coffee table. He had been very grateful for the interruption which had put an end to that tiresome conversation with his son and daughter-in-law, and now he hoped to finish his cup of tea and join his grandson in the Land of Nod while they all sorted themselves out at the other end of the house.

Scratch, sensing something he wasn't allowed to touch, jumped up onto the brochures and began to paw them about. The result was disappointing. They didn't make the satisfactory rustling noise of a proper newspaper, they were hard to chew pieces off and, worst of all, didn't seem to produce any reaction from William.

When Lesley and Stephen came in, things were much better. Lesley shrieked and clapped her hands, and Stephen snatched the brochures up and tried to straighten them out.

'Wretched cat! Where were we?' he said, moving William's cup out of reach and sitting down beside him.

'"Green Banks", I think,' said Lesley. 'These rooms look comfortable, don't they, Father? You can take some of your own furniture.'

William had no desire to take his furniture to 'Green Banks' or anywhere else. His eyes narrowed thoughtfully.

'…and this one's really quite reasonably priced, considering all the facilities they offer. Look – it's even got a swimming pool.'

'So it has,' said William, who had never been near a swimming pool in his life and didn't intend to start now.

'It's only at Henley, so it wouldn't be far for us to visit.'

'Nor would it.' William had always had an aversion to Henley, since being taken to visit an elderly lunatic aunt there at a tender age.

'We could ring up and make an appointment for you to visit after the holiday.'

'Isn't it a good thing that Julia decided to bring the family for Christmas?' William remarked. 'Young Posy will be such good company for your Tobias!'

'Yes,' said Lesley, a hint of doubt in her voice.

'They'll be able to play some of the games she taught him last time,' William went on.

'Er … yes. We weren't entirely sure…' Stephen trailed off.

'I seem to remember them having a high old time in the shrubbery! Did Posy find his room, by the way? I'm sure she will. She seems a very determined child.'

Lesley got up. 'I think perhaps I ought to see what's happening.'

'Of course they may take some finding,' said William, as Stephen didn't move. 'So many places for children to hide in a house like this!'

'I'd better come with you,' said Stephen.

'Shut the door on your way out,' said William. 'Oh – and I should put these things away somewhere. You wouldn't want them to get spoiled.'

♣ ♣ ♣

'Oh, but this is a *sweet* little room!' said Julia. 'Do you know, it was where my nanny used to sleep when I was a little girl! Posy, come and look at…'

'We ought to let Shelley and Frances have it then,' said Tony, throwing himself down on the narrow bed. 'Christ, this is uncomfortable!'

'Well, if you want to swap?' said Frances guiltily.

'Oh no, darling!' said Julia. 'It's lovely and peaceful up here. The nursery wing's quite cut off from the rest of the house. Shove up a bit, Tony.'

'We'd never prise Shelley out of there now, anyway,' he said. They had left her en route, admiring the multi-mirrored dressing table. 'The room we give her in Wimbledon just isn't going to seem the same. I'm afraid we'll have to move in here with William, Julia. It's so hard to keep a good nanny these days!'

'God forbid!' laughed Julia. 'This is a ghastly house – don't you think so, Frances? All those bare boards and freezing corridors! It made boarding school seem positively luxurious. I can't imagine why Stephen's so keen to live here.' She patted the end of the bed for Frances, as there was no chair. 'Sit down and tell us all the gossip.'

'Er … I think perhaps I ought to check on Tobias,' said Frances, uneasily aware of Posy's disappearance.

'Oh, he'll be fine. Posy and he'll be having a wonderful game somewhere. I must say, we wouldn't have your job for anything! Aren't Stephen and Ratso simply horrendous to work for?'

'Ratso…?' Frances blinked.

'Lesley. Everyone calls her Ratso – everyone in the family, that is – didn't you know? Oh, I suppose you wouldn't!' Julia shook back her red curls and pushed a pillow up behind her. 'Their last nanny only stuck it a fortnight, and she gave Ratso a real earful before she went – reading between the lines. We were hoping you'd be able to tell us all about it!'

'No, I … er…'

'Oh, we were *counting* on you! Couldn't you make discreet enquiries?'

'Oh come on, Julia! I can't see Ratso having intimate little chats with her nanny over the teacups. In fact, you can't imagine Lesley being intimate with anyone – nor

69

Stephen. It's a family mystery how Tobias was ever conceived ...'

'Shh, Tony! You'll embarrass Frances! You can tell us, do they actually... I mean, do they share a room?'

'Er ... yes.'

'With a double bed?'

'No way!' interrupted Tony. 'Two chaste singles, pushed together once a year!' He sat up, and leant back dubiously against the single bedhead. 'How on earth did you come to get saddled with that pair, Frances? Or rather, however did Stephen and Ratso manage to get hold of such a very classy nanny?'

Frances, blushing, explained how the advertisement for a well-educated, 'well-spoken' nanny in *The Lady*, seemed to hold out the promise of a glittering new life among intellectual Oxford society.

'And you found yourself landed with Lesley and Stephen and Tobias!' Tony chuckled. 'I'm surprised you didn't take the first train back.'

'Well ... it was a bit difficult.' She described the grand send-off, how her brother Joe had moved into her room, and what a fortune her salary as a full-time live-in nanny seemed compared with what she'd been earning at the doctor's.

'And that's important to you?'

'It means I can help out at home...' Somehow, with these sympathetic listeners, her whole life story came pouring out – how her father's death had left her mother with four children to bring up on a small pension, her own decision to leave school instead of going to art college, and how the new job would at last enable her to make a real contribution to the family income.

'So you're absolutely trapped – how ghastly!' Julia rolled her eyes. 'It's like Jane Eyre, or something. In fact, you do look a bit like Jane Eyre, doesn't she, Tony? Sort of old-fashioned – oh, in a lovely way, I mean! It's having your hair up, and that long skirt – it is pretty! – and you've got those wonderful classical features one sees in old paintings …'

Frances blushed again. She wasn't used to being described in terms that suggested she was beautiful.

'I suppose you've left a string of broken hearts behind you in … where was it?'

'Ludworth. But I haven't.' She could hardly count John Rowington, whom she'd dated since school, and who'd accepted the news of her departure with depressing equanimity.

'What? No men in your life?' Tony raised his brows at Julia.

'Oh, what a change from darling Shelley! She's man-mad. We never know who's going to appear at breakfast.'

Frances gaped at her. Surely they didn't really allow their nanny to have men staying overnight?

Julia's eyes dropped. 'It's so hard to get hold of a decent nanny in London,' she said. 'Even when one can offer them *everything*! I mean, we have this ridiculously large house – all the gadgets and things. Two cars – though Shelley doesn't drive, of course. Only one little daughter, and she virtually looks after herself…'

'You'll make Frances sorry she isn't working for us.'

'Yes, it's an awful pity … but we can't exactly… Anyway, Shelley's a darling really.'

She broke off. They had all heard Lesley's shrill voice in the passage.

'Oh dear! She's calling Tobias,' said Frances.

There was a sharp rap at the door and Lesley opened it, glaring at the three of them crammed together on the bed as if she'd caught them taking part in an orgy.

'Tobias and Posy are missing,' she said dramatically. 'If you've finished showing Mr and Mrs Britwell to their room, Nanny, perhaps you would help us search the house.'

🌲 🌲 🌲

'Oh, you don't want to worry about them!' Shelley was lying on the bed with her legs apart, in a way Frances found faintly embarrassing. 'Pose'll have taken him off somewhere. She loves having another kid to push around.'

'Mrs Shirburn's a bit worried…'

Lesley and Stephen were turning the whole place upside down for their missing heir and his cousin, and a good few remarks had been passed about Frances's dereliction of duty in failing to keep track of her charge.

'She's a right old fussy-knickers, isn't she?' Shelley shifted herself into a more comfortable position. 'I reckon she doesn't get enough, that's her trouble. Should have seen the carry-on when they came over in the summer – all because Posy took her pants off in the paddling pool. He's a tight-arse 'n all. Not a flicker when you try it on a bit, just to see if he's human.'

'You've no idea where Posy went, then?'

'Ain't been no sign of them here. This room's OK, isn't it? I had a go with your lippie – hope you don't mind.'

'I'll try downstairs, then.'

'Oh yeah. They'll be lurking somewhere.'

🌲 🌲 🌲

'I can't think where they can have got to!' Lesley wailed for the umpteenth time. 'Have you looked in the garden, Stephen?'

'Oh, for heaven's sake! It's pitch dark.'

'So you haven't. I suppose it's too much trouble to search for your son on a cold winter's night… *Such* a pity you couldn't keep an eye on them, Nanny, when we were so busy downstairs!'

Frances bit her lip, forbearing to remind her employer that her nannying duties had been eclipsed by those of parlour maid.

'Is there a cellar or something?' she ventured.

'The cellar! Oh my God…' Stephen and Lesley bolted downstairs as one.

Frances hovered where they had left her, in the passage outside Julia and Tony's room. Those wretched children could be hiding anywhere in a house this size, and to be honest she wasn't really sure what all the fuss was about. What exactly was Lesley afraid Posy would do to Tobias if they weren't caught in time?

She began to call again, half-heartedly, knowing that if Tobias was in earshot he had no intention of answering.

'Hello, there!' Tony emerged from their room looking dishevelled. 'Not found the terrible twins yet? I hope your Tobias isn't leading our Posy astray.'

'Tony, stop teasing Frances!' Julia peered round the door. Frances got the impression she hadn't many clothes on. 'Have you tried the cupboards in the attic?' she said. 'Some of them run under the roof for miles.'

'That's where they'll be,' agreed Tony. 'Come on, Julia, let's finish our … er … unpacking.'

🌲 🌲 🌲

William was beginning to feel a bit peckish. It was about the time he usually had his tea.

Scratch was restless too. There were muffled noises coming from the big china-cupboard next door that he rather thought might be rats, and he welcomed the opportunity to investigate the dining-room side of the wall.

The house was momentarily quiet as William headed for the kitchen. Someone had left the cellar door open, and he pushed it to as he passed. He had a feeling he'd seen a tin of salmon that would make a nice sandwich.

Scratch gave up on the dining room as soon as he heard the tin being opened. The noises sounded less like rats on this side, and he didn't want to risk encountering anything which might start grabbing at him again.

William shut the kitchen door behind them and turned on the wireless, loudly, because everyone on the BBC tended to mumble. Scratch jumped on a chair to watch the progress of the salmon.

Chapter Six

'Leo, I suppose you did let William know you were coming,' said Hilary with sudden awful foreboding, as they turned in at the gates of Haseley House.

'Yes … well …'

He hadn't.

'… you know what a rude old bugger he is when you phone.'

'But you told Margery?'

'God no! Mother can't stand me turning up anywhere she's going to be. Too much competition, I suppose. She likes to rule the roost, and with a strong personality like mine …'

'Leo! You mean you didn't tell anyone?'

'Well … I rather left it up to you – as I'm your guest, in a manner of speaking …'

Hilary closed her eyes in anguish. She sat still as the car drew up, hoping to disassociate herself from the moment of disclosure when Leo's family opened the door.

Never, never again would she submit to three unadulterated hours of Leo's company. The drive had been interminable and, as darkness gathered, there had been nothing to do but listen while he rabbited on. If only he would let you sit there in peace while he told you how clever he was it would be one thing but, no, Leo had continually to test, to ask probing questions to prove one had been attending, and that one had an opinion – the correct opinion – on the subject he'd been pontificating about. It reminded Hilary of English tutorials back at Oxford, with a particularly exacting tutor determined to extract the full potential from a bright but idle student. And, despite the way Leo kept going on about her intelligence, if she did venture to enter into a discussion to alleviate the boredom, he would dismiss whatever she said with a patronising air that made her want to shoot him.

They were a long time answering the door, and she was forced to get out and slowly climb the steps.

'Ring again. They can't have heard the bell.'

'This is ridiculous,' he said at last. 'I don't believe anyone's going to answer.'

A little flutter of panic rose in Hilary's breast. She had been so looking forward to the end of this awful journey, to having someone take Leo away and offer her a cup of tea …

'They can't be out. William knew *I* was coming.'

Why did she get the feeling that the door would have been answered if Leo hadn't been with her?

Perhaps something of the sort occurred to him too. He set his mouth grimly and banged hard on the door, then stepped back to scan the dark crenellations and leaded panes above them.

'Someone's bloody there! There's a light on in the attic.'

Hilary looked wistfully up at the gingerbread-cottage dormers, with a fleeting idea of hauling herself up the ivy. 'I don't suppose they can hear us from there.'

'It's iniquitous keeping us standing about like this!' Leo slapped his arms with an exaggerated shiver, although the evening happened to be unseasonably muggy. 'Especially you, Hilary.' He turned on her suddenly. 'They can treat me like dog-shit. Good God, I've had to learn to be thick-skinned where this family's concerned – but it's quite unforgivable to force you to hang about on a cold winter's night!'

'I don't see why I should get any more favourable treatment than you,' said Hilary, then, realising she'd fallen into the trap of his paranoia, added quickly, 'Anyway, I'm sure they're not keeping us out here on purpose.'

Leo gave a knowing smile. 'We'll go round the back,' he said, as one making a triumphant discovery, then hesitated.

The pathway that led into blackness round the side of the house did not look inviting.

'Have you got a torch in the car?' asked Hilary.

'No.'

Surely Leo must be the only man in the world not to keep a torch in his car.

'Well feel along the wall. You'll probably find there are lights on further round.'

'You're coming, aren't you?'

Hilary smiled at the unmistakable note of pathos that had crept into Leo's 'no bars are going to keep me out!' tone.

'I thought I might wait here.'

'You know the house better than I do.'

'Of course I don't, Leo! You must have been coming here ever since you were a child.'

'No I haven't. William's never liked me. Ben used to visit him much more than I did. Surely you came with him?'

Hilary sighed. The times she had come with Ben had always been in daylight. The sitting room with its big turret window must be round to the right. Someone was bound to be in there. 'You go ahead, then.'

'Better take my hand.' Leo failed to specify whose protection he had in mind.

'I'm OK,' Hilary said untruthfully. Beyond the range of the porch light, the darkness was almost total. The path they were on was narrow and felt slimy, and she daren't put out a hand to balance, for fear of meeting Leo's.

When they finally reached the turret, it was unlit. Only a faint gleam from the open door made it clear that the room inside was totally empty. Leo banged on the window nevertheless.

'Try the French doors.' said Hilary, with little hope. She was right. They were locked.

Leo rattled the handle aggressively, then carried on along the terrace, peering in at windows, with the desperation of the wolf trying to get in to the three little piggies.

Hilary rested against the dining-room wall and gazed out over the invisible lawn, fantasising about seizing Leo's car and driving off to the nearest hotel. He disappeared round the corner of the East wing, and she suddenly realised she didn't want to be left on her own.

'There's a light on here,' he said. 'William must be in the kitchen.'

'Thank goodness!'

The curtains were drawn and no one responded to their knocks and calls.

'There'll be a side door somewhere,' said Hilary.

'I dare say.' The shrubbery had encroached right over the path at this neglected corner, making it almost impossible to get through.

'Why doesn't William cut some of this stuff back?' Leo growled, flailing at an overgrown privet branch, and slapping it into Hilary's face in the process.

As she ducked to avoid it, something caught her eye at the bottom of the house wall – a movement. Something pale had moved!

She jumped, and steeled herself to look again. A dark frame was set low against the path, and within it … no, it couldn't be! For a moment Hilary could swear she'd seen a face – a white face, its mouth open in a silent plea for help…

'Leo!'

'What?'

'Nothing. Is this the back door?' She pushed past him and began to hammer at it – violent, panic-stricken blows.

'Oh why is William so deaf?' She heard a sob in her voice. This was ridiculous. She'd come to Haseley out of the goodness of her heart, and now she was in some kind of Haunted House scenario – a bad B film.

'We might as well go back to the car,' said Leo.

'No, not that way!' Hilary shrieked as he made to go back the way they had come – past the face. 'I mean, it'll be quicker to go straight on,' she finished lamely.

On the last side of the house was a small window, dimly lit from the hall. 'I suppose he locks all the windows,' said Leo.

He stepped onto the remains of a rockery, reached up and gave the sash a half-hearted push. It shifted.

Frances decided that she wouldn't make a good burglar. She felt embarrassed creeping about other people's homes. It wasn't really likely that William would climb all the way up here and ask her what she was doing in his attic, or that she would suddenly find herself invading the privacy of some previously undisclosed occupant behind one of the numerous doors, but she still felt uncomfortable searching the upstairs bedrooms.

Julia had been right about the cupboards. Nearly every room seemed to have one close under the eaves – black, musty holes ideal for keeping skeletons in, or worse. She decided it wasn't in her job description to explore each one to the end, and she limited her investigation to a quavering call in the doorway which nothing, to her relief, responded to.

At last she felt honour had been satisfied, and made her way slowly down the back staircase to see if Lesley and Stephen had had better luck with the cellar.

She turned the last corner, and froze. Someone was climbing through the window at the bottom of the stairs! Talking of burglars, here was the real thing – taking his chance on a large house at Christmas time. He probably knew William lived alone, or might even have heard he'd planned to be away. Whatever ought she to do?

As she hesitated, the man glanced up and saw her. His appearance was suitably unkempt, with hair that looked as if he'd just climbed through a bush, heavy-lidded eyes, a big nose and a weak mouth. An expression of irritation and embarrassment crossed his face, appropriate to a burglar caught in the act.

Frances had no idea what to say. Her social skills did not extend to addressing someone found half way through a window in somebody else's house. 'Go away' was a bit tame. She might scream for help, but that seemed rather unnecessary when hers was so obviously the position of advantage. By rights the burglar should have run away of his own accord once discovered, but he seemed to be having problems with the window. In fact, as she watched, the sash suddenly gave, trapping him on the window sill.

His arms flailed as if he were practising swimming. 'I suppose you wouldn't think of giving me a hand?' he said tetchily.

Frances was clear about this. 'No,' she said in as firm a voice as possible, and returned rather hurriedly back up the stairs.

♣ ♣ ♣

Hilary saw the window drop and managed to reach up and just lift it high enough to free Leo. To her annoyance, he wriggled back out instead of in.

'There's a girl there,' he explained when she protested.

'Good! Is she going to let us in?'

81

'I … er … expect so.'

'Well we'd better go round to the front.'

'There's no one there now,' said Tony.

He was right. The window was shut. It was as if Frances had dreamed the whole thing.

'But there *was* a burglar! I saw him.' Her cheeks flamed. It was bad enough having disturbed Tony and Julia in the middle of what was apparently a nap, without Tony thinking she had got him down here under false pretences.

But he put a reassuring arm round her shoulders. 'Never mind – he's obviously gone now. Come along with me and we'll see if we can't find out where William keeps his whisky. Nothing like it for post-burglar shock.'

'My God, what's that?' gasped Hilary. The black darkness had been suddenly lit by the arc of a powerful beam. Had William installed some hitherto unsuspected security system? Were they about to be attacked by ravening Alsatians? She didn't feel her overstretched nerves could take much more.

'It's a car. Cor – nice Mercedes!'

They could see it now, resting panther-like on the drive. A man in a long winter greatcoat climbed out and went round to open the passenger door.

'Do you think William has Secret Service connections?' Hilary whispered a little hysterically. 'No wonder he didn't want anyone here for Christmas! This is probably a safe house, and …'

'It's Mother,' said Leo.

'Oh, so it is! How wonderful!'

'I suppose so.'

Hilary ran up and embraced her mother-in-law. 'Thank goodness you've come! We can't get in. No one seems to hear.' She broke off, making an effort to control herself in front of the stranger.

'William's a deaf old fool,' said Margery. 'Ought to be in a home. Wasn't I telling you, Oliver? This is my daughter-in-law, Hilary – married my elder son, before … well, you heard about that. This is Oliver Leafield, the architectural historian. You'll have read those fascinating articles of his in *Country Life*.'

'Yes … er … ' stammered Hilary.

'If you've been to the dentist lately,' he rescued her, with an understanding twinkle.

He was disconcertingly tall, and she found herself mumbling 'How do you do?' into his coat buttons as his hand enveloped hers. When she craned her neck back the extra few inches, she met a sensitive, intellectual mouth, finely sculptured nose, and eyes that seemed disturbingly perceptive in this half-light.

Hilary felt suddenly shy, dominated by the size of his hand, and that huge coat. She turned away with the excuse of introducing Leo, and found that he wasn't there behind her.

'Who's that lurking in the shadows?' said Margery. 'Have you got someone with you?'

'Hello, Mother.'

'Leo! What are you doing here? You weren't invited, were you? Of course not! William can't stand you. Hilary, why on earth have you brought Leo? … Oliver, this is my younger son. I don't know what he's doing here.'

'Mother, please…' Leo shook Oliver's hand, trying to indicate his mother's eccentricity with a grimace and a twist of his head.

'I expect you'd like to know what he does for a living,' Margery continued remorselessly. 'We all would!'

'I'm a novelist, as Mother knows perfectly well – Leo Watlington. And I do write under that name, before you ask.'

'He wasn't going to,' said Margery tartly.

'I gather you met Margery at a dinner party, Oliver.' Hilary decided it was time to intervene.

'Yes indeed,' he said warmly. 'You can always be sure of meeting someone interesting at Nigel's. And when Margery discovered my thing was architecture, she very kindly invited me down to see Haseley House.'

Leo gave an exaggerated cough and attempted to engage Hilary in a meaningful look, but she refused to catch his eye.

'Mother's good at issuing invitations to other people's houses,' he was forced to murmur.

'Not kind at all,' said Margery. 'Write a decent article about the place and you'll be doing William a favour – put Haseley on the map, so to speak.'

'Not to mention whoever he leaves it to!' Leo assured himself of Hilary's attention this time by digging her sharply in the ribs.

'We've always found it rather hard to take seriously,' she confessed. 'It's so like the set for a horror film.'

'Not take it seriously?' Oliver raised his eyebrows at her. 'One of the most important works of Joseph Watkinson of Oxford?'

'It's dark now,' she grinned. 'Wait till you see it in daylight!'

'I must say, I'm already staggering from the effect of that magnificent porch. Hardwick Hall meets Strawberry Hill – amazing!'

'We were brought up to think all this Victorian stuff was impossibly ugly,' said Margery, waving an arm dismissively at her ancestral home, 'but I gather it's fashionable now. Oliver says people write theses about places like Haseley.'

'It never ceases to amaze me what so-called students are permitted to waste their time on,' said Leo, forgetting that his anti-academic hobby horse wasn't the best way to impress Oliver.

'Leo didn't make it to university.' said Margery.

'I chose not to go. There is a difference…'

'Why don't you make yourself useful? Go and fetch the cases from the car.'

'But how are we going to get in?' asked Hilary.

'Oh that's all right,' said Margery. 'I've got a key.'

'A key to William's house? How did you manage that?'

'I've always had one,' was Margery's answer. 'Let's get where I can see … yes, this is it.'

'I don't believe it,' muttered Leo, as he and Oliver went to unload the luggage. 'Keeps us all hanging about in the cold, and she had a key all the time…!'

♣ ♣ ♣

Frances felt rather guilty, reclining on the sofa with a large glass of William's whisky in her hand, while the search for the missing children was presumably still going on without her.

'Oh, stuff that!' Tony reassured her, sitting down beside her with his own glass. 'They'll have found them ages ago. Anyway, it's after six o'clock – well past your knocking-off time – unless Stephen and Lesley were very canny with your contract!'

Frances frowned, embarrassed to realise she couldn't remember exactly what that complicated document had said about hours. It had been very hot on things like paying for her own phone calls and not leaving without due notice – a legacy of the previous nanny, no doubt. But what about the actual hours of work? How stupid of her not to have checked!

Tony must have seen her expression. He turned to look at her, resting his elbow on the back of the sofa. 'Seriously, Frances, they're not the most benevolent of employers, and they may not have the sense to realise what a gem they've found. You mustn't let them exploit you.'

'Oh no – I don't!' said Frances quickly, glad that Tony hadn't witnessed the parlour-maid incident that afternoon.

He was still regarding her earnestly. 'Well, I hope you realise you have friends here now. If things do start to get too much, and you feel you want someone to confide in, you will come and talk to me – or Julia – won't you? I'd really hate to see you taken advantage of.'

Frances felt a warm glow that wasn't entirely due to the whisky. Of course she couldn't really go whingeing to Tony about the Shirburns, but how nice of him to go out of his way to be so friendly to her! One might have expected him to be on the other side, after all.

'Terrible luck about their damp-proof course,' he was saying, 'going wrong just before Christmas. I thought those things lasted for ever.'

'Yes,' said Frances, a little awkwardly in view of Lesley's hint that the damp might not have been the Shirburns' only reason for deciding to spend Christmas at Haseley.

'Particularly hard on you, Frances. I expect you were hoping to see your family, weren't you, instead of being stranded out here in a gloomy old house in the middle of nowhere? I don't know how long Stephen and Lesley are planning to stay…'

'Oh, it's only for a few days, I think.' said Frances, realising that they hadn't said exactly how long. Now Tony pointed it out, she supposed the Shirburns had effectively got her trapped here, with no means of escape, until they decreed that it was time to go home. Thank goodness the Britwell family had decided to join them!

'Just as well we decided to come along and cheer things up.' Tony read her mind. 'We love Christmas! All that silly sentimental stuff. Julia decorates a mean Christmas tree. William hasn't got one, has he? We'll fetch one in tomorrow. And I have a secret recipe for stuffing…' He touched his nose conspiratorially. 'Say no more, except that the bottle of Courvoisier in the cupboard must remain unviolated until the day! It makes the whole difference to

Christmas, doesn't it? Having a house full of people? I bet you and the Shirburns were relieved not to be stuck with just old William for company!'

'Oh yes, I was!' said Frances, not wanting to disclose what Lesley's reaction had been when she'd heard about all the other visitors.

But Tony must have been too perceptive. He put his head on one side, eyeing her quizzically. '…were Stephen and Ratso not as pleased as you were, perhaps?'

'Oh no … it's just … er … I think there was something they wanted to discuss with your father-in-law,' stammered Frances, anxious not to let him think it was anything personal against him and Julia, 'and they were rather hoping to talk to him on his own.'

'Oh, I see,' said Tony, making a wry face. 'I thought our welcome wasn't as enthusiastic as it might have been! We obviously interrupted some important *tête-à-tête*.' He indicated the tea things, which no one had bothered to clear away. 'I wonder what it was all about.'

Frances realised that she was able to throw some light on this now. She found the pile of brochures Stephen had hastily gathered together and passed them across to Tony. 'I think it was something to do with these.'

'Aha!' He examined the brochures and raised his eyebrows at her. 'I scent a plot! What do you say, Nanny Frances?'

Frances grinned back. Somehow it was OK for Tony to call her Nanny.

'They're retirement homes, aren't they?' she said. 'Mr Shirburn must be planning to move into one.'

'Or having it planned for him.' The sudden grimness in his tone startled her.

'You mean – he doesn't want to go?'

'I can't imagine William agreeing to leave this place of his own free will, can you?'

She remembered Lesley's pink angry face, William's scowl. 'But why should they try to make him move if he doesn't want to?'

Tony glanced round meaningfully. 'Fine old mansion, this – if you like that sort of thing.'

Frances stared at him aghast. Surely Stephen and Lesley weren't trying to push William into a home just to get their hands on Haseley House?

'… fetch a good bit if it were to come on the market – provided it was sold with vacant possession.'

'But they can't be intending to sell it!' she objected. 'Mrs Shirburn said something to Tobias about living here when he grows up…'

'Did she indeed?' Tony looked at her with narrowed eyes. 'On the other hand, it would of course make a very nice country retreat for an Oxford don. How do you fancy it, Frances – Nanny to the Lord of the Manor of Haseley?'

What, live permanently in this sinister old house, with its inexplicable creaks and groans, and all those empty derelict rooms upstairs? There was a weird scratching noise in the wall at the moment that sounded horribly like rats! Frances shuddered, and moved a little closer to Tony.

'No, you're not part of the plot, are you Frances?' his warm smile returned. 'I'm glad. Anyway – what am I thinking of, gossiping to you about your employers like this? Most improper! Let me get you another drink…'

Chapter Seven

The rest of them hung back as Margery pushed open the front door, mutually conscious of the awkwardness of walking into someone else's house unannounced.

'The hall's in a dreadful state,' she observed to Oliver. 'You'll have to ignore all the missing tiles – and that perfectly ghastly wallpaper. I expect your expensive camera's capable of cutting out that sort of thing, isn't it?'

The familiar smell of Haseley – mould and polish and old stone caught Hilary unawares, sweeping her back in time so vividly that for an instant she assumed it was Ben beside her.

But it was Oliver who met her instinctive glance of affection, saw her drop her eyes immediately and look away embarrassed.

'William must get this place done up,' said Margery decisively. 'Then he can sell it for a packet instead of leaving it to that ghastly son of his… What's the matter, Leo? Stop wittering!'

'There's somebody coming,' he moaned.

'Well what if there is? Oh, it's Julia. Don't say *they've* all descended on poor old William as well! William's daughter,' she explained to Oliver. 'Married Tony Britwell – bit of a spiv. Makes a good thing out of other people's money – you know the type.'

'Aunt Margery – how lovely!' said Julia, who had been well within earshot. 'Have you been ringing the bell? William's put us in the attic and you can't hear a thing. Hilary, darling!'

Julia's powerful scent enveloped her as she kissed her on both cheeks. Hilary tried to return the embrace without embarrassment. She was sure Julia genuinely liked her, and had never been able to work out why she didn't feel the same way.

Margery introduced Oliver, and Hilary saw him visibly recoil as Julia seemed about to kiss him too, but she confined herself to one of her almost sexual handshakes.

'*Super* to meet you... Oh – Leo!'

'Yes, I don't know why he came. *I* didn't bring him.'

Leo emerged from where he had been trying to efface himself against the coat-stand. 'I came down with Hilary, actually...'

'Oh dear!' said Julia, giving Hilary a reproachful look that set her teeth on edge. 'Don't let Daddy see you, for heaven's sake! We'd better put you in the dining room. There's no one in there.'

'This is ridiculous!' protested Leo as Julia hustled him through the door. 'I can't stay in hiding for the whole of Christmas!'

'I'll get Tony to find you a drink,' she promised him. 'He's gone off somewhere with the nanny...'

'Where's William?' demanded Margery, ignoring Julia's attempt to relieve them of their coats. 'In the sitting room? Come on, Oliver. We'll go and give him a rocket for not answering his bloody front door!'

Hilary followed them, feeling the combination of Margery and William was too much to ask a sensitive man like Oliver to face alone. He was already looking rather stunned by Margery's uninhibited appraisal of her brother's house, which she took up again as she threw open the sitting-room door without bothering to knock.

'...This room's not quite such a slum. Newish carpet and some fairly decent furniture ... ah, Tony! What are you up to in here? Trying your luck with the nanny, apparently.'

Tony had been caught with his arm round an attractive little blonde girl, who leapt up guiltily, her cheeks flaming.

'Julia's husband,' Margery explained to Oliver, 'the one I was telling you about.'

Tony somehow managed to keep his composure. 'Hello, Aunt Margery. How splendid to see you. Hello, Cousin Hilary.' There was something caressing about the way Tony said 'cousin' that made Hilary wince slightly, as he took the opportunity to kiss her full on the mouth. He held out his hand to Oliver.

'This is Oliver Leafield,' Margery introduced him. 'He's a friend of Nigel Rofford's.'

'Oh yes, the ... er ... architectural historian.' Tony dropped his hand rather suddenly and placed it on the girl's shoulder instead. 'Frances and I were just discussing her unenviable job. She's young Tobias's nanny.'

'Ah, the *Shirburns'* nanny, are you? That's right, Tony – no sense in fouling your own nest. There's a pleasure in store for you, Oliver – my nephew Stephen and his wife. Awful snobs, with a quite horrendous offspring. Only to be expected, I suppose, when you bring a child up as if he were a research project...'

Frances was interested to discover that one couldn't actually die of embarrassment. She must have run it as close as anyone when that terrifying old lady had come in and got totally the wrong idea about her and Tony. She would have liked to explain that they were only discussing how to protect William – her brother, surely – from a dreadful plot, but Tony had obviously decided it was better not to say anything. Perhaps he didn't trust this Oliver Leafield, standing there so huge and silent in that great black coat. He had certainly given him a funny look when he found out who he was.

Tony seemed to be fond of his cousin Hilary, though, and she wasn't at all the sort of languishing person Frances had expected. She had bright, intelligent eyes and a firm mouth and lots of dark curly hair, and when William's sister started going on about the Shirburns in that horrendously forthright way, she caught Frances's eye with a really kind smile.

'I expect you'll be wanting to get Tobias's tea or something, won't you, Frances?' said Tony.

She knew he was offering her the excuse to escape and seized it gratefully, wishing everyone wouldn't watch her go as if they were waiting for her to be out of earshot. Oliver held the door open, and Margery followed her with those eagle eyes. 'I give that one a week!' she heard her say, before the door was quite closed.

To do William justice, he hadn't heard the front doorbell. He was busy preparing a delicious sandwich of tinned salmon, pickled onions and a few letters of cold alphabet spaghetti. Scratch, who *had* heard it, took the precaution of sliding under the dresser until he realised William wasn't going to answer, and he could go back to the juice from the salmon tin undisturbed.

William did hear the banging on the back door, but equated it with the similarly irritating noises someone was making from the direction of the cellar – the inevitable result of having a horde of people in the house.

He looked up unenthusiastically as Julia bounced in, leaving the door ajar.

'There you are, Daddy! What's that disgusting mess you're eating?' Julia poked at his sandwich and made a face. 'Aunt Margery's arrived, with the architect guy. Such a shame he's gay – he's got a lovely sensitive face! Oh – and Hilary's here as well.'

William brightened. He liked Hilary. She had pretty hair and twinkly, sensible eyes, and she'd been married to his nephew Ben, of whom he'd been particularly fond. Best of all, she wasn't always trying to get him to do things, unlike most of his relations.

'Why don't you put a bit of salad on that?' said Julia. 'You really ought to eat more vitamins.'

Scratch, who had finished his meal already, took the opportunity to slip out for further investigation of the rats. The dining-room door was closed, but a moment or two later Frances came into the hall, and a pathetically raised paw easily persuaded her to open it.

Inside – joy of joys! An infrequent visitor to Haseley, but one of his favourites – Leo!

Maybe it was his particular smell, or a kindred feline nature the cat detected, but probably it was because of the way Leo utterly froze whenever he approached him. Scratch could impose his will on most people to a greater or lesser extent, but with no one was his domination so totally, satisfyingly complete as with Leo. He could do whatever he liked: jump up; claw his toes; knead him mercilessly; and still Leo would hold his stiff, stricken pose until rescue came or the cat condescended to leave his victim voluntarily.

On sighting this appealing visitor, Scratch leaped forward with a cry of delight.

'Aargh!' said Leo.

The sound startled Frances, who'd thought the room was empty. She put her head inside – and froze. That burglar hadn't escaped after all! He was here in the dining room! Whatever should she do? The cat was making a valiant attempt to pin him down, but it wouldn't be able to hold him for long. She would just have to go and fetch Tony, even if it did mean facing those people again.

Hilary pretended to be listening to Margery instructing Oliver about architecture, because otherwise she knew that Tony would collar her and make her look into his eyes and tell him all about her life. She surreptitiously felt the teapot on the table, but it was cold, and she was just wondering whether she could follow the nanny's example and escape, when the girl herself came bursting back into the room.

'Tony – I'm sorry – but that burglar … he's still here – in the dining room… ' she gasped.

'A burglar? Nonsense!' retorted Margery. 'We've never had burglars at Haseley! There's a fine stucco ceiling in there. You must make a point of seeing it, Oliver.'

'I will. But … er …' He was looking at Hilary, an amused question in his eyes.

Her mouth dropped. Hadn't Julia put Leo in the dining room? And one of the nannies had seen him trying to get through the hall window!

'Don't worry, Frances!' Tony was squeezing the girl's arm. 'We'll go and sort him out for you.'

'Please hurry!' she said desperately. 'I've left the cat holding him down.'

'This I must see,' said Oliver.

Hilary, remembering Leo's antipathy to cats, let the others go in front of her, then slid past them towards the kitchen. The accusations and explanations were more than she felt she could take without a good strong cup of tea.

A peculiar knocking sound from the cellar reminded her for a moment of that face. She had imagined seeing it, of course – a trick of the dim light – and the knocking could be anything in an old house: death-watch beetle probably … like those odd noises she had noticed just now in the sitting-room wall.

The kitchen seemed warm and welcoming. William had the kettle on, and was engaged in some ludicrous argument with Julia about lettuce. It was reassuring to see that, despite his professed horror of eating anything 'good for him', he looked just the same as ever. He sat hunched over his meal, addressing imprecations to Julia's heedless backside as she rummaged in his fridge, apparently searching for ice to put in a gin and tonic. With his bright eyes and rather beaky nose, he reminded Hilary of a grumpy little robin defending its territory. Neither of them noticed Hilary until she laughed.

For an instant William's face was transformed by a beam of delight.

'I heard you were about the place. So you've condescended to come and say hello to me, have you?'

'No.' She kissed his forehead. 'I've come for a cup of tea. Good God, what *are* you eating?'

'My supper,' said William, with a belligerent look at Julia.

'What would you do with him, Hilary?' Julia gave up on the ice and came to lean against the kitchen table. 'If Daddy's determined to get an ulcer…'

'I thought it was scurvy you were threatening me with.'

'Posy's just as bad. Refuses to go near a vegetable! Children seem to exist on crisps and chocolate bars nowadays, don't they? You can't ever get them to eat a proper meal.'

Very likely, Hilary thought, if you let your child fill itself up on junk food. Obviously Julia and Tony still had the *laissez-faire* attitude to Posy's upbringing that had made her the pudgy, self-centred little girl Hilary remembered.

'Where *are* the children?' she said aloud. 'I haven't seen Posy or Tobias yet – or Stephen and Lesley, come to that.'

'Lucky you!' muttered William.

'Oh, Daddy! Isn't he naughty? They're around somewhere. Posy took Tobias off for a game, and Stephen and Ratso went to look for them – oh, ages ago! Wouldn't you rather have a decent drink? I was just getting one for … anyone who wants one.' She cast a meaningful glance towards the dining room that William might easily have seen.

'No – tea!' said Hilary firmly. 'Do the bags still live in the toffee tin?'

'Why wouldn't they?' said William.

'I don't know what we're going to do about supper,' said Julia. 'Daddy says Aunt Margery and her friend were supposed to be eating out, but I expect we'll have to feed them. Have you got anything planned, Daddy?'

'No,' said William.

'Of course you have! Mrs Arncott will have got something in when she heard we were coming.'

William's smile suggested otherwise.

'There'll be a few more than she expected. Let me see – *two* more, isn't it, Hilary – or thereabouts?'

Hilary still refused to rise to the bait. It wasn't fair to blame her for Leo's arrival, when Julia herself had let slip the news about the gathering at Haseley.

'I'm having *my* supper,' said William smugly. 'I didn't invite anybody else here, and I don't see why I should feed them – there's some bacon in the fridge,' he added as a dispensation to Hilary.

She had just been to the fridge for milk and seen that it was crammed with food. William also admitted, under cross-examination, that there was a turkey in the larder and plum pudding in the cupboard. Mrs Arncott had been to Sainsbury's the day before.

'I don't think food will be a problem…' she began, wondering why Julia had tried to make it one.

'Whatever's going on in the dining room?' Julia interrupted suddenly.

In fact, the sounds had been so faint that Hilary doubted if William would have noticed them unprompted.

'Poor Daddy! You can't get any peace, can you? I suppose you'll want to go and see what's happening.'

♣ ♣ ♣

Tony paused at the dining-room door, put a finger to his lips and winked at Frances before flinging it wide.

'Oh!' He drew up short. 'Leo!'

'Is that who's causing all the trouble?' Margery clicked her tongue. 'Bloody typical!' She pulled Oliver into the room. 'This is the ceiling I was talking about…'

'But … do you know him then?' said Frances, considerably taken aback.

'Yes, it's Julia's cousin Leo – Aunt Margery's son,' said Tony.

'Her son?' Frances stared from Leo to his unconcerned mother, busily showing Oliver the tiles round the fireplace. 'Then why on earth was he climbing…? I mean…' Was the whole family mad?

'Will somebody get this blasted cat off me?' interrupted the 'burglar' through gritted teeth.

'Leo rather likes to be unconventional,' Tony explained. 'I expect he thought the front door was a bit too mundane…'

'It wasn't like that at all. None of you would answer the damn bell! If this stupid girl hadn't decided to act so hysterically…'

Frances, not for the first time that day, found herself wishing she could have spent Christmas somewhere quite, quite else – Antarctica, perhaps. That awful misunderstanding about her and Tony had been bad enough, but then to have taken Margery's son for a burglar! Now that he stood in full light she could see that Leo had the Shirburn nose so prominent in his mother and William, and to a lesser extent in Stephen, but she really didn't know how she could have been expected to recognise a member of the family climbing unannounced through a window.

'You can't blame Frances,' Tony chuckled, moving to put an arm round her. She stepped out of reach, thankful that Margery was preoccupied with Oliver at the other end of the room, and Hilary didn't seem to have followed them in.

'What a splendid cat!' said Oliver suddenly, bending down to click his fingers at Scratch.

'Do you like cats?' said Leo hopefully. 'Perhaps you could get this one to go away.'

Scratch looked from one to the other, weighing up the possibilities. He hadn't had time to exploit the full potential of Leo, and people who professed to like cats were in danger of sweeping one up and subjecting one to undignified excesses of affection. On the other hand, this man was new and was wearing a very attractive coat...

'Thank Christ for that!' said Leo, getting up and stretching. 'It's been a nightmare in here, I can tell you. There's the weirdest of noises coming from that cupboard.'

'What are you lurking about in here for, anyway?' Tony asked him.

'It's all Julia's fault. She said I had to hide from William,' said Leo, with an air of grievance. 'I can't think why the old bugger's taken it into his head he doesn't like me! I suppose it's because I can't help speaking my mind. Old people always think they can be as rude as they bloody well want...' He lowered his voice so that Margery wouldn't hear. '...and they can't stand it when they come up against someone who just isn't prepared to be intimidated ... Oh hello, Uncle William!'

'Harrumph!'

William surveyed the scene in his dining room and was not pleased. Margery had promised him Leo wouldn't turn up and there he was, hopping about in that irritating way of his, embarrassed yet attention-seeking. Julia's husband was ogling the poor little nanny. Margery was prodding the woodworm in the shutters and had a stranger with her who must be that pansy friend of Rofford's. He was perched on the edge of the table letting the cat take ecstatic liberties with the corner of his coat.

The man stood up when he saw William and held out his hand. William backed away.

'Don't look so grouchy,' said his elder sister. 'I didn't bring Leo. He came with Hilary, I gather. This is Oliver Leafield. We've started to look round, but the place is even worse than I remembered. Did you know that there's woodworm in these shutters?'

Tony sidled up to Hilary with a grin. 'So you're responsible for Leo, are you?'

'No, I'm not. I only...'

'We mustn't be horrid to Hilary about it.' Julia squeezed her waist. 'There's no reason on earth she shouldn't pal up with Leo, just because the rest of us are so beastly.'

'But I haven't. He only gave me a lift...' It was so unfair! Even the nanny seemed to be eyeing her reproachfully.

Tony winked, and Julia frowned at him. 'Not another word! It's a pity we couldn't keep the dread news from Daddy, but you were all making such a noise in here. I really don't know how he's going to manage Christmas with all these people,' she went on, in a voice only just subdued. 'He shouldn't have let everyone dump themselves on him like this! What with Margery's architect friend, and Stephen and Ratso insisting on bringing their nanny...'

'Hi...!' Everyone turned to the doorway. The single syllable was long drawn-out, a little plaintive, designed to attract the full attention of everybody in the room. A girl in an outrageously short tight skirt was posing with an arm against the door jamb, like the guest star in an American sitcom waiting for her entrance to be applauded before carrying on with her scene. 'What's going on?' Her eye ranged across her audience, pausing speculatively at the most eligible-looking man.

Hilary nearly laughed out loud. Leo's expression couldn't have been more horrified if the girl had offered him a good time behind Kings Cross Station.

Oliver's lips twitched, as he was dismissed in one assessing glance. Margery's mouth curled in undisguised disgust. Tony said, 'Hi there, Shelley! Been having a snooze? You've missed all the fun.'

102

A flicker of something in Shelley's eyes – a kind of smug recognition – gave Hilary a flash of insight. *She's had him already*, she thought.

'This is Posy's nanny,' said Julia. 'Our wonderful Shelley! You haven't found Posy have you, darling? Hilary's longing to see her – and dear little Tobias, of course.'

'No,' said Shelley, eyeing Hilary without interest – a mere woman, and middle-aged at that. Hilary smiled ruefully.

Despite her conversation with Tony, Frances felt a pang of conscience at the mention of Tobias. It was past his bedtime now, and Lesley must have been coping with the trauma of bathing him in the cavernous bathroom, finding him something he would eat and settling him into bed, all without the assistance of his nanny.

On the other hand they might have been calling for her for ages. She wished she could catch Shelley's eye, or get to the door, but it meant either crawling under the dining-room table or pushing past the waspish Leo.

'I wouldn't open that if I were you,' he was saying to Oliver, who was about, at Margery's invitation, to investigate the china cupboard. 'There've been the most extraordinary noises coming from it – rats or something.'

'Have you got rats, William?' asked Margery accusingly.

'Of course not! What do you think I keep that great cat for?'

Scratch, who'd had to abandon the coat when Oliver moved, looked up guiltily from Leo's shoelaces.

'I tell you, there's something frightful in there.'

'Oh, don't be so melodramatic, Leo!'

'Open it, someone, for heaven's sake!' said Julia. 'I can't stand the suspense.'

Oliver, apparently without fear, opened the double doors of the cupboard. He revealed Posy and Tobias, a picture of innocent childhood, in the process of holding a tea party with some of the little coffee cups.

'Oh, Posy, you naughty girl! We've been searching for you everywhere,' said her mother untruthfully.

'I was in here with Tobias. Who's that man?'

Tobias, blinking in the sudden light, eyed the assembled company and found them deficient. 'Where's my Mummy and Daddy?'

'They went to look for you – in the cellar...' Frances tailed off. If the children hadn't been there, why had Lesley and Stephen never come back?

From the look of amusement on Tony's face, she saw that the same awful possibility had just struck him. He whispered in Julia's ear and winked at Frances.

'Oliver,' he said, 'we'd like you to open another door for us!'

Chapter Eight

Hilary recognised the face at once. Pale, gaunt and desperate, it bore all the signs of long and hellish incarceration. Stephen looked no better. Hilary stepped back a little as the pair emerged, grubby and dishevelled, and scanned the crowd for someone to blame.

'You *stupid* girl! You knew we'd gone down to the cellar. What on *earth* possessed you to shut the door?' The poor nanny was first in line.

'But I didn't...'

'Why doesn't it have a *handle* on this side, anyway? This place is an absolute death trap!' exclaimed Stephen, thumping the door frame irritably. 'Father shouldn't be living here, if he's going to let everything go to rack and ruin ... It isn't *funny*, Julia. We could have been in that cellar for days!'

Julia and Tony were succumbing to a justifiable, but untimely, fit of the giggles. Hilary turned to frown at them, but only succeeded in attracting unwelcome attention in her own direction.

'Hilary, I'm sure it was you wandering round outside!' Lesley accused her. 'Didn't you see us calling for help? You must have done! Oh for God's *sake*! Can't anybody keep that animal under control?'

Oliver stepped forward and seized the cat by one protesting leg, just before he disappeared into the exciting new domain behind the usually closed door. Lesley, suddenly conscious of a stranger in their midst, broke off her tirade with an embarrassed cough and looked at the rest of them for enlightenment.

It was left to Hilary. 'This is Oliver Leafield, Margery's friend.'

She felt for Lesley, faced with this attractive man caught in such a ridiculous situation, with smuts on her forehead and cobwebs in her hair.

'Oh – the journalist.' She dealt with it by shaking hands churlishly, and resuming her role of outraged victim. 'I suppose the very *last* thing you've all been doing is trying to find poor little Tobias while we've been shut down there! He could be lying *dead* somewhere, for all we know…'

But her son gave the lie to this by appearing at that moment, hand-in-hand with his cousin Posy. He squeaked as his mother swooped forward and swept him up in a possessive embrace.

'*There* you are, Mummy's precious boy. We was so wowwied about you… How *could* you let her take him away like that?' She glared at the young seductress's parents, who were breaking into renewed giggles at the bizarre sound of baby language coming from Lesley's thin lips. 'You *know* Tobias isn't old enough for Posy's rough games! And now it's well past our bath-time – if you wouldn't mind, Nanny.'

'Hope you're up to the job, Frances,' said Tony, with a mischievous lift of the eyebrow in Lesley's direction.

'I'm going to have my bath with Tobias,' announced Posy, taking his hand again.

'No, I don't think that's a very…' But Lesley was too drained to put up much of a protest, and Posy was already leading the way upstairs.

♣ ♣ ♣

After a derisive 'Pah!' at their stupidity, Margery hadn't stayed to watch Stephen and Lesley's release from the cellar. Hilary found her in the kitchen, hectoring William.

'…What? No, of course I didn't say we wouldn't want feeding! You can't invite someone like Oliver Leafield, and not offer him a decent meal.'

'*I* didn't invite him,' William was quick to remind her. 'And I've already eaten, thank you.'

'Well *you* may not be hungry, but the rest of us are. We're certainly going to want dinner. And something proper, not those tins of muck you keep in your store cupboard … has Mrs Thing gone? Oh never mind – here's Hilary.'

She must have seen her mouth drop, and flapped an impatient hand. 'No, I didn't mean you had to do it all. There's no reason Julia and Lesley can't help. Are they still messing about in the cellar? They must come and make themselves useful … And you can't skulk in here, William, with visitors to entertain! You men must come and be polite to Oliver. He'll want to hear all about the house…' She shepherded him away, a relentless force.

Hilary grinned as she heard her giving orders to the troops outside. Margery would be outraged at any suggestion that she wasn't at the forefront of women's rights, but the concept of equal allocation of domestic chores would simply not have occurred to her.

'Isn't she an old bossy-boots?' said Julia, duly coming into the kitchen with a sulky-looking Lesley. 'Never mind. Let's make a lovely meal, shall we? ...I wonder if Daddy's got any candles, and there must be some napkins somewhere.' She began to rifle through drawers.

'The question is what to cook,' said Lesley, raising Hilary's hopes that she had more practical priorities. She opened the fridge, and sighed with irritation. 'There's absolutely *nothing* here that Tobias is going to be able to eat. I suppose these fish things might do at a pinch, but they're full of colouring...'

'I don't think we can feed everyone on fish fingers!' said Hilary.

'No, there wouldn't be enough.' Lesley hastily snatched the packet and clutched it to her. 'And he's got some frozen peas. Thank goodness...'

'Now, I'm going to make the table look absolutely beautiful!' declared Julia, as if it were a favour, and disappeared with an armful of draperies. Lesley snorted, and began to search William's cupboards for a saucepan, tutting at what she found.

Hilary, realising that it was going to be left to her, mentally began to count up the number of people in the house who might be expected to want dinner, and groaned aloud.

'What on earth are we going to give them all? Loaves and fishes?'

'No, Tobias needs those, I told you.' One would like to think Lesley was being funny, but Hilary knew better. Had *she* been so one-track minded when her own child was small? It was hard to believe... Daniel! God, he would be halfway up a mountain by now. Would anyone have William's number, if there had been an accident? Was there any point in trying to reach his mobile on top of a Cairngorm? This was the age when one really worried about them – no longer under one's constant eye, still young enough to seek danger, and too old to be ordered not to.

'Margery isn't seriously expecting us to get a meal for everybody, is she?' Lesley was suddenly back on the planet. 'I don't know what with. We can hardly start on the turkey!'

'William's got plenty of potatoes,' Hilary had discovered, 'and some onions, and lots of that nice strong cheddar. What about a cheesy potato pie?' It wasn't exactly Christmas fare, but Hilary had always found it a useful dish when a horde of Daniel's hungry friends descended unexpectedly. She only wished he was here to eat it now.

'Yes, that sounds fine,' said Lesley, not in the least interested so long as it didn't involve fish fingers.

'Lovely, darling,' said Julia, when Hilary had taken the trouble to go next door and ask her. 'Do you think the big candelabra looks best here on the sideboard? We could do with some holly.'

There didn't seem much point in asking for help peeling the potatoes.

'Oh, that's a good idea!' said Lesley a few minutes later, turning from the grill to see Hilary at work surrounded by bowls and mounds of peel on a corner of the kitchen table. 'If you do a couple extra, Tobias can have mashed potato with his fish fingers.'

'He could have had some of this with the rest of us,' said Hilary.

'Oh no, I don't think so… What is it you're making?'

'Cheesy potato pie. It's Daniel's favourite.'

Lesley shook her head. 'No, Tobias has never had that. He doesn't like things he hasn't tried before.'

'Oh dear, how very inconvenient,' said Hilary, trying not to sound too sarcastic.

'We don't find convenience an issue, when it comes to bringing up a child.'

No, one couldn't accuse Lesley of that. Hilary watched as she prodded the fish fingers with the tip of her own, cut one in half to make quite sure it was cooked, and turned them carefully onto a plate. Now she was bending down to … oh hell!

'Hang on, Lesley – you can't use the oven. We'll need it for the pie.'

'Oh … but I need to keep Tobias's meal warm until he's finished his bath.'

'Yes, but the rest of us have got to eat too!'

Lesley stared at her, struggling with the concept that the requirements of her child might not take first priority in this household.

'Your thing isn't nearly ready,' she concluded at last, pointing to the pile of potatoes yet to be peeled. 'It'll take you ages to do the rest of those, and I'll have finished with the oven by then.'

Julia swept in at that moment with an armful of holly. 'Look at all this? Isn't it lovely? I remembered the tree from when we were children, and it's twice as big now. What a shame that good berries are supposed to mean a hard winter! Sorry, Hilary darling, but I'll just have to have the big table. You don't mind moving your stuff, do you? I can see that you're making us something wonderful. Aren't you lucky to be able to cook!'

Hilary resisted the temptation to pick up the bowl of potato peelings and add them to Julia's holly arrangement with some considerable force.

🌲 🌲 🌲

Having disposed the sexes to her satisfaction, Margery had gone for a rest, leaving the men in uncomfortable non-camaraderie in the sitting room. William was damned if he was going to make polite conversation to Oliver, whom he didn't know, or Tony and Leo, whom he disliked, and he sat down and picked up the paper. Leo coughed at his choice of reading material and tried to include the others in a superior grimace, but Oliver was busy tickling the cat, and Tony had obviously been about to grab the *Daily Express* himself.

Stephen came in, a little cleaner but no better tempered, having been forced to wash in the downstairs cloakroom. 'You'd think a house the size of this would run to more than one bathroom, or at least a basin in one's bedroom... Oh – Leo!' he broke off with a surprised frown. 'What on earth are *you* doing here?'

'Everyone asks me that!' complained Leo. 'I don't know why I *shouldn't* come to Haseley for Christmas – everybody else has!'

'Yes, well. We were rather hoping for a quiet family time.'

'I *am* family,' objected Leo. 'And I've as much right to visit the family home as you, or Tony, or...' His sweeping hand had reached Oliver, and dropped in embarrassment.'Let alone all these nannies and people,' he finished lamely.

'I'd hardly call Haseley House your family home,' said Stephen drily, frowning at the cat fur covering the only remaining chair. 'You and Ben were brought up in Highgate, I seem to remember! Julia and I are the only people who can rightfully call Haseley home.'

William looked up from his paper.

'Apart from Dad, of course,' Stephen added hastily. 'Oh dear, is that a flea?'

'Talking of homes,' Tony had picked up one of the brochures from the table and was leafing through it. 'There's some real belters in here! Right up your street, I should imagine, Oliver, a period piece like this.' He tapped the page.

Oliver, who couldn't possibly see from there, gave a polite smile of assent.

'Sweeping lawns, splendid architecture – just the sort of stately pile we could all fancy passing our declining years in.'

'Yes, indeed!' Stephen leant forward eagerly. 'Ideal, I might say, for someone who was no longer entirely capable of looking after himself, but who still wanted the prestige of a larger home.'

'Perfect for elderly snobs.' Leo's sarcasm went unheeded.

'…I really think you should have a proper look at these, Father.'

'Yes, William, perhaps you should…' Tony laid the page across his paper, an irritating replacement for the article he was immersed in comparing different brands of leg wax. 'Everyone in this family would want to be sure that *you're* not going to be taken in.'

'I beg your pardon?' Stephen stared at him.

'We all know what those places are really like, of course,' Tony went on blithely. 'Most of these so called "retirement homes" are just an excuse to house people in appalling conditions while charging them through the roof.'

'Oh, I hardly think so…'

'It's all over the media. You can't open a paper or turn the TV on without seeing another old people's outfit exposed as a gang of crooks, out to make a fast buck. As well some of us know the score – eh, Leo?' He winked at his cousin, who gave a start of surprise, and murmured uncertainly, unsure which way to jump in an argument which meant supporting either Tony or Stephen.

William, undoubtedly the greatest media devotee among them, dropped the brochure in the basket beside him and went back to his article.

Scratch, deciding it was his social duty to fill an awkward silence, jumped up onto the bureau and proceeded to entertain the company with an attempt to get round the room without touching the floor. 'Can't you stop him?'

moaned Stephen, as his claws skidded on the polished surface. 'That's a valuable piece of furniture!'

Leo cringed as he used the back of his chair as a springboard, inches from his head, and there was a hiss of intaken breath as he picked his way through the ornaments on the mantelpiece. Only William was unfazed, having seen this trick before.

The gap across the doorway was the awkward bit. Oliver gave vent to a 'Bravo!' as he made it with a carefully judged leap from the bookcase to the piano. A back leg caught the music stand as he descended, but it was an otherwise faultless performance, fully deserving of the cheers and groans which greeted his arrival back on *terra firma*. With the attention still on him, he chose the moment to demand exit from the stage. Oliver obliged by opening the door, and slipped out at the same time.

♣ ♣ ♣

'Nice guy,' said Tony, with a nod towards the door.

'Yes, he seems reasonably intelligent,' conceded Stephen.

William snorted, not so much in condemnation of Oliver Leafield, but aware that neither of them had exchanged more than a word with the man.

'It depends how you measure intelligence, doesn't it?' said Leo significantly, but no one obliged by asking what he meant.

'I wonder what he's making of Haseley,' Stephen went on. 'It's a great pity the house has been allowed to fall into such a state! I'm sure you could afford to keep it in better

114

repair, Father, if you only made the effort ... Still, I imagine a professional will be used to seeing past that kind of thing.'

'A professional!' Leo infused the word with irony. 'Yes, I suppose it's a profession of sorts. On the other hand, one *might* be tempted to call someone who enjoys other people's hospitality on no very good pretext a parasite.'

'A *parasite*, Leo? Yes, I suppose one might,' said Tony, winking at William in a way that annoyed him intensely.

'Nonsense!' said Stephen, having missed the point to this. 'The man's obviously a busy academic. It was very good of him to make time to visit Haseley, especially at this season ... I imagine it reflects the high standing in which the house is held in architectural circles,' he added with a hint of self-satisfaction.

'Let's hope he writes an article that sends its value rocketing, then,' said Tony, 'and we'll forgive him any other little foibles... What about you, William?' he went on, ignoring Stephen's puzzled frown. 'What did you think of Oliver Leafield?'

William considered the matter. He'd been predisposed to take against a man who'd been invited to his home against his will in order to criticise it. But in the event, Oliver hadn't turned out to be the male version of Margery he'd imagined. All his comments about the house had been enthusiastic, and he'd made no attempt to pressurise William into making unnecessary repairs or selling up. What was more, he was one of the few people to appreciate his cat, and one of the even fewer that Scratch was prepared to unbend to. Yes, William gave a little nod of approval. 'He was all right.'

'I'm glad you liked him,' said Tony, with a gleam that suggested he was enjoying a private joke.

'Why shouldn't I?' said William crossly.

'You're not bothered by his … er … supposed proclivities, then?'

To be honest, William had forgotten all about them – but they could be dismissed at once with the rest of his preconceptions. There was nothing pansy about Oliver Leafield.

'What do you mean?' Stephen and Leo both exclaimed sharply.

'Oh…!' Tony affected surprise at getting the reaction he'd no doubt intended. 'Well … I don't know quite how to put this, but rumour has it that our friend Oliver … um … bats for the other side, so to speak.'

'Huh! Gay, is he? I might have known.' The contempt in Leo's voice barely hid his delight at finding something to place to Oliver's supposed discredit.

'Well I don't know why that should count against him!' said Stephen, with a glance of dislike at his cousin. 'We are supposed to live in a tolerant society, after all.'

'Oh yes, quite,' said Tony, taking the opportunity to raise his eyes despairingly in Leo's direction himself. 'Some of us, anyway! Nothing to sneer at, nowadays. It's a biological thing, isn't it? People can't help the way they're bent.'

'I'm not saying that!' Leo realised he had gone off line, and was struggling to get back on course. 'Good heavens, as a creative artist, I'm the *last* person to indulge in small-minded bigotry.' He glared at the rest of them, daring them to disagree. 'I merely meant that Leafield is typical of a certain kind of man…' He tailed off, quite unable to find any way of following this through.

'Well I'm sure we've nothing to worry about where Oliver is concerned,' said Tony. 'They're not all paedophiles, are they? Despite what one hears?'

'Of course not,' said Stephen with some irritation. 'Many of my academic colleagues are … er … bachelors in that way, and most eminent men.'

'And it's good that William feels able to welcome someone like that into his home without prejudice.' Tony turned to him, with an approving smile. 'It must be reassuring for the guy that you trust him around your grandchildren.'

'Tobias, you mean?' said Stephen sharply.

'Well, he's not likely to go after Posy – given his preferences!' said Tony. 'Why – do you think Tobias could be in any danger?'

🌲 🌲 🌲

'Scar-ee!!' said Shelley. It seemed to Frances a fair summing up of the bathroom at Haseley House.

Tobias, who had run in with Posy, now hung back, cowed by the sudden echoes of their voices against the cavernous ceiling. He eyed the massive bath, the huge taps and a cylinder instead of a bathplug, its claw feet set on a chequered stone floor which made no concessions to bare feet.

'I don't wa-ant to!' His cry resounded back to them, assuming the horrifying dimensions of a prisoner condemned to the torture chamber.

'Oh come on, Tobias,' Frances tried to pull herself together. 'Posy's going to have a go in Grandpa's big bath, aren't you, Posy? ... Let's see if this funny plug thing works.'

Warily she stepped forward and found out how to lower the porcelain cylinder so it did indeed stop the plughole. Posy broke her stunned trance to run up and help by turning the hot tap on full force. No steam rose from the water. Frances put her hand under the flow and felt it slowly change from icy cold to lukewarm.

'That's as good as it's going to get,' she concluded. 'Better make it a lick and a promise tonight. We don't want you catching pneumonia.'

'Trendy now, these old-fashioned bathrooms,' observed Shelley, looking round the room more kindly. 'Which bit's the shower, do you think?'

'I don't expect William's got one,' said Frances, who was trying to encourage Tobias out of his clothes. Posy had already got rid of hers and was dancing up and down on them in lieu of a bath mat.

'That's a bugger. Tony always likes to strip off for a shower before bed,' said Shelley, with a reminiscent expression that made Frances wonder how she knew.

'*I* want a shower!' announced Posy.

'Well you ain't,' said her nanny. 'Get in that bath with Tobias before I smack your bum!'

Posy yelped and scrambled over the side into the bath, where Tobias was already sitting gingerly. 'It's frigging cold,' she declared.

Shelley didn't seem to have heard, and Frances thought it best to ignore the word, rather than draw Tobias's attention to it. She found some soap and his flannel, but it was snatched out of her hand.

'*I'm* going to wash Tobias,' said Posy, and began scrubbing at her cousin as if he was a bad stain on a favourite dress.

'No, that's a bit rough...' Frances rescued him, and distracted Posy by persuading her to attend to her own grubby knees. When had the child last had a bath?

Shelley was more interested in redesigning William's washing arrangements. 'Don't suppose there's a jacuzzi either. Waste, really, when he's got all this room. Tone and Julia were going to put one in last year, but then the money thing happened ... Oi, Posy! You'd better come out of there, if you're just going to splash about!'

'When I grow up I'm going to have a swimming pool with bubbles in it,' she told them, 'and a big pink car, and a pony like my friend Becky.'

'Better find yourself a rich bloke like Becky's dad then!' Shelley winked at Frances. 'Where's the old man keep his towels?'

'This looks like the airing cupboard.' The pile of linen inside didn't seem to have been disturbed for years. She pulled out a couple of thinning, grey-white towels, handed one to Shelley and wrapped Tobias in the other.

He stood shivering on the bare floor. 'It's friggin' cold,' he said.

Chapter Nine

At least in a house this size, there was always somewhere else to go. Hilary had found herself a retreat and settled down again, not altogether sorry to have escaped the frenetic atmosphere in the kitchen.

The old butler's pantry had a large stone sink, and smelled faintly of the contents of the miscellaneous jam jars and bottles of wine that William kept stored on its shelves. Stephen and Lesley would no doubt have it converted into some grim utility room, if and when they moved in ... What a waste of a wonderful house like this, with its secret nooks and atmospheric crannies, to treat it as mere bricks and mortar, instead of the historical entity it had matured into over the years! Despite herself, Hilary couldn't help returning to Leo's speculations. *Was* William really intending to leave his home to his unbeloved son and daughter-in-law? More likely he just hadn't pushed himself to thinking about the matter, and hadn't made a will at all. Haseley would go to Stephen and Lesley by default. But just supposing...? No, better not to imagine what she herself might do with this house, or let Leo's insidious poison seep even into her daydreams.

She jumped guiltily nevertheless when there was a knock at the pantry door. To her surprise, Oliver Leafield came in.

'Do you need any help?'

'Oh! Er ... yes, thank you. That would be marvellous.'

She'd spoken without thinking. What could an eminent architectural historian possibly be given to do in the role of kitchen maid? He was only being polite, and she should have politely refused his offer, not fallen on his neck with gratitude.

'You seem to be getting on pretty well with the potatoes,' he said, before she could think of a way of retracting. 'Shall I start on these onions? I presume you want them all peeled and chopped.'

'Oh yes – if you're sure you don't mind ... I've somehow become solely responsible for feeding the five thousand, and panic's beginning to set in.'

Oliver had already picked up the knife, and was divesting an onion of its skin with startling swiftness. She watched him chop it into neat slices as rapidly as a machine, and start on the next one. 'Blimey! You've done that before.'

He looked up and smiled. 'Cooking's one of my hobbies.'

'I wish it was one of mine,' Hilary sighed.

'I expect you do more interesting things with your time.'

Did she? Hilary thought about it. The trouble with not very well paid freelance work was that you had to keep at it most of the day. By the time she'd tossed the last red-pencilled manuscript aside, all her brain was fit for was mindless television. Better not admit this to a man who doubtless frequented art galleries and concerts, when he wasn't writing articles for *Country Life* or cooking.

'Not at all. It must be lovely to be able to make nice meals for your family.'

'Well, I live on my own, so it's more for friends really.'

Oh Lord, had he thought she was fishing? Of course Oliver couldn't be married, if he'd been happy to come to Haseley for Christmas.

'I've got a son,' said Hilary, as if it absolved her from being interested. 'I'm sure Daniel would have loved me to be a domestic goddess when he was growing up ... He's climbing in Scotland at the moment.'

'And you're worried about him.' Oliver looked at her with a sympathy that made her realise how much her face must have given away.

'Yes I am a bit ... I know it's silly. He's a man now, and I've got to learn to let go.'

'It must be hard, though, when you've already lost your husband.'

So he knew about Ben ... shit! She didn't want him to see her as a pathetic widow, neurotically clinging to her grown-up son to give her life meaning.

'I sure Daniel will be fine. Anyway, I'm going to stop worrying about what he's up to, and just enjoy Christmas,' she lied. 'Thanks for doing those. I expect I can manage now, if you want to go back to the sitting room.'

'Oh, please – no! Do let me grate the cheese.'

Hilary giggled at his desperate face. 'Is it awful in there?'

'You wouldn't believe!' he grimaced. 'Not to speak ill of your relatives, but I got the impression everyone in that room had it in for everybody else, and was determined to make them feel as uncomfortable as possible. I had to duck several tim es to avoid getting caught in the crossfire.'

'Oh dear! Tony and Stephen don't really get on and they do tend to snipe at each other, and of course William has no time for either of them,' Hilary explained.

'And as for your friend – Leo, is it? He seems to hate everyone indiscriminately.'

'He's not my friend,' she said quickly. 'I just had a lift in his car... Yes, Leo despises humanity in general, I'm afraid.'

'An interesting stance for a writer,' he observed. 'Anyway, it was all a bit much, and we made our escape.'

'We?' Hilary was puzzled.

'Me and the cat.' He described the high-wire performance Scratch had treated them to, making her laugh.

'So what are your plans for dessert tonight?' he asked when he'd dealt with the cheese, after pausing to admire the antiquity of William's grater.

'Dessert? Oh, I don't know,' Hilary shrugged. 'We could open some tins of fruit.'

'Oh, I think we can do better than that... Would there be eggs?'

'Yes, dozens of them.' What William *did* decide to stock, he kept in plentiful supply, she'd noticed.

'And flour?'

'We'd better look.'

They went back into the kitchen, where Lesley, still guarding the oven, gave a nervous look over her shoulder.

There was flour next to a tin of mustard powder and some Worcester sauce. William was obviously partial to Welsh rarebit.

'Better taste it,' said Oliver, bravely sticking a finger in the packet and licking it. 'Yes, that's fine … and I presume he's got butter and sugar.'

'Pancakes?' Hilary was trying to guess what he had in mind.

'Actually, I was thinking profiteroles.'

'Good God!' She and Lesley gaped at each other. 'Do you know how to make them?'

'It's not very difficult.'

'You'll need chocolate, won't you, for the sauce?' Lesley began to scan the shelves herself.

'Drinking chocolate … that'll do at a pinch.' Oliver pulled it out. 'Let's see if he's got a baking tray. The secret is to run it under cold water first, and to have the oven really hot. Can we turn it up a bit, do you think?'

'Oh, of course!' Lesley leapt to obey. 'I'll take out these fish fingers.'

🌲 🌲 🌲

Frances and Shelley brought the children downstairs, to find the kitchen a hive of culinary activity. Hilary was at the table, scattering grated cheese over a huge potato pie, with Lesley beside her decanting things from a baking tray onto a plate. Scratch was engaged in the task of clearing some stray curls of cheese from the floor, while Oliver stirred an exotic-smelling pan on the stove.

'Hello, darling? Did you have a nice bath?'

'No, it was fri…'

'The water wasn't very hot, I'm afraid,' Frances put in quickly. 'But we've got some nice warm clothes on now.'

'We' couldn't be said to include Posy, who had refused to don anything but a skimpy T-shirt and some flip-flops. 'Dressing gown? That's not something kids wear, is it?' had been Shelley's response when Frances had suggested that this might not be adequate for the rigours of Haseley House. 'And she grew out of her slippers years ago!' They might have been talking about rompers.

'Would you like some nice fish fingers for your supper?' Lesley asked her son. 'Mummy's got them all ready here, with some mashy potato.'

'I don't know.' Tobias wasn't going to make it as easy as that. He surveyed the kitchen to see what else might be on offer. 'What are those round things?'

'They're profiteroles, darling. I'm not sure you like them.'

'Oh, I think he might!' said Hilary, clearly irritated by this pre-closing of doors. 'Oliver's made them specially for our pudding,' she explained to Tobias. 'They're going to have chocolate sauce on and cream in the middle – if we can find it. Why don't you try one?'

'*I'm* going to have lots and lots.' declared Posy. She bounced up to investigate the pan, rubbing herself sinuously against Oliver at the same time.

'You'll go pop then, and we'll have to scrape your insides off the walls!' Shelley told her, making Tobias giggle and Lesley frown.

'Are they going to eat in here?' asked Frances, looking doubtfully at the cluttered table, and wondering if she should start trying to make some space.

'Good lord, no!' said Lesley. 'Julia's set the table in the dining room. You can take these in, if you like.' She handed her Tobias's plate of fish fingers, peas and mashed potato, a neat meal for one. Presumably some other provision was being made for Posy – and the rest of them, come to that.

The dining room looked stunning. Julia was putting the finishing touches to a scene that wouldn't have been out of place illustrating Christmas in one of those 'perfect home' magazines. Every available surface was decorated with candles, sprigs of berry-laden holly and artistic trails of ivy. At the table, each place was set to perfection, with matching china, linen table napkins, rows of silver cutlery and bone-handled knives, and an intricate centrepiece had been concocted out of pine cones and ribbons and gold-painted leaves – Julia must have brought a spray-can with her.

She turned when she heard Frances's gasp of admiration, and pointed gleefully to the Christmas crackers she was laying beside each plate. 'Aren't these fabulous? We got them in this gorgeous little shop in Wimbledon – you'd love it! …Don't worry, there are plenty more for Christmas Day.'

Worry about the supply of crackers wasn't chief among Frances's concerns at the moment. She hovered uncertainly with Tobias's fish fingers, reluctant to introduce such a prosaic note onto this splendid table.

'What have you got there? Your supper?' Julia enquired kindly.

'No, it's Tobias's. I was just wondering where to put it. Have you set him anywhere particular?'

'Oh, the littlies won't want to eat in here with us old grown-ups!' Julia assured her. 'Posy won't want more than a biscuit anyway. She never does.'

'It's just that there isn't room at the kitchen table, and Mrs Shirburn thought…'

'Oh dear, trust Lesley!' Julia made a comic face at Frances. 'Well there isn't room at this one, either, I'm afraid. I've only just managed to fit everybody round we're such an awful crowd!'

The news was not received well in the kitchen.

'And whose fault is that? Nobody *asked* her to bring their mob down to Haseley!' said Lesley, perhaps forgetting that two of the Britwell contingent were among her audience. 'I really don't see why Tobias should be excluded from his own family dining table, as if he were some kind of second-class citizen!'

'Perhaps we could make a bit of room at this corner,' suggested Frances, aware that Tobias's meal was getting cold.

'No of course we can't!' snapped Lesley. 'Not with all this cooking stuff around. It's unhygienic.'

Frances saw Hilary and Oliver exchange a glance of wordless amusement, and was a little puzzled. It wasn't that Lesley's remark hadn't been amusingly silly, but she'd been under the impression that the two of them had only just met, and here they were looking as if they'd known each other for years.

'Sorry about the mess. We'll clear some of it away.' Oliver turned off his pan and came over.

'No, no!' Lesley flapped an embarrassed hand. 'It's *extremely* good of you to undertake the cooking. We're all most grateful.'

'Oh, I'm only the under-chef,' Oliver protested at once. 'It's Hilary you need to thank.'

Lesley didn't waste more than a nod in that direction. She had opened her mouth to resume the debate, when Stephen came in, and hovered near the door looking anxious.

'Could I have a word with you, Lesley, do you think? ...In the dining room.'

'Oh ... um ... yes.' She followed him out.

'Wonder what's got his pants in a twist?' Shelley expressed the thoughts of all of them. 'Come on, Tobe. You going to eat them fish fingers before the cat gets them, or what?'

'Can I have one?' asked Posy. 'I'm *starving*!'

'You can have some of this pie as soon as it's hot,' said Hilary, who was putting it in the oven. 'But I don't know where you're going to sit. Is there really no room next door?' she asked Frances.

'I'm afraid not. Actually I could only see eight chairs.'

'So where are me and you supposed to eat?' Shelley, like her, had realised this barely covered the remaining adults.

Oliver looked across at Hilary, a questioning gleam in his eye.

'Oh yes!' she exclaimed. 'There's a table in there ... come on, guys. Bring your plate, Tobias. Oliver and I have got a secret hideaway, but we'll let you use it as a dining room.'

'Is it the china cupboard?' asked Tobias, obediently picking up the plate.

'No – a bit bigger than that, so you can all sit down. It's called the butler's pantry.'

'The butler used to keep his underclothes there,' Oliver told them as they followed her out, but only Frances grinned.

Lesley met them in the passage. 'Where are you taking Tobias?' she demanded sharply, apparently addressing Oliver.

Frances explained, and waited for her to find some reason to veto it. But to her surprise, having ascertained that only the nannies would be present, Lesley now seemed to like the idea of the children being separated from the other adults. She shooed Oliver away almost rudely when he offered to fetch more chairs, hustled the rest of them into the pantry and shut the door behind her.

🎄 🎄 🎄

Only one of William's irritating visitors now remained in the sitting room. Stephen, having grown increasingly fidgety, had eventually given in and left, muttering something about having 'a quiet word' with Lesley. Tony, not wanting to miss the fun, had made the excuse of seeing whether Julia needed any help. But the most irritating person of all seemed determined to stay and give William unwanted company. He buried his head in his paper, hoping Leo would get bored and go away.

'So, what has the *Express* got to tell us about the world?'

William hadn't failed to notice the slight ironic emphasis on the name of his newspaper. He gave a non-committal grunt, but unfortunately this was enough conversational interchange for Leo.

'You don't find their political comment a trifle lacking in impartiality, shall we say?'

William wouldn't say anything on a subject in which he had no interest at all.

'Myself, I prefer to stick to the jolly old *Grauniad*.' This must be some kind of joke, by the way he tittered, but it was lost on William. 'You would have been interested to read an article in there the other day about author-funded publishing…'

William doubted it. In fact, by the time Leo had imparted every detail, he was quite sure he wouldn't. He abandoned his paper, and put the TV on, turning the sound up a little higher than even he usually had it.

'You don't really want to watch *that* rubbish, do you?' William had found one of those rather amusing quizzes. 'The News is on Channel 4 now.' Leo had to shout to make himself heard. 'If you press the button saying '4' on the remote…' He came over, as if to do so. William swept it out of his reach.

'I know how to work my television, thank you very much.'

'Pity you don't know where the volume control is,' Leo muttered, sitting down again.

William proved him wrong, by turning it up a little more.

After a while Leo stood up and began to pace the room. 'It's a sad reflection on modern life the way technology has killed conversation.' William didn't respond. 'I said, it's a sad reflection on modern life...' he began to repeat more loudly. 'Oh, never mind! Perhaps I'll go into the study. One might get a bit of peace in there.'

William waited till he heard the door close, then turned the TV back down to a reasonable level.

♣ ♣ ♣

Hilary, too, had been surprised that Lesley hadn't put up any opposition to the idea of the children eating in the pantry. She left her settling them down at the table, and went to see how the pie was doing.

Oliver smiled as she came into the kitchen. 'I think this is nearly hot actually. Shall we put some in a separate bowl for the nursery contingent? You'd better take it in though. I don't seem to be very popular in there.'

'Oh don't be silly!' Hilary began to protest. But it was true. Lesley *had* been acting rather strangely. One minute she'd been all over their distinguished visitor; the next she seemed to be anxious to keep him at more than arm's length. Hilary was sure that she and Stephen had now realised how advantageous a flattering article might be to whoever inherited Haseley House, and had resolved to be charming to Oliver. So why, so soon after her 'word' with Stephen, had Lesley virtually thrown him out of the pantry?

'Ah! I get it.'

'What?' Oliver was spooning potato pie into a dish.

'I've suddenly realised why Lesley's so keen to keep you out of there.'

'Well, I'd love to know.'

But before she could get a chance to tell him her theory, Stephen came in with Julia and Tony.

'We must have wine,' Julia was saying, 'and I know Daddy'll have nothing decent in ... Oliver, darling, I bet you're an expert, aren't you? Why don't you and Stephen pop down to the pub in the village and see what you can lay your hands on?'

Hilary wasn't surprised to see Stephen's mouth drop in dismay. She was sure he knew nothing about wine. Why send him?

'We're just about to serve dinner,' she warned Julia. 'If you and Tony want to zip down to the village…'

'No, we can't go. We're busy doing the table ... You don't mind, do you, Oliver? Stephen knows where the pub is. He'll hold your hand.'

'Um – I'm actually in the middle of helping Hilary,' said Oliver, with an eye on Stephen, who looked as if someone had just despatched him to Antarctica without an overcoat.

'Yes, we can't do without the pastry chef,' said Hilary firmly. 'And I really don't think there's time for anyone to start disappearing now.' Why did Julia always make these elaborately inconvenient plans?

'What's all this?' Lesley came in. 'I thought we were about to have dinner.'

'Julia wants me to go down to the village and buy wine,' Stephen had found his voice at last, '…With Oliver.'

'What? No, of course you can't go!' Lesley glared at poor Oliver as if it was his fault. 'We don't need wine. There's plenty of fruit juice.'

'It's not quite the same.' Tony was trying to engage Hilary in a conspiratorial glance, but she wasn't having it.

'I bet you'll find William's got wine anyway,' she said. 'Why don't you have a look in the pantry, Oliver? There are all kinds of bottles in there.'

'Oh no, I'll go!' said Lesley at once, satisfyingly confirming Hilary's suspicions. Lesley clearly didn't want the architectural expert to get too good a look at the butler's pantry, with that nasty patch of damp behind the door.

🎄 🎄 🎄

William wasn't left in peace for long. Margery emerged from her nap, fully refreshed and keen to take issue with him about the state of the upstairs rooms. She wasn't as easily dispatched as Leo.

'Turn that thing off! It's very rude to watch TV when you've got visitors.' She snatched the remote and did it for him. 'No, don't pick up the paper! Listen to me. You've got to get in a good firm of builders – one of these specialists that are used to dealing with broken-down old houses. Oliver probably knows somebody. It won't cost you more than twenty or thirty grand, and it'll be money well spent...'

She carried on remorselessly, brushing aside any of William's objections with a peremptory 'Rubbish!' There was nothing to be done. He knew as well as anybody that once his sister was fired up, one had little option but to wait until she ran out of steam.

But well before that happened, rescue came in the form of Julia, announcing that dinner was ready.

'Oh bother!' said the woman who had been so insistent on its preparation. 'We can't come now. William and I are busy talking.'

'It'll get cold if you don't. Come and finish your talk in the dining room.'

'Oh all right.' Margery stood up to obey. '...If you really think the building work would be too disruptive, you'd better book into a hotel for a month or two.'

But William didn't want to hear the rest of Margery's plans for his discomfort, or eat a meal he didn't need. He settled down, and reached for the remote control.

'Buck up, William, I'm holding the door!'

'You go ahead. I've had supper already.'

'Oh no, Daddy, you've got to have dinner with us!' pleaded Julia. 'Hilary will be so hurt if you don't. She's cooked it specially.'

'Of course you must come and show your face! Good heavens...' Margery hurried across to chivvy him out of his seat. 'What are your guests going to think, if you don't bother to turn up to your own dinner party?'

William scowled when he saw the way that his dining room had been taken over by the Spirit of Christmas Present. It wasn't a room he used much, but he still didn't like to see it decorated with all those silly painted leaves and things. And there was a perfectly good electric light, so why fill the place with candles? ...Crackers, though. William had a bit of a weakness for crackers.

134

The room was already crowded with people, hovering uncertainly behind the chairs, waiting to be told where to go. William was about to take his place at the head of the table, but Julia touched his arm.

'I'm afraid Hilary and Oliver rather seem to have taken over tonight,' she murmured apologetically, 'so they'll have to sit at either end and play host. It means you and Aunt Margery being squashed up in the middle, unfortunately, but what else can one do?'

William didn't quite see her logic. Being a thin person, he wasn't particularly bothered by the lack of elbow room, though he would have preferred not to be seated next to Lesley. But Margery was plumper, and didn't look at all pleased to find herself jammed between Stephen and Tony. Why couldn't Julia have put her on the outside in Stephen's place? And wait a minute … William grinned to himself. One member of the family was missing altogether!

Chapter Ten

'No, of course you must sit there! You're in charge tonight.'

Hilary was absolutely horrified. She'd brought the pie in, to find everyone else squashed up along the sides of the table, leaving a huge empty space at either end. Julia was patting the place beside her determinedly.

'Nonsense! We're only the cooks.' Hilary exchanged a desperate glance with Oliver, who was following with warm plates. 'There's no need for us to sit anywhere special. I really think William and Margery should be at the head…'

But Julia wouldn't have it. 'No, you're the stars of the evening, cobbling together a meal for all us dreadful people! You must sit here and be Mother.' She pulled Hilary down onto the chair. 'Pass the plates up, Oliver darling.'

He obeyed and sat down at the far end of the table, looking equally embarrassed, especially when both Lesley and Stephen tried to shift away, giving him even more room.

It was almost as if Julia had calculated her seating arrangements to give maximum annoyance, Hilary thought. Why put Margery between Stephen and Tony, two people she couldn't stand, instead of next to her friend Oliver?

Lesley was all but sitting on William's lap now – and what was he doing in here anyway, adding to the crowd in the dining room, when he'd so firmly told them he'd already had his supper? She herself had been placed as far as possible from the person she would have chosen to be near, but at least Julia hadn't seated her next to Leo… Come to think of it, where *was* Leo?

'Isn't this lovely?' said Julia brightly. 'A proper family meal! Perhaps we ought to say grace or something first, as it's Christmas.'

Everyone stared at her in consternation, then glanced round covertly at their neighbours to see who had religious inclinations.

'Shame to let this get cold,' said Hilary, who was quite sure none of them had, least of all Julia. She picked up a serving spoon.

'Yum yum!' said Tony. 'What's it going to be, I wonder?'

'It looks wonderful!' Julia eyed the dish dubiously. 'Now you mustn't worry a bit,' she assured Hilary in a confidentially lowered tone. 'We all know you've done your best, and no one's going to blame you if you haven't been able to manage anything very nice.'

Hilary wanted to say that on the contrary, her cheesy potato pie was delicious as well as nourishing, and if Julia had any complaints she could have helped with the cooking, instead of buggering about with decorations! But she decided to let the pie speak for itself.

'Mm, this really *is* yummy!' Tony's surprise gave him away.

'Very decent,' Margery paused in some argument she was having with William to acknowledge.

'Superb!' Oliver raised a forkful in salute.

'I think perhaps Tobias might have liked this after all.' The final accolade.

'Wonderful, darling! It's not as if we were expecting high-class French cuisine, after all.'

🌲 🌲 🌲

Frances could have confirmed Lesley's notion. She'd put a spoonful of the pie on Tobias's plate when she doled it out to Posy, and after a tentative poke round, he'd finished it and demanded more. Luckily Hilary had been generous with their share. They were also the first to sample Oliver's profiteroles, and could have informed the dining room party that they were in for a treat.

'Cor, I'm busting!' Shelley announced, pushing away the remains of a big bowlful. 'You're going to have to carry me up them stairs, Pose.'

'I'm too full as well,' giggled Posy. 'And so's Tobias. You'll have to carry us all, Nanny Frances!'

'No way – not with all those profiteroles inside you! I might have managed otherwise… Do you think we should clear this up a bit?' she added to Shelley.

'Nah! We're not paid to skivvy. He's got somebody comes in, hasn't he?'

Frances could imagine the forthright Mrs Arncott's reaction to finding a load of dirty plates in the pantry next morning – if she ever did find them.

'Perhaps we'd better take things through anyway… Come on, kids. Pile the plates up.'

The children looked at her in bemusement, but soon got the idea of this new game of clearing away after a meal. Even Shelley helped by carrying the profiterole dish into the kitchen.

They caught out Scratch.

He too had given the menu his warm approval. Oliver had put the cream carton down for him, and when he'd disposed of every drop he could reach without jamming his nose in the bottom, he'd leapt onto the draining board and found the bowl Hilary had used to mix in the cheese. There was an embarrassed clatter as he swiftly regained the floor, and began to wash as if he'd been there all the time.

'I did see you,' Frances told him, wondering what Lesley would say about hygiene.

'Where's the dishwasher?' said Shelley, opening and shutting cupboards with increasing puzzlement.

'Same place as the shower,' Frances grinned.

'What? … Oh bleedin' hell! He hasn't even got a dishwasher.' Shelley shook a despairing head.

Frances was prepared for trouble getting Tobias to settle down in a strange room in the company of his boisterous cousin, with his mother out of reach. She made sure a drink came up with them, and encouraged the children to race each other up the stairs and see who could get into bed fastest. They were both under the covers when she and Shelley arrived, Posy shrieking her triumph. But Tobias looked at Frances doubtfully and started to climb out again.

'I need a drink … Oh, you've got one.' He took two mouthfuls and put it down again. 'I think I need a wee.'

'You *can't* do! You just went to the loo downstairs,' Posy reminded him.

'Try to snuggle down now, Tobias. Look, Posy's nearly asleep.'

'No, I'm not,' said his unhelpful cousin, sitting up and wriggling out of the covers to prove it.

'Get back in there this minute!' The bellow startled them all. 'You too, Tobias. There are big green monsters under them beds, and they'll grab any feet they find on the floor. There's nothing they like better than kids' juicy little toes for their supper … Yes, better keep them under the covers as well.'

Frances gasped in horror – but she had to admit it worked like a charm. Posy's giggles suggested that she was used to her nanny's flights of fancy, and Tobias took his cue and joined in. Both sets of feet remained firmly under the bedclothes though.

'Right then,' Shelley built on the ground gained, 'this light's going off in a minute. France and me are going downstairs for some peace. We don't want to hear no more talking – and *certainly* no laughing…'

'Aren't I going to have a story?' Tobias looked at Frances pathetically.

'He usually does,' she told Shelley. 'You go down, if you want. I'll read them a quick one.' She searched for the book.

'I can read,' Posy reminded them.

'Well of course you can – big girl like you!' said Shelley. 'Tell you what, you can read Tobias his bedtime story. Save us the trouble.'

'Oh yes, *I'm* going to read it!' Posy snatched the book out of her hand and began to ruffle through the pages. 'Here's one about a wicked goblin. I'll read that one.'

Frances looked to see how Tobias was taking this, but he seemed quite content with the turn of events. He nestled up against Posy, where he could see the pictures in the storybook, and didn't even raise his head when Frances said they'd be back later, and they slipped out of the room.

'That's got you off the hook!' Shelley nudged her cheerfully. 'Posy's reading isn't as hot as she thinks, and she'll start making it up as soon as she gets to a difficult word. She'll be telling him stories for hours!'

'We'd better not leave them too long,' said Frances, a little worried at where Posy's imagination might have led her. 'His mum'll be up to kiss him goodnight as soon as she's finished dinner.'

'Let her take over, then,' was Shelley's advice. 'Time you and me knocked off for the day. I'm going to put my feet up. You coming?'

'In a bit. I want to make a phone call.'

Shelley went into their bedroom, and a moment later music blasted through the wall ... 'Knocking off' didn't include any question of listening out for the children apparently.

Frances sighed. She and Shelley were chalk and cheese. Even their taste in music was different. She wished things hadn't been arranged so they were forced to share a room. Far from making her feel less lonely, the unrelieved presence of someone she had so little in common with was only adding to her sense of isolation ... Still, she'd better get used to Shelley's company. It had been made pretty clear that a distinct social line had been drawn at Haseley House and, kind though some of the family had been to her, the nannies weren't going to be encouraged to find friendship across the divide.

She moved further away from Shelley's pulsating music, and pulled out her mobile. Whether or not it would make the homesickness worse, Frances felt an overwhelming need for contact with people who loved her. They'd have finished tea now. Mum would have settled down by the fire in front of *Corrie*, trying to shut the boys up as they squabbled over a computer game. Everyone would race for the phone when it went, hoping it was her, longing to know how she was getting on, just as she longed to hear their news … no signal. She went a bit nearer the window … still nothing. Perhaps it would be better in the attic.

She hurried up the stairs, past the children's door, only vaguely aware of the chatty tone that suggested Posy had already given up on the text of the story. There was a chair in one of the unused bedrooms. She climbed onto it and pointed her phone towards the ceiling. This was as high in the house as she could get. Please, please… It was no good.

With hammering heart she tried shaking the phone, but she knew perfectly well there was nothing wrong with the battery. Mustn't panic. Get down off the chair. Oh why was this dreadful house so determined to deny her any contact with normal humanity? … Outside. There'd be a better signal outside. Down, down, down all the stairs. Kitchen.Back door… Hell, it was bolted! She forced them away, top and bottom, and ran out into the darkness.

No signal. There was *still* no bloody signal! She ran on down the path at the side of the house, seeing nothing but the display on the phone…

It was useless. She'd known it would be really. Here she was, out in the dark and cold, cut off from friends and family, who she'd probably never see again… And now – oh lord – something was moving, crunching on the gravel at the front of the house! Frances hurried back inside and re-bolted the door.

And then, as she sat at the kitchen table, taking great breaths, she remembered that not everyone relied on mobiles. *Stupid girl*! She knew William had a telephone in the hall… It was even possible that it contacted the outside world in the normal way! She could offer to pay for the call…

But even as she went to pick it up, she realised this was no good. Voices came from the dining room close by. Any moment someone would come out, and she certainly didn't want anyone else at Haseley House to overhear what she had to say to her family. Was there an extension somewhere? She opened a door.

'Oh … sorry!'

She'd been so sure they were all at dinner, but no, here was that wretched man again – the 'burglar', Leo Watlington. Why did he make such a habit of sitting in rooms on his own?

She would have retreated instantly, but he called her back. 'Yes? What do you want?'

Awkwardly she explained about the phone.

'God, no! You won't get a signal in this place – hills all round, and the yokels wouldn't think of defiling them with anything as progressive as a phone mast!'

'I suppose not. Anyway, I'm sorry for disturbing you…'

But Leo seemed unwilling to let her go. He asked about her family and education, and having learnt that she'd hoped to have gone to art college if things had worked out differently, revealed that he himself was a writer. The pause for her to insert a suitably admiring comment was the only one he gave after that.

'I don't have to explain to *you* the problems a creative artist has in getting recognition. The moguls of modern publishing have no imagination. All they're interested in is so-called "popular fiction" – pap to fill the station bookstalls. And when you present them with a work of – yes, I have to say it – real literary merit…'

Frances listened in ever-increasing amazement as Leo held forth on the subject of his own talents. How desperate must the poor man be, if he felt he had to impress the nanny?

She was trying to think how to get away and find a phone, when something caught her eye – a movement at the window … God, someone was out there! No, not another burglar! She really didn't think she could take it.

With pounding heart she watched as a figure loomed up out of the darkness and pressed its nose against the glass, making a ghastly distorted face. It spread its hands in a claw-like action and slowly slid down the pane, like something in a horror film. From there the creature dropped to its knees, and clasped its hands together in a pleading gesture. It wanted to be let into the house!

Leo at last realised her attention was elsewhere, and turned to see what she was looking at.

'What on earth…? Oh, for heaven's sake!' Somewhat to her surprise, he seemed to be expressing impatience rather than fear.

'Let me in!' The voice came clearly through the glass now. Leo, one burglar colluding with another, found the catch on the window and threw it open.

A lithe young man climbed through, and stood on the carpet grinning mischievously at Frances. He had curly brown hair and thick eyebrows, which might have looked fierce if it wasn't for the twinkle in the green eyes beneath them.

'Well – just in time to rescue a damsel in distress, it appears! Is this man annoying you?'

'Oh no…' Frances began to stammer politely, although the stranger seemed to have summed up the situation quite well.

Leo looked sour. 'What on earth are *you* doing here, Daniel?'

'I might ask the same of you.'

'Well you needn't,' said Leo pettishly. 'I'm here for Christmas, with the rest of the family – I brought your mother down with me, as a matter of fact.'

'Oh Lord, did you?' Daniel pulled a horrified face. 'She'll never forgive me!'

'Didn't you realise she was here?' Leo was puzzled.

'Yes, of course. That's why I came. I was supposed to be climbing in Scotland with some mates, but someone made a balls up and we'd nowhere to stay … I've been on the road all day, arrived at last, shattered and starving, and then no one would answer the door!'

'Would you like some dinner?' Frances came to her senses and spoke for the first time. 'The others are all in the dining room. They started some time ago but…'

'*What*? You mean everyone else is having dinner, and nobody bothered to fetch me?' Leo's expression was so appalled, it was hard not to laugh. Frances caught Daniel's eye and looked away quickly.

'Oh dear, Leo. They must have forgotten you existed!' he said with a naughty grin. 'Never mind. Let's go and see if there's anything left.'

♣ ♣ ♣

Poor William, thought Hilary – he didn't stand a chance. As soon as Stephen and Lesley realised that Margery was trying to persuade him to undertake a major repair programme, they jumped on the bulldozer and added their weight.

'That's an excellent idea, isn't it, Father? It's only sensible to protect a valuable asset like Haseley by investing a little bit now for the future…'

Whose future, she wondered? Eighty-year-old William's, or the people who hoped to inherit the house?

'You could always move into a care home while the work's being done – on a temporary basis, of course.'

No one else seemed to have noticed that Oliver had been left rather isolated at the end of the table, with his neighbours' backs so firmly turned in the other direction. He caught Hilary's gaze and gave a rueful smile.

She was just wondering how offended Julia would be if she suggested swapping seats with Lesley, when Julia spoke instead.

'So what are everyone's plans for tomorrow? Last chance for Christmas shopping! Tony and I have a few little things left to get, and we simply must have a tree, mustn't we?'

'A bit more booze wouldn't come amiss,' Tony added. 'What do you say, Lesley?'

Lesley looked startled at the implication that she was a drinker, then realised what he meant. 'Oh, shopping! No, Stephen and I have got everything we need ... I think we'd prefer to find a rather more mind-stretching activity for Tobias tomorrow – something educational. Isn't there a museum at Cirencester?'

Julia made a face. 'Well, if you're sure the poor little lamb would rather do that than McDonald's...'

'Sounds like your kind of thing, Oliver – a museum?' said Tony. 'Why don't you show young Tobias what's what, while the rest of us hit the shops?'

Stephen glanced at Lesley in alarm. 'Oh no, I don't think...'

'What? No, Oliver doesn't want to go to Cirencester tomorrow,' Margery broke off her argument to inform them. 'William's going to give him a tour of the house, so he can write his thing for *Country Life*.'

'I could do that,' said Hilary. 'Not write the article. Take Oliver round the house, I mean.'

She flushed. Was she being too pushy? But Stephen and Lesley had looked so appalled at the idea of him joining them – presumably afraid of being upstaged by his superior knowledge of antiquities, and she was sure William wouldn't want to spend his time traipsing up and down the stairs ... Oh, sod it! Why not just admit to herself that she would enjoy a morning in Oliver's company? She would love to show him all the little eccentricities that made her so fond of Haseley – the unexpected rooms and oddly placed cupboards and bits of old wallpaper hidden behind doors. She knew he'd appreciate them just as she did.

'Thank you. I'd be very grateful.'

He smiled at her, and for a moment she felt ... what? She wasn't entirely sure, so instantly had it been succeeded by a pang of guilt. Christ, how could a man who wasn't Ben cause her to feel anything like that spark of delight? ... No, of course it wasn't wrong to be happy. She'd had to tell herself this numerous times, when the cloud of her bereavement began to lift and let in the occasional ray of sunshine. But to find enjoyment in the normal little pleasures of life again was one thing – this sudden soaring of her heart quite another!

'What's going on outside?' said Julia suddenly. Sounds could be heard from the hall. 'That's not one of the nannies – it's a man's voice. But I thought they were all in here ... oh dear! *Surely* we can't have forgotten somebody?'

The glint in her eye reinforced Hilary's suspicions regarding Leo's omission from the table.

The door opened, and everyone turned to see, not Leo, but – *Ben*!

'Hi Mum! Hi, Gran! I thought I'd come and check up on you all.'

For a second Hilary really had thought her husband had come to haunt her! Guilty conscience, of course, and the total unexpectedness of seeing Daniel here, when he was supposed to be hundreds of miles away. She recovered, and joined in the babble of laughing questions and explanations ... no dreadful accident, just a mix-up about accommodation. Yes, he really was staying for Christmas – if Uncle William didn't mind, that is. Mind you, he had thought he'd have to drive all the way back to London when he couldn't get anyone to answer the door.

'And where's that pretty girl who let me in? Who is she?'

'Oh, nobody,' Stephen assured him, 'just one of the nannies. I expect she's gone back upstairs.'

Leo, following in Daniel's wake, hadn't a hope of getting attention for his own misfortunes.

'Did I really forget to call you? Oh, how dreadful! Never mind, come and sit next to Hilary.' Julia revealed that there was plenty of room for two chairs at the head of the table. 'Daniel, darling, you go down to the other end.'

Why that way round? Hilary wanted to catch up on all Daniel's news, not be landed with a sulky Leo! Now she was faced with the sight of her son and Oliver sitting side by side, shaking hands and introducing themselves. She found herself watching anxiously. What did the two of them think of each other? How well were they going to get on?

'I suppose that's cold now,' said Leo, wrinkling his nose, 'but you might give me some anyway, rather than just sit there with the spoon in your hand! I am quite hungry.'

♣ ♣ ♣

Scratch the Cat was debating where to spend the night. The tiny room they'd found for Leo had been his first choice, but unfortunately he'd taken the precaution of shutting the door. Oliver's door was closed as well, and he could sleep with William any time, so that was no fun. Up in the attic, though, he was more successful. The door of the children's room had been left ajar so they could be heard in the night, and Scratch remembered he'd once got a very good reaction from sleeping on Tobias's face when he was a baby ... two for the price of one here! Scratch jumped softly onto the bed and settled down.

Chapter Eleven

The scream woke Frances. She lay there, heart hammering, trying to persuade herself she'd imagined it. After all, her whole night had been disturbed by uncomfortable dreams – most of them featuring a big old house, with hundreds of doors, where she was desperately searching for something. But she was pretty sure that the scream had been real. She turned to see if Shelley had heard it, but she was dead to the world, head buried in her pillow, just as she'd been when Frances had come to bed.

It had been ages before she could get to sleep last night. Her overtired brain had insisted on replaying images from her long, eventful day: fields on the journey; that first startling sight of Haseley House; and the exhausting procession of new faces, critical or curious or friendly, culminating with the one that most particularly lingered in her mind. If the owner of those mischievous eyes was going to be staying here, perhaps Christmas wasn't going to be so miserable after all!

Hilary heard the scream too, more faintly, but she'd been lying awake some time, trying to make sense of her feelings.

Of course she'd been delighted when Daniel turned up so unexpectedly yesterday evening. It was a huge relief to know that she no longer had to worry about him risking his life mountain climbing, and she could look forward to having his company for Christmas after all. If she'd been granted a wish by some benevolent fairy that's exactly what she would have asked for ... so why, for that instant of subconsciousness before her rational mind kicked in, did she feel a tiny sinking of the heart?

She was still trying to pin it down, when she heard the scream. It came from somewhere upstairs, where the children were sleeping – but it didn't sound quite like a child.

The scream woke Scratch with a most unpleasant start. He leapt off the bed and dived for cover. Tobias and Posy woke more slowly, rubbing their eyes and wondering what was wrong.

Stephen appeared, in bare feet and pyjamas, and seeing both children safe, also looked round in puzzlement for the source of the disaster.

'That animal ... that dreadful creature ... was trying to *smother* Tobias!' Lesley, still hysterical, explained her reason for rousing the household. 'Yes, he was,' she insisted, as Stephen made dubious noises. 'I found him asleep *right* on top of the children!'

Curiosity brought Kath Arncott in to work that morning. She had every excuse not to come in on Christmas Eve – public holiday, wasn't it? And anyway, the old man wasn't supposed to be there, if things had gone to plan, never mind with a house full of people! Yes, she'd be quite within her rights to take the day off, as she'd make clear to him later.

But there wasn't much going on at home – nothing to do but try to keep the kids from killing each other. They were a pain at holiday time ... and there was so much going on at Haseley House! She'd missed the late arrivals, with having to go back last night, and she was longing to see what they all made of each other, and how Lesley had enjoyed sleeping in that room, and whether the poor new nanny had stuck it out, or already fled the scene. She settled the boys in front of the TV, with strict instructions not to switch to any of those unsuitable channels their dad had installed before he went away, and set off up the hill, prepared to play grudging with William.

There was only one person in the kitchen – a stranger, but he appeared to be making himself quite at home. He had already found William's frying pan, and was getting eggs and bacon out of the fridge.

'Aha,' said Kath, making him jump, 'you must be Mrs Watlington's journalist!'

'Oh ... er ... yes ... Oliver Leafield.' He came over to shake hands. 'And you must be Mr Shirburn's housekeeper.'

Kath nodded her acceptance of the title – better than 'char', which she'd heard herself referred to as by Lesley ... nice manners, one had to give him that.

'So how is Mrs Watlington?' she asked, when she'd given him her name. 'Got down here all right, I take it?'

'Yes, thank you. She's fine.'

He would have gone back to his cooking, but Kath decided she could prod a bit more.

'What do you make of her then? Get on with her OK, do you?'

He looked a little taken aback, but then replied warmly. 'Yes, I think she's charming.'

'Well that's a turn up! Some of us reckon she can be a bit starchy.'

'*Starchy*? Hilary Watlington?'

'Oh lord, not her! I was talking about the old lady.'

He flushed. 'Oh yes, of course you were. Well, I like Margery very much too.'

This interesting line of conversation was interrupted by the entrance of William, who greeted her in his normal affectionate manner.

'You here? I would have thought there were enough people in the house to make my life a misery.'

'Well, that's the thanks I get for coming in to work on my holiday!' Kath rolled her eyes at Oliver.

'Any proper mother would be at home, looking after her children.'

'So I should be. God knows what those kids'll be up to with me away! But how would you manage, may I ask, with all your family staying and no help in the house?'

They could have happily carried on like this all morning, but the door opened, bringing a surprise for Kath.

'Hul-*lo*! …It's young Daniel, isn't it? Well, I never!'

Daniel grinned. 'Hello, Mrs A. How are you?'

She looked him up and down, delighted with what she saw. Who would have thought the gangly teenager could have turned into such a hunk?

'Haven't *you* grown up well! ...And the image of your father, bless him. Come and give me a kiss.'

'Pah!' exclaimed William, as Daniel obeyed her. 'A boy hardly older than your two! Cradle-snatching, I call it.'

'Who's for bacon?' Oliver stood with spatula poised.

'If you know how to cook it,' said William, looking dubiously at the dry pan. 'You need plenty of fat in there.'

'Not if you get it really hot to start with.' Daniel went over to advise.

'I could use the grill, if you prefer.'

'Blimey! A load of men, and you reckon to know all about it,' exclaimed Kath, but realising the next step in this argument, picked up a duster and quickly made herself scarce.

🌲 🌲 🌲

'Lesley, I'm sure Scratch didn't mean any harm,' said Hilary, trying to keep her irritation at bay. 'Cats like sleeping with people – it keeps them warm. Can't you think of him as an extra cuddly toy?'

They were on the landing now, Frances shivering in her dressing gown, the children still bemused, Stephen trying not to yawn, Lesley red-faced and breathing sharply.

'Tobias's toys are made under hygienic conditions, and *washable* when they get dirty. You can't possibly compare them to a filthy creature like that,' she pointed to Scratch, who now that the screaming had stopped, had come out to join them, 'which has never been washed in its life, as far as I know!'

Inevitably, Scratch stretched out a leg, and began to wash himself all over with some care.

Hilary bit back a smile. 'Well, no one's been hurt, and it's rather chilly on the landing. Wouldn't it be sensible to get everyone dressed, and go and find some breakfast?'

'Yes, Nanny, I don't know why we're all standing out here!' Lesley decided to transfer the blame to Frances. 'Tobias'll catch his death. Can you put some clothes on him, please? And I still don't understand what the children were doing asleep in the same bed...'

Hilary had rather hoped to be first downstairs, though she knew William was an early riser. She wanted to get a cup of tea and sort her head out quietly, before she was required to play her part in the tumult of the household. What she hadn't expected was to find the two people foremost in her bewildered thoughts sitting at the kitchen table having breakfast together ... for a moment she almost drew back.

But they both looked up and smiled to see her.

'Hey, Mum, come and have some eggs and bacon. This guy's not a bad cook – even if he isn't quite up to Uncle William's exacting standards!' He shot Oliver a grin, suggesting a shared joke ... *sharing jokes already*. That was a good thing, wasn't it? Why did she find it somehow disconcerting?

Oliver had picked up a plate and gone across to the stove, ready to serve her. He turned and raised his eyebrows – nothing more, but for that second her heart lurched. *Not a good thing*! She tried to greet him in a natural way, and the words wouldn't come out ... *a very bad thing*. She glanced anxiously at Daniel, but thank heaven he didn't seem to have noticed.

'I'm not that hungry really,' she managed to stammer at last. 'I'll just get a piece of toast.'

'Here you are, I've done some.' Oliver foiled her plan to hide over by the grill, by handing her a neat rack of uniformly golden slices.

'Just as well,' Daniel chuckled. 'Mum always burns it.'

'I do *not*!' She sounded like an aggrieved child, but it annoyed her that he was giving Oliver the idea she was incompetent.

Daniel made as if to duck, with a grin at Oliver that made her really want to hit him.

'I'll have you know that I had a lot of compliments on my cooking last night!' Oh dear – defensive – not attractive.

'Yes, Mum, that was a really good cheesy potato pie.' And gave her son the opportunity to patronise her.

'It was indeed.' No better coming from Oliver.

'And as for those profiterole thingies!' Daniel rolled his eyes. 'It truly worries me that I nearly arrived too late and missed them.'

'Well they're not hard to make.'

'If you gave Mum the recipe, we'd be forever in your debt.'

No, she wasn't going to point out that Daniel was old enough now to make his own profiteroles, that there might be a bit more to her life than supplying her son's domestic needs.

'Better still, I'll give her a tutorial.' Oh dear, he mustn't look at her like that, though! Not with Daniel there. She busied herself with the toast, trying to think of some normal topic of conversation – something to suggest the totally neutral relationship between herself and a man she'd met for the first time only yesterday.

'So, what's everyone going to do this morning?' Good. That sounded suitably impersonal.

'I rather think I might check up on little Cousin Tobias,' said Daniel, with a twinkle. 'Make sure he's being looked after properly, you know?'

'She's called Frances,' Hilary told him. 'But don't get her into trouble with Lesley. There's already been a bit of a do upstairs.'

' And you're going to show me round the house.'

'Oh my God – I'd completely forgotten!' Hilary looked at Oliver in consternation. That had been last night – but things had changed.

'Well, if you'd rather not…'

'Rather not what?' asked Margery, entering in time to catch this interchange, and helping herself to some toast.

'Hilary said she'd give me a guided tour of Haseley this morning, but needless to say she doesn't have to…'

'No, of course she doesn't! William can do that – it's his house, after all. Hilary would much rather go on a jaunt somewhere… What about that bird place at Slimbridge? We'll get Stephen to take us. Your car's too small, Daniel, and Leo's such a God-awful driver.' Margery munched her toast, at her happiest making plans.

✿ ✿ ✿

Shelley had slept through the whole thing. She didn't wake even when Frances, after suffering a most unjust lecture on the 'impropriety' of having permitted the two little cousins to share a bed, came back and hastily put some clothes on.

But Frances was blowed if she was going to undertake the task of getting Posy ready as well as Tobias. Shelley could darn well do her job, and when there was still no sign of movement, she went over and shook her shoulder. 'Come on, Shelley, time to get up.'

'Shurrup. Sod off. Wazzamatter?'

'Everyone else is awake. Lesley found the cat on the kids' bed, and had hysterics … come on! She's on the warpath now. I've got to take Tobias down, and you need to sort out Posy.'

'Oh bleedin' hell! Leave me alone, can't you?'

✿ ✿ ✿

In fact, Frances found that Posy had dressed herself, and Stephen and Lesley were just emerging from their bedroom, so it was a party of four that escorted Tobias down to his breakfast.

They made a bit of a jam in the doorway. Frances, peering past Stephen's arm, saw that there seemed to be several people in the kitchen already. Were any of them…? Yes, he was there – sitting beside his mother at the table, with scary Mrs Watlington.

'We've finished the bacon, I'm afraid,' Oliver Leafield was saying, 'but I can do some more eggs, and there's plenty of fried bread in the pan.'

'Oh, yes – splendid!' Stephen stepped forward eagerly, just as Lesley was saying 'Oh no, I don't think so!' She put a protective arm round her son, as if to defend him from evil. 'We don't allow Tobias to eat fried food.'

'Well he's not the only pebble on the beach!' said Margery Watlington tartly. 'Stephen's never been a fussy eater – or wasn't till you came along. And your nanny could clearly do with a proper breakfast, judging by the size of her!'

Everybody turned to look at Frances, who felt her cheeks flame red.

'Oh hello! I didn't see you there.'

She couldn't even return Daniel's friendly greeting. What did that terrifying old lady have against her? This was the second time she had made her want to die!

Posy spotted a favourite cousin and ran forward to greet him, drawing the eyes with her, to Frances's great relief.

'Hello, madam!' Daniel hugged her in return. 'You've grown a bit since I last saw you.'

'Yes, I'm grown up now.' She pressed herself against him, batting her eyelashes – an eight-year-old siren. Frances happened to catch Margery's expression of extreme distaste.

'Now, Nanny, where's Tobias's muesli? Is that skimmed milk?' Lesley declared herself in charge. 'Oh dear, there's not much room at the table, is there?'

Hilary and Oliver took the hint and began to clear their plates away. Daniel gently detached himself from Posy and stood up to help. His grandmother stayed in her seat.

'I can't think where Tobias's box can have gone,' Stephen was saying. 'I remember bringing it in last night.'

'Well we must find it!' Lesley's voice rose. 'It's got all his food in – and his special plate and mug.'

Margery gave a disgusted exclamation. 'William's china not good enough? It should be. He's still using the stuff we were brought up with – been in the family for God knows how long.'

'Oh – I *thought* it looked interesting!' Oliver pounced on one of the plates and turned it over.

'For heaven's sake!' exclaimed Lesley. She pulled out a chair and lifted Tobias onto it. 'I don't know what you're going to eat, darling. This isn't even wholemeal bread!' She glared at the remains of the toast.

But Frances, scanning the room, believed she'd noticed something on top of one of the cupboards. 'Isn't that the box up there?'

'Oh yes! What on earth's it doing there? I believe your father must have hidden it deliberately, Stephen … er … thank you.' Oliver was tall enough to reach and had handed it down.

'You're not giving the child that parrot food?' Margery wrinkled her nose, as she watched a helping of Tobias's special organic muesli from the health food shop being poured into his special bowl with rabbits on. 'Good God, if I'd put that sort of muck in front of Ben and Leo when they were little…'

'If we've finished our breakfast, perhaps we'd better leave them to get on with theirs,' said Hilary, smiling at her mother-in-law and indicating the door.

'Oh – yes, you'll want to put some glad rags on, I dare say,' said Margery, although Hilary looked nice already, and it was she who was still clad in an old dressing gown. And, Oliver, you must find where William's hidden himself, and remind him he's got guests to entertain.' She chivvied them out in front of her, like a dog with a couple of recalcitrant sheep.

'Haven't you finished as well?' Lesley asked Daniel.

'Actually, I thought I'd have another bit of toast.'

He sat down, grinned at Frances, and began to spread a piece with butter and marmalade. To her surprise, he passed it to her. She took it gratefully. Lesley's veto on fried food was taken to apply to all of them – though Frances suspected Stephen would have broken it if he'd known what to do with a frying pan – and no alternative had been offered. Lesley, as usual, was only concerned with Tobias, and they were now both occupied in trying to persuade him to eat his cereal. Posy, having been told to wait till her nanny came down for her breakfast, had got bored and was wandering about the kitchen poking into things.

'I never got a chance to thank you properly – Frances, isn't it?' said Daniel. 'I'd have been waiting out there all night, if you hadn't spotted me. Once Leo's into one of his rants, he wouldn't notice if there was a horde of pillaging Vikings outside!'

'Oh no – that's OK.' Frances remembered with some guilt her reluctance to let the frightening apparition into the house.

'I bet he was boring the pants off you, wasn't he? God knows what persuaded him to come down to Haseley! It certainly won't have been Mum's doing, whatever Julia says. She finds him just as much of a pain as the rest of us – more really, because he quite obviously fancies her. Do you think that's why he came?'

'Would you like a banana with it, Tobias?' said Lesley, finding an excuse to nip this interesting conversation in the bud. 'I'm sure that would help it down … perhaps you could fetch him one, Nanny, if you've finished gossiping.'

'Oh, but she hasn't started yet!' objected Daniel. 'I'm just giving her the opening, so she can reveal what she really thinks about us all. Aren't you longing to know?'

'There are some in the fruit bowl, if you don't mind… I'm afraid she has a job to do, Daniel.'

Frances passed a banana that Lesley could easily have reached herself, and watched her peel it and 'take all the nasty black bits out' at Tobias's direction, before slicing it into his muesli. Was Daniel really interested in her opinions – or was it just a way of teasing Lesley? She had to admit that this seemed the more likely.

'Good lord! What have you got there?'

Posy was settling herself down at the table beside them, bringing with her an enormous packet she must have found in one of the cupboards.

Tobias's mouth dropped in jealousy.

'I want *tho-ose* for my breakfast!!'

Lesley and Stephen shot round to see what had caused the outcry, and were in time to see Posy reach for a bowl and pour herself a good helping of Coco Pops.

'Oh my God, she's found some of that awful junk your father lives on!'

'I wa-an't...!'

'No you don't, pet. One more mouthful of nice muesli for Mummy!'

The door opened and Shelley came in, still looking half asleep. 'Mornin' all! What you got there, Pose? Cor blimey, it's early!' She started to give a huge yawn – and at that moment spotted the stranger sitting beside Frances at the table. She stood there, eyes goggling, forgetting to shut her mouth.

A second later she was beside them, swinging out a chair that had its back set to Frances and its front so as to almost interlock her legs with Daniel's. 'Hel-*lo* there! Don't think I've seen you before, have I? Are you one of Julia's cousins come to stay as well? ...Oh, that's brilliant! Someone to knock around with at last. Everyone else round here is either a kid or geriatric!'

Frances might well have been invisible. She couldn't help admiring Shelley's technique. With little wriggles that hitched her short skirt even higher, leaning forward to make the most of her low-cut top, and totally impervious to Stephen and Lesley's disapproving frowns, she dropped Julia and Tony's names into the conversation as family friends for whom she worked as a favour, while dismissing Frances herself as 'Tobias's new nanny. Only been with them a few days.'

Frances's heart sank as she watched her. Never in a million years could she have approached a guy in that up-front way – particularly somebody she fancied – but Shelley seemed to have no fear of rejection. Frances could

164

only envy her uninhibited confidence in her power to attract, and wish that the previously lively Daniel wasn't staring at her as one bewitched.

'Here we all are. Good morning, darlings!' Julia and Tony breezed in.

'Oh good, a fry-up!' Tony marched straight to the pan.

'Hello sweetheart, I see you've found some breakfast.' Julia kissed her daughter, making a face of sympathetic disgust as she caught sight of Tobias's bowl. 'Oh how horrid! Wouldn't you rather have Coco Pops, darling?'

'Who's for an egg?' said Tony. 'Come on, Shell. I know you're always up for a bit of protein!'

Shelley giggled and glanced at Daniel, who woke from his trance.

'Not for me, thanks, I've eaten … and I think I'd better go and check on Uncle William.' Suddenly he wasn't there. Frances and Shelley caught each other looking wistfully at the door.

As usual, things cheered up with the Britwells around, and Tony was soon handing round a plate piled high with delicious cholesterol.

'So who's coming shopping this morning?' said Julia, when everyone except Lesley was tucking in to fried bread.

'Me, me!' said Posy, banging her spoon on her bowl.

'Me!' echoed Tobias, picking up a knife to imitate her.

Lesley snatched it quickly. 'No, darling, you're not shopping. We're going to the museum instead.'

He turned to her doubtfully. 'Do I like museums?'

'Museums are *boring*!' Posy informed him. 'They're full of old stuff used by dead people, and you're not allowed to touch... *I'm* going shopping for lots of presents for me!'

'Of course you like museums, Tobias!' said Stephen, frowning at his niece. 'Remember that book you've got about the Romans? A lot of them lived here in the Cotswolds. If I remember rightly, there are some very nice reconstructions of villa buildings at Cirencester, complete with well-preserved mosaic floors.'

'You'll enjoy seeing all the nice Roman things with Mummy and Daddy,' Lesley cut in, before Stephen could launch too thoroughly into lecturer mode.

'Is Frances going?'

They turned to look at her. Frances could see Lesley weighing up a reluctance to let her escape any duty against the fact that she and Stephen didn't necessarily want her with them, and something told her she was waiting to see which option Frances would least prefer herself.

So what *did* she want to do? Trail round a museum with the Shirburns, or check out the Cirencester shops with the Britwells, and possibly Daniel as well, where one could probably get a signal for the mobile? No contest!

All she had to do was to look eager.

'No, I think perhaps we'll make this a family occasion.' Lesley rose to the bait. 'In fact why don't we ask your father to come?' she added to Stephen. 'It would be nice for him to spend some quality time with Tobias.'

'Oh, of course Daddy must come to Cirencester!' exclaimed Julia. 'I bet he hasn't got presents for anybody. We'll make him do his Christmas shopping.'

'Yes, yes! Grandpa must come!' Posy got the import of this.

'Oh – I'm sure he'd rather go to the museum with us,' said Lesley, with an anxious glance at her husband. 'William's not all that fond of shopping, is he, Stephen?'

'If he's fond of museums, it's the first I've heard of it!' said his daughter dryly.

'It'll be such a squash for him in your car, and there'll be plenty of room in ours now, as Frances isn't going.'

Frances's mouth dropped. It hadn't occurred to her that she'd contrived to be left behind altogether!

'No problem fitting him into the Discovery either,' Tony pointed out. 'Shelley doesn't mind a bit of a squeeze in the back seat, do you?' he added with a suggestive leer that made her giggle.

They were still arguing politely when Margery Watlington came back, dressed ready to go out, and her opinion was immediately sought on whether her brother would prefer Christmas shopping or Culture.

Her answer pleased nobody.

'Good lord, no! Children have far too much rubbish at Christmas, without people buying more for them. And he certainly won't want to visit a dreary old museum! Anyway, William's not going anywhere. Hilary wants to go to Slimbridge now, so he's got to stay and show Oliver round the house.'

Chapter Twelve

Back in her room, getting ready for an expedition she didn't in the least want to go on, Hilary wondered how, yet again, she'd managed to let herself be bulldozed by Margery. Yes, she had been momentarily unnerved when Oliver had reminded her of last night's promise – but only because, with Daniel there, she had slipped back into being that other person, his mother: sensible; reliable; and so steadfastly attached to his late father that there was no question of her ever having feelings for another man.

The next moment common sense had told her that of course Daniel wouldn't see it as a betrayal if she spent the morning showing Oliver round Haseley! It wasn't as if they were going to leap into one of the beds or something. She'd only met the man yesterday, for God's sake, and she'd no reason to suppose that the frisson of attraction was on anything but her side. But by then Margery had come charging in to her rescue, and like a well-meaning whirlwind, swept up all her plans and rearranged them before she'd had time to draw breath.

Damn! She hadn't the slightest desire to visit the reserve at Slimbridge. Pleasant enough in the summer, but Margery must have forgotten how cold it would be on the Severn estuary at this time of year. She put on thick tights, jeans and a big knitted jersey, hoping to strike a balance between keeping off hypothermia and looking vaguely respectable, and left the bedroom still feeling grumpy.

To her embarrassment, she found Oliver emerging from his room at the same time.

'Oh God! I thought you said you were going to find William.'

His face dropped, and she realised she'd sounded curt – if only he wouldn't keep taking her by surprise!

'Yes, I know,' he said sheepishly, 'but I'm afraid my nerve failed me. Much as I love Margery, she doesn't quite understand that one can't really march in and start ordering one's host about as if he were a younger brother. I thought perhaps I'd look round on my own.'

'Well you mustn't miss the linen cupboard, in that case – I'll show you.' Hilary led the way down the passage. 'The trouble with Margery is that she's a pathological organiser, and she can't always be made to realise that people don't necessarily want to do what she's arranged for them.'

'That came from the heart!' He'd noticed her sigh. 'Do I gather you're not that keen on visiting this bird place?'

'Not in the slightest! If I have to go out, I'd rather shop in Cirencester with the others. At least the shops'll be warm.'

'But you didn't really want to go at all?'

'Well I had actually planned to take you round the house. There are bits even William's forgotten about, or he wouldn't think to point out ... look at this amazing cupboard. There's a hatch at the top, so that the maid could throw clean towels down without having to compromise anyone's modesty.'

'That's what I call gracious living! The whole bathroom's fabulous, especially that wonderful bath. Good God, is that an original Crapper?'

'You mean the loo? It *can't* have been called that!'

'Oh yes,' he grinned. 'Old Thomas Crapper was a pioneer of sanitary ware… I wonder when this system was installed. One could do with a look at the tanks, but I suppose they're in the roof space.'

'There's a tank in one of the attic cupboards,' Hilary recalled. 'It makes the most unearthly noise if anyone flushes the loo in the night, I can tell you from bitter experience!'

'Oh great! Do you mind if we…?'

'No, of course not – if I can remember which one it was…'

♣ ♣ ♣

Meanwhile, William was making his own plans for the day.

He and Kath were in the sitting room, following their usual routine of her pretending to clean while she had a moan, and him pretending to read the paper. However this morning she had an additional listener, and ever since Daniel had come in, Kath had been taking full advantage of his politely sympathetic ear.

She was well away on the problems of What to do with the Children during the Holidays, when Leo appeared in the doorway.

'Would it have been too much to wake me? I gather that everyone's had breakfast, and there's nothing left in there now!'

'Sorry, mate, but I got up hours ago, and you were sleeping like a baby.'

'Hullo, Mr Watlington! I didn't know *you* were coming to join the party.'

Leo looked defensive, before realising that here was one person who apparently did not find the surprise unwelcome. Kath, for some reason unknown to William, held his nephew, 'the writer', in great respect, and was simpering delightedly at the prospect of adding him to her audience. 'I was just saying to young Daniel here, it's not easy, what with me having to work, and nobody to keep an eye on what those lads are up to. Things'd be different if their dad was still at home, but of course, now that I'm all on my own …' She looked at him under her lashes to drive this point home. 'It's so difficult finding something for kids to do, when they're not in school… Don't get me wrong – they're lovely kids, but they can be a bit of a handful.'

'Yes, I remember!' said Daniel, with a little shudder. He'd had experience of Grime and Brine.

The childless Leo nodded wisely. 'Modern children don't seem to have any inner resources of their own, which means that they need constant entertainment. Personally I blame the lack of intellectual stimulation in the home environment. So many parents think it acceptable to sit back and let the television do their work for them!'

'Yes, you don't like to leave them parked in front of the TV all day, do you?' William knew that's just what Kath *did* like to do, whenever she could get away with it. 'Even though lots of those things are educational – at least, they seem to have a fact sheet you can send for afterwards … not that my two would bother. Get enough of that stuff in school. They'd rather have a good cartoon, or one of those things with girls in.'

'We boys like those.' Daniel was trying to keep his face straight.

'There's far too much unsuitable programming on the box these days,' declared Leo, the man who claimed never to watch it. 'And the nine o'clock watershed is a joke!'

'Oh yes, isn't it?' Kath probably thought he was talking about a comedy show. 'I can tell that you're the sort of person who understands children, Mr Watlington,' she told him, ignoring Daniel's derisive snort.

'Oh, I don't know about that.' Leo made a brief concession to modesty. 'But, the fact is, most people have simply no idea how to treat them. They make the mistake of talking down to them, and one thing young people hate is being patronised.'

'Good heavens! Do they really?' said Daniel.

William was listening with only half an ear, but then Kath said something that caught his attention.

'I dare say little Posy and Tobias get a bit bored in the holidays too – specially being down here, with none of their friends around… Shame, isn't it, Mr Watlington, to think of my boys on their own in the cottage, and those poor kids with no one to play with up here?'

It was the sort of hint-dropping that William would usually have refused to pick up on principle. He knew Kath was an inveterate snob, who would love an opportunity for her boys to mix with the children at the 'big house', and he also knew just what their parents' reaction would be to such a suggestion. He put his paper down and looked at her thoughtfully.

172

'Yes – what a good idea!'

'What?' Kath stared at him.

A slow smile spread over William's face. 'Why don't you invite your boys to come and have a game with Julia and Stephen's children? I'm sure their parents would be delighted!'

Daniel raised an appreciative eyebrow. 'Grime and Brine? Come to play with Posy and Tobias? Oh, excellent! And I'll tell you what, Leo, everyone else is going out, so they'll want someone to supervise them, and since you're so good with children…'

He didn't need to say more. 'Oh yes, *you'll* help to look after them, won't you, Mr Watlington? I know they couldn't be in better hands!'

It was rather chilly in the garden. They had been sent out here on the pretext that 'it would be nice for the children to get some fresh air' – really, Frances suspected, so that the adults could continue arguing without the inhibiting presence of them or their nannies. Tobias had been fastened into his winter coat, and after rejecting all her suggestions for imaginative or warming games, was hurtling round the rose beds in a rather manic way, chased by a hysterical Posy. Shelley, having egged her into this state with a 'Go on, *get* the little sod! You're letting him escape!', had suddenly vanished, no doubt to indulge in a fag behind one of the bushes.

This must once have been a lovely garden, when someone who cared was alive to look after it – Stephen and

Julia's mother perhaps. The roses were straggly and unpruned now, and the soil beginning to spread over what should have been neat paths between the beds. One branch of the climber on the old brick wall at the end had become detached and was shooting along with a life of its own. She would like to paint the mixture of reds and pinks and browns in that wall – a summer view, with the roses out against it.

She wondered who was winning the Battle for William. It hadn't seemed to occur to his family to ask him what *he* wanted to do, any more than they'd consulted her own wishes about going to Cirencester… God, how stupid she'd been to shoot herself in the foot like that! Now she'd be staying behind, quite possibly all on her own – or else stuck with the dreadful Leo, who seemed to make a habit of being forgotten by everyone else… She wasn't sure which would be worse.

'Hi!' She jumped to feel a hand on her shoulder. 'I saw you through the window. Thought I'd better come out and warn you that you might be about to be collared by Leo again.'

It was Daniel, apparently reading her mind.

'Oh no! Why?'

For the bearer of bad news, he looked curiously cheerful. 'I think he might want to ask for your professional advice.'

Frances blinked at him, unable to imagine what Leo could possibly wish to consult her on, or why Daniel should find it so amusing if he did.

'Uncle William has invited Kath Arncott to bring her boys over to play with Posy and Tobias this morning,' he explained, 'and Leo, who's apparently the world's greatest expert on childcare, has volunteered to supervise them all!'

'*What*?'

'I know! Isn't it fabulous? I have to admit that the volunteering wasn't entirely his own idea, but he absolutely walked into it – you should have heard him boasting how wonderful he is with children! And Grime and Brine, Kath's kids, are *horrendous*. They were completely out of control when I last saw them, a couple of years ago, and they're that much older now. Stephen and Ratso will go up the *wall* at the thought of them mixing with dear little Tobias. I don't think Julia will be all that pleased either.'

'But…' He was looking at her, clearly expecting her to appreciate a joke which Frances just couldn't find funny. Was the idea that she and Leo be left to deal with this horrific scenario while the others went to Cirencester?

Before she could think of a way to explain her concern, Shelley re-emerged from behind the laurel bush – and spotted Daniel.

'Looking for me? Just having a quick one. Old fussy-pants here turns her nose up if I smoke in the bedroom! Getting more like her boss every day, if you ask me – don't they say that about dogs?' Frances was grateful he didn't join in her broad chuckle. 'Can't say I'm looking forward to this shopping trip,' she went on, surprisingly, since she'd talked of nothing else. 'It's not going to be much fun squashed up in the back of the Discovery with a load of old wrinklies all the way to Cirencester… Say, Dan, you've got a car, haven't you? What about giving us a lift?'

'Yes, sure…' He glanced across at Frances.

'Oh, Frankie's not going – Tobias's mum and dad don't really count her as one of the family, they said, and they told her to stay behind … so it'll just be you and me, all cosy.'

'Oh, I see! I didn't realise.' Daniel was looking at Frances with understanding now, but before he could say more, Kath appeared round the corner of the house. She winked at Daniel, and hollered at the children.

'Hey kids! Who wants to hear about the treat they're having this morning?'

✦ ✦ ✦

'There you are!' said Margery. 'We wondered where on earth you'd got to.'

So much for discretion! There seemed to be a sea of faces in the hall, all looking up at them, as Hilary and Oliver came down the stairs.

'Sorry – did we keep you waiting?' said Oliver. 'Hilary and I got a bit carried away, I'm afraid.'

Oh great! She waited for Tony to make some ribald comment, but for once he failed to leap on a potential innuendo.

'So are we ready to roll now? What about the kids?'

'You'd better fetch Tobias, Stephen. Make sure he's wearing his scarf.'

'And what happened to Daddy? He's supposed to be coming shopping with us.'

'Oh, but I thought we'd agreed that he'd rather visit the museum.'

'No, no! William's staying here to show Oliver round, and you're driving me and Hilary to Slimbridge.'

'Then who's taking us to Cirencester, may I ask?'

'Actually,' Oliver confessed, in the moment's silence that followed Lesley's aggrieved question, 'there's no need to bother William now – I've had a tour of the house.' He smiled at Hilary.

'Oh … well all right, you'd better come to Slimbridge with us. I dare say Stephen can fit you in.'

'But I've already explained, Aunt Margery, *we're* going to Cirencester.'

'But Hilary wants to go to Slimbridge …'

'No,' Hilary interposed gently, 'I don't.'

'What? Of course you do!'

'Not really.' She felt a little conscience-stricken to see her mother-in-law so taken aback. 'I'd rather go shopping. But if you're keen, of course I'll come with you…'

'Oh good Lord, *I* don't want to go to Slimbridge!' exclaimed Margery. 'I just thought it would be a treat for you.'

'Looks like we're all off to Cirencester then,' said Julia, after the stunned pause that greeted this disclosure. 'What fun! You'd better come with us and Daddy…'

'No, William's going with us.'

'Fine,' said Tony unexpectedly. 'And I expect you can find room for Oliver on the back seat as well, can't you, if he squeezes up next to Tobias?'

'Oh, I'm not sure…'

This was the moment William chose to come in search of a little mid-morning refreshment. He was startled to find so many people in the hall, especially when they all rushed towards him and began to jabber about museums and shopping and the relative comfort of their cars.

He waited until the hubbub died down and they were looking at him expectantly. Then he delivered his news.

'I've invited Kath Arncott to bring her children up here this morning to play with Posy and Tobias – we thought they'd be such good companions for each other! And Leo has kindly volunteered to supervise them... Oh dear, I do hope you haven't made any other plans? Little Grime and Brine would be so disappointed!'

The effect was everything to be expected, and William felt a momentary pang. Daniel should have been there to see the expression on Lesley's face.

Margery was the first to speak, and did nothing to calm the waters. 'Aren't those boys a bit rough? Never mind, it won't do Tobias any harm to have the corners knocked off him. Leo will be hopeless, of course, but at least it'll keep him out of everyone else's hair.'

'Oh dear, no, I don't think that will do...' Stephen looked anxiously at his wife, but she was still incapable of speech.

'Oh, Daddy,' exclaimed Julia, 'we're all supposed to be going into Cirencester! And anyway ... I mean, one doesn't want to sound snobbish, and I'm sure Kath's boys are darlings – but would they be comfortable, playing up here with ours? I'm thinking of them as much as anything.'

'It's a *preposterous* idea,' Lesley found her voice at last. 'I'm surprised at you even considering anything so unsuitable, William... God knows how a creature like Mrs Arncott brings up her offspring! Do you *want* your grandson mixing with the type of delinquent one reads about in the *Telegraph*?'

Not being a *Telegraph* reader, William wasn't qualified to say, but at that moment the prospective delinquent ran into the hall, followed by his cousin Posy and a beaming Kath.

'Mummy, Mummy, we've got a *treat* happening!' He could hardly get the words out for excitement.

'Grime and Brine are coming to play – they're *boys*!' Posy jumped up and down in delight.

'They're bigger than us, but they won't mind – and they've got 'puter games!'

'But darling, we've planned a treat for you already. We're going to the museum, remember?'

'Museums are boring! Posy says so ... I want to stay and play with Grime and Brine!' His face began to work. There was going to be a scene. William put off going to make his coffee.

'But it really isn't suitable ... oh dear!' Lesley looked at her sister-in-law with a hopeless gesture.

Julia weighed in, at her most bright. 'Tell you what! Why don't we go to Cirencester this morning, and then perhaps, if there's still time, Grime and Brine could come over this afternoon.'

'Yes – if there's time.' Lesley clutched at this lifeline, looking anxiously to see how it was received by Tobias.

'That way you get *two* treats,' Tony pointed out.

'Why can't we play with Grime and Brine now, and go shopping later?' enquired his sagacious daughter.

'All the shops'll be shut by then,' Julia improvised. 'It's Christmas Eve.'

'In my day,' declared Margery, as the verdict hung in the balance, 'young people were told what was happening and expected to get on with it… Come on, we're going to Cirencester. Has that child got a coat?'

Hilary was amused to see how this broke the spell. Posy ran off to find one, terrified of being left behind. Kath muttered, 'I'll bring them along this afternoon then,' and hurried away before anyone could argue.

'You'd better have a coat too, Daddy,' said Julia. 'Oh – where is he?'

'He must have gone back to the living room. Never mind, we'll collect him on the way.' Lesley saw an opportunity to snatch victory. 'Come on, Hilary, if you're ready… I'm afraid we can only take one, Oliver.'

'That's all right,' he came to her rescue. 'I've got my car. Hilary can come with me.'

'Are you sure, Hilary?' Oh dear, why was Tony looking at her in that quizzical way?

'I expect Daniel would like a lift as well. I'll go and find him.' God forbid anyone should think they were contriving to be alone. She hurried off in search of third-party cover.

She eventually tracked her son down to the garden where he was, as so often, surrounded by women. Shelley was gazing soulfully into his face – in as much as that girl could be said to have a soul – and Frances was standing a little apart, also looking rather wistful. Daniel hadn't been in the place five minutes and he was already breaking hearts, it seemed!

'Everyone's off to Cirencester now. Are you coming? Oliver kindly says we can go with him.'

'Oh no,' Shelley shot her a look of dislike. 'Daniel and me are going in his car – aren't we Dan?'

'No, you're going with the Britwells,' Hilary nipped that one in the bud. 'Hurry up, they're waiting for you … Frances, there's plenty of room with us.'

'Oh! But…'

'Don't you want to come?'

'Of course she does!' said Daniel.

'Dad's not out there, is he? We can't find him.' Stephen met them as they came back inside. 'Oh well. He must have gone with Julia and Tony.'

But Julia appeared a moment later. 'Funny – I thought Daddy was in the kitchen. Bother, he must have gone with Stephen and Ratso after all.'

🌲 🌲 🌲

William waited till he'd heard three sets of tyres go off down the drive, before emerging from his hiding place in the pantry. Scratch appeared from a cupboard at the same time. They looked at each other, mutually appreciating the sudden silence in the house. Even Mrs Arncott had gone home.

But what was that? Oh no! One person had inevitably been left behind.

'Where *is* everybody? … I say! Hello? … Where on earth have you all got to?'

William and Scratch slipped back into the pantry until Leo had vanished upstairs.

Chapter Thirteen

Frances could hardly believe her luck. Here she was, being whisked off to Cirencester after all, seated like a movie star in the back of Oliver's posh car, with Daniel beside her! The winter sunshine had struggled through the mist now, bathing the fields and stone walls and silhouetted trees in a magical golden glow. What a contrast from her drive through this same countryside with the Shirburns yesterday! She felt like Posy, wanting to bounce up and down with delight.

'Does anyone know the way?' enquired Oliver. 'I take it I start by going back to the village. What happens after that?

'Haven't a clue, mate,' said Daniel cheerfully. 'Just about made it here from London – but I think Cirencester's in the other direction.'

'Oh dear, we did go once, but Ben was driving and I didn't take much notice.'

'There's a signpost.' Frances pointed ahead. Oliver drew up at the little crossroads and they scanned each arm in vain. 'We could go to Ready Token instead.'

'Or Ampney Crucis,' said Hilary.

'Sounds painful!' Daniel made a face. 'I fancy Meysey Hampton.'

'Nice girl,' Oliver grinned. 'I'll try Barnsley. If we end up in Yorkshire, I can always find the M1 and come back.'

Hilary was beginning to feel that, in this company, she wouldn't greatly mind if they never found Cirencester and were destined to meander round these pretty Cotswold lanes for ever. Any awkwardness there might have been if she and Oliver had been alone in the car was dispelled by Daniel's light-hearted presence, and she liked his friend, the gently humorous Frances... How different from that awful journey with Leo last night! She'd always loved this part of the world, and Oliver pointed out things she'd never noticed before: the grassy hump of a prehistoric tumulus in a neighbouring field; an ancient boundary marching across the landscape, its ragged hedge made up of a dozen different kinds of shrub; a weathered milestone almost buried in the verge. 'This must have been a turnpike road. Did you see that little toll-house at the crossroads? And I think that lane could be Roman.' He pointed to a track bordered by tall trees, which continued the line ahead when their own road swerved away. 'Not just because it runs straight – you can get that with later Enclosure roads – but those old oaks must have taken centuries to grow. Pity about the mud! It would probably lead us to Cirencester.'

'Well, we're on the right road now,' said Daniel a few moments later. 'That's Stephen's car in front.'

'Oh no!' Frances sank down in her seat a little.

'You're quite safe,' he grinned. 'Stephen doesn't make a habit of using his mirror, from what I remember – anyway, what's the problem? They didn't forbid you to come to Cirencester – they just didn't want you to come with *them*!'

Nevertheless Frances was relieved when they watched the Shirburns turn into one car park, and Oliver deliberately drove on to the next.

'No sense in following at their heels... Good lord, what a fabulous church!' he exclaimed, suddenly spotting it towering over the neighbouring houses as they drew up. 'We must take a look at that.'

They headed in that direction at a leisurely pace, pausing to examine the shops or gaze up at the picturesque buildings they passed. With everything decorated for Christmas, the old town had a quaintly Dickensian feel – all it needed was snow and a horse-drawn carriage or two.

'I'm going to buy myself one of those shawls!' declared Hilary, pointing to a tempting display in one of the windows. 'Come on, Frances – they've got bags as well.'

Oliver stayed outside with Daniel, taking photographs of the old building opposite. Frances bought a scarf for her mother, and then spotted some shirts with silly slogans on she knew the boys would love... Dare she get a present for Daniel? No, of course not – good heavens, she'd only known him a day – but she bought an extra shirt anyway.

'Gosh, this is fun!' said Hilary, as they pressed each other into buying embroidered purses. 'It's years since I've had a really girlie time! That skirt would be lovely on you. Why don't you try it on?'

'Oh right!' said Daniel, eyeing the bags as they emerged. 'Like you only went in for a shawl?'

The church was even more impressive at close quarters, flanked by a massive porch flamboyant with traceried carving. 'You'd take it for a cathedral, if you didn't know better,' said Hilary. 'To be honest, it reminds me of parts of Haseley.'

'Me too,' grinned Oliver. 'In fact I think I'll use a photo of the stonework to illustrate possible influences… Let's look inside.'

'Actually,' said Frances, 'do you mind if I stay here? I want to make a phone call, and you can't get a signal at Haseley.'

'I'll wait here too,' said Daniel. 'Monuments and stuff aren't really my thing.'

Hilary might have said the same, but it would seem unkind to let Oliver go on his own. She followed him into the dark passage that led inside, prepared to be a bit bored.

'Nice fan vaulting,' he pointed upwards. 'I think you go through this little door here … wow!'

It was indeed spectacular. They found themselves facing an arcade of delicate pillars, reaching up and up to a roof they seemed barely strong enough to support. In the dappled light from the stained glass windows, they gave the impression of a silent forest of tall saplings, turned to stone by some ancient spell. The echo of footfalls and hushed voices seemed out of all proportion to the small number of people in the building, making one imagine that they must be underlain with other voices and other footsteps, layers from older times. Hilary shivered, momentarily overwhelmed by such unnerving venerability.

But Oliver was totally unfazed. He darted about delightedly between tombs and brasses and carved pews, stooping to examine the painted tiles on the floor, or draw her attention to a fine old chest or a quaintly worded memorial. 'What an exceptionally fine pulpit! Good heavens, I believe that's a sermon timer! Do you think they still use it? Come and see this cup! It belonged to Anne Boleyn.' Oliver had the gift of making everything interesting, because he was interested in everything, and Hilary found she was enjoying herself.

Meanwhile it was a very different telephone conversation from the one Frances would have been having if she'd managed to get through last night, with Daniel standing tactfully out of earshot, if not out of smiling distance ... yes, she was having a lovely time! There were a lot more people staying than the Shirburns had been expecting, but they were mostly very nice – particularly a lady called Hilary, and her son, Daniel ... Frances tried to keep her voice impersonal, but her mother knew her too well.

'Yes, I do mean *that* sort of nice, but I can't talk now... We're in Cirencester. It's really pretty, and it's got some lovely shops ... no, not the Shirburns – I'm here with Daniel, as a matter of fact.'

He came over when he saw that she'd finished. 'Everything OK? It must be tough, not being with your mum and dad at Christmas.'

'Just Mum. My father died three years ago.'

'Bloody hell – so did mine!'

'Oh!' They stared at one other, stunned by the coincidence ... of course she'd known Daniel's mother was a widow, but somehow she hadn't connected it with Daniel losing his father ... just as she'd lost her own. 'Pants, isn't it?'

'Sure is. Made me the warped little individual I am... Actually it probably is what made me want to be a doctor,' Daniel observed more seriously. 'Trying to cure people because I couldn't save him, kind of thing. Not that anyone could have done much for a brain haemorrhage.'

'And I suppose that's why I've ended up as a nanny.' Frances told him about missing out on art college, then wondered if it seemed like showing off. '... Though I probably wouldn't have been any good.'

'Why not? Of course you would!'

They could see Hilary and Oliver coming out of the church now, laughing at something. It made her look younger and more carefree, and it occurred to Frances that she was really rather pretty.

'The worst thing about Dad dying,' said Daniel, lowering his voice a little, 'is the effect it had on Mum. I ranted and raged and dealt with it, but she sort of retreated into herself... It wasn't that she didn't talk to anyone, or cried all the time – in some ways that would have been better. She just ... stopped enjoying things, I guess. It's ages since I've seen her really laugh like that.'

'The church was good. You should have come. Where are we heading now?'

'Down here, to look at this wonderful row of old houses – sixteenth century, surely.' The other three grinned at each other. Oliver was nothing if not decisive.

'All right, mate. Don't get run over,' pleaded Daniel, but he'd already taken his photo, with a charming smile to the van driver who'd been too startled to hoot. 'The man's a liability! Why are we going round with him?'

'I can't think,' said Hilary happily. She'd caught the affection in Daniel's tone.

Enjoying Oliver's enthusiasm, and content to follow in his wake, they wandered after him down the lane, until he suddenly stopped in front of a stone archway.

'Oh! Do you mind if we…?'

'No, Oliver, we can't go in there!' Hilary had seen poor Frances flinch.

'Shirburn Alert,' Daniel reminded him. 'You are entering a potentially contaminated zone.'

His face fell. 'Oh yes, of course. They were going to the museum, weren't they? And I suppose we'd be bound to bump into them – even if we just popped in for a moment.'

'It's not really fair on Frances…' said Hilary, torn by his looking as if a toy had been snatched away.

'That's all right. You go in,' she responded at once.

'Oh come on, live dangerously!' Daniel grinned at her. 'We'll hide you behind an urn or something if they are still about, but I bet old Tobias was carried out kicking and screaming ages ago.'

Even Frances had to admit that the museum was fascinating. After a while she forgot to look for the Shirburns round every corner, and became enthralled by the various displays. Daniel found her gazing wistfully into a case holding an intricately patterned gold pendant that would have formed part of a Saxon woman's dowry.

'It's so beautiful! …I'm not sure it wouldn't have been worth living in one of those miserable dug-out huts and having to weave all your own clothes, just to wear something like this every day.'

Daniel insisted on having his photograph taken wearing a suit of Roman chain mail meant for kids. Oliver found he was too big for it, and Daniel said that he ought to use his status as a top academic to complain to the museum authorities.

It was the mosaics that entranced Hilary. 'You'd swear they were painted! How could they possibly get such detail with bits of flowerpot and pebbles?'

'I'll pop in here and buy a postcard, I think,' said Daniel as they passed the giftshop on the way out. 'Don't wait.'

'Wouldn't mind a look at the books,' said Oliver. 'They might have one on mosaics, Hilary...'

Frances picked up some tourist leaflets from the desk and was soon engrossed in the delights of Bourton-on-the-Water and Arlington Row... There were some brilliant places in the Cotswolds! It would be nice to come back, in the summer perhaps, and explore them with someone who had a car, and who'd enjoy going round the Wildlife Park as much as she would.

She was only vaguely aware of people coming out of the door that led to the toilets on the other side of the foyer – until she heard a piercing little voice.

'I thought you said that Nanny Frances wasn't coming to the museum! ... Yes, she is – she's sitting over there.'

It was too late to hide. Lesley was looking in her direction with a mixture of surprise and disapproval. Stephen emerged at the same moment, and saw her pointing. Frances stood up to face the music, wishing they hadn't happened to catch her on her own.

'Oh dear, Nanny! I thought we made it clear we weren't expecting you to join us.'

'No – I wasn't,' she hastened to explain. 'I didn't realise ... I thought you'd gone.'

'You haven't come to find us?' Stephen was puzzled. 'Then what are you doing here?'

'The Britwells brought her with their nanny, I imagine.'

'Oh no – I came with Daniel.'

As soon as she'd said it, she realised her mistake.

'Oh *did* you indeed?'

'And his mother, and Mr Leafield.' It was too late. Lesley wasn't listening … oh hell, where were the others? For a moment Frances wondered if they weren't deliberately hiding.

'Well, since you *have* turned up, Nanny, you might oblige us by minding Tobias – if it wouldn't be too much trouble. Stephen and I have a piece of rather important shopping to do.'

'Ah! Yes, indeed.' Her husband responded to her meaning look.

'I'm coming with you…'

'No, this is grown-up shopping. You stay with Nanny.'

'I don't wa-ant to!' Tobias followed them through the glass door and out into the street.

Frances grabbed his hand. 'Perhaps it's to do with Christmas presents,' she suggested. 'They always have to be kept secret, don't they?'

'Yes, well – we won't be long.' Lesley and Stephen hurried away, and disappeared into a shop at the other end of the road.

Frances acquitted the others of hiding, as soon as she saw their expressions of horror when they came out to find Tobias sitting beside her. She couldn't help grinning.

'God almighty! Where did he spring from?' Daniel looked up, as if he might have dropped down from the gallery above their heads.

'His mummy and daddy have gone to buy something private – so we're looking after Tobias for a little while … at least, I've got to. You don't have to wait.'

'You mean they just commanded you to babysit, and buggered off? I don't believe it!'

'But they'd already said they didn't need you, surely? They can't have it both ways!' Hilary was appalled.

'It's all my fault,' said Oliver. 'You said we shouldn't go into the museum… Tell you what, *I'll* look after Tobias, while you three go shopping or whatever.'

Although they laughed, Frances was very touched.

'*I'd* like to go shopping,' said Tobias. He sounded a little wistful.

'Would you, mate?' said Daniel kindly. 'Not got all your presents yet then?'

'I'm having my presents on Christmas Day,' Tobias told him. 'That's tomorrow.'

'I don't think he's *quite* got the concept…' Frances smiled.

'That's a pity,' said Hilary. 'Buying presents for other people is much the nicest part of Christmas.'

'Yes, isn't it?' Frances met her eye, both with the same sudden thought. 'I'll go and see if Mummy will give you some money to spend, Tobias. Wait here.'

She'd noticed which shop Lesley and Stephen had gone into – a stationer's – and found them at the counter, paying for what they'd bought. They didn't look very pleased to see her.

'Tobias wants to do some Christmas shopping,' she explained. 'Do you think he could have a little bit of money to buy presents with?'

'Er … yes, of course …' Stephen handed her some of the change he'd just been given, at the same time trying to cover their purchase guiltily with his other hand. Naturally Frances glanced to see what it was … *how odd*!

Lesley too looked furtive. 'We'll be out in a minute. Don't take him far.'

'What a brainwave!' Hilary murmured to Frances. She could see that Tobias was really enjoying choosing little presents for everyone, and it was doing him all the good in the world to be made to consider what people other than himself might want for once. She even got the chance to take him aside and encourage him to buy a little sachet of bath oil for Frances. He was so pleased! Lesley, to do her justice, stayed tactfully in the background, and expressed suitable delighted surprise when Tobias told her that he'd been doing 'real Christmas shopping'.

They were just debating whether it was worth taking all the parcels back to the car, when there was a loud coo-ee from across the street.

'There's Posy! … Posy, I've got you a present – and you, Auntie Julia – but you can't open them now 'cos it's a s'prise!'

'Darling, that *is* exciting. I can't wait! Have you been wondering what had happened to us? We stopped off at a garden centre to get a Christmas tree. It's in the car. Poor Shelley's covered in pine needles, aren't you, pet?'

That explained Shelley's grumpy expression – but not another mystery. Margery was with them, stopping to talk to Oliver as he photographed the Corn Hall, and Tony was there, laden with bags and pretending to mop his brow…

The same question must have been on Lesley's mind, as Hilary watched her scan the group. 'So what have you done with William?'

'Daddy? We thought he was with you!'

Lesley and Stephen looked at each other, then, rather accusingly, across at Oliver. 'Did he come in *your* car?'

'No, of course not,' Hilary replied for him. 'Oliver brought me, Daniel and Frances. Do you think we smuggled William in the boot?'

But to her surprise, Oliver came over, looking a little self-conscious. 'Um – actually, I'm afraid he must have accidentally got left behind. I saw him disappear into the pantry just as we were all about to go.'

'Silly bugger!' said Margery. 'He missed a good morning out. Not that he would have appreciated having a Christmas tree rammed up his backside in your car, Tony! Now what about lunch?' she went on. 'I'm ready for a sit-down, myself. The Woolpack used to be good. They know me there.' Margery set a fast pace down the road.

'A pub? Oh, I don't know.'

'Doesn't Tobias like pubs? Posy loves them! It's a pity she's just had a Big Mac.'

As Frances had feared, Shelley grabbed her arm at the first opportunity, and pulled her out of earshot of the others. 'How the *sod* did you wangle that one, you jammy little cow? Riding in the back of Mr Leafield's car, all cosied up to Daniel, when I was stuck between that old crone Margery and a bloody Christmas tree! I suppose you gave them a Cinderella story about being left behind and conned them into taking you, as soon as you saw Daniel was going – and you knew perfectly well I fancied him! Well it's not over yet, I'm telling you. You wait and see!'

♣ ♣ ♣

The Woolpack turned out to be in a pretty, half-timbered building. Its series of small bars, with their odd-shaped corners and uneven floor levels, was packed with Christmas Eve drinkers and couldn't have been much less suitable for a large family group of mixed ages. They didn't know Margery there as well as she'd thought – the place had changed hands twice in the twenty years since her last visit – and nobody spoke very good English. Nevertheless they seemed to think they could provide a meal, if the party was prepared not to sit all together.

Shelley saw her chance and manoeuvred Daniel into a niche with one tiny table, pulled her top slightly off one shoulder, flicked her hair back, and set to work. Frances, now firmly restored to Nanny mode, and recruited to ensure that her charge was kept away from the polluting influence of empty beer glasses, was unfortunately positioned just where she was forced to watch the performance.

She wasn't the only spectator.

'Will you look at that tart, trying to play the vamp with poor Daniel!' Margery barely kept her voice down. 'As if he's going to fall for that sort of cheap trollop's tricks! Does she really think an intelligent young man like him is going to be interested in some common little piece employed as his cousin's nursemaid?'

Frances felt her cheeks grow hot. She could only be thankful that Margery hadn't seen her and Daniel together this morning, or overheard Shelley's accusation of using similar tactics herself... What if his nice mother had been secretly thinking on the same lines? Daniel was going to become a doctor. Obviously they wouldn't want him forming a relationship with someone who hadn't even been to college. How stupid of her to have imagined, even for a moment, that he was being anything more than kind to Tobias's nanny!

Hilary was having a much better time. For one happy moment, it had looked as if she and Oliver were going to end up sitting by themselves, but Tony wouldn't allow that. 'Come on, you two, we can pull these tables together ... get another chair. You move round, Julia.'

Posy skipped between the tables, poking her fingers into her mother's parcels one minute, the next hopping across to advise Tobias what to eat, or go and make sheep's eyes at a strange man at the bar.

Julia and Tony were in good form, and the food, when it eventually came, was excellent. Oliver, prompted by relics of the wool trade displayed on the walls, entertained them with the story of how he and Margery's friend Nigel, a historic-buildings inspector, had visited a historic and very rundown farmhouse, and nearly been shot by the farmer.

There was only one jarring moment.

'Hullo, hullo! Looks as if Daniel's getting well in there.' Tony indicated the alcove where he was sitting with Shelley.

'Oh! A budding romance, do you think?' Julia nudged Hilary coyly. 'Wouldn't it be lovely if your Daniel got together with our Shelley! We must have him over for a meal, when we're back in London.'

No one argued when Margery declared that they'd all seen enough of Cirencester and wouldn't want to carry on after lunch.

'Yes, we must get home. You need your nap, don't you, precious?'

'Oh yes, we have to go back now,' Lesley received unexpected support from her niece. 'Grime and Brine are coming to play!'

'Yes, yes! Grime and Brine are coming to play,' echoed an already drowsy Tobias.

'I think you're too tired, darling. We'll make it another time.'

'You can sleep going back in the car, Tobias,' said the resourceful Posy. 'Then you'll be awake enough to play when we get there.'

'Well, we'll see. Stephen, are you going to pay our bill? ...Come on, Nanny.'

'No, Frances must come with us,' Hilary intervened. 'She left all her things in Oliver's car, didn't you, Frances?'

The Shirburns turned off to the other park, rejecting Posy's offer to go with them and 'make sure' Tobias went to sleep, and the rest of them made their way back in loosely scattered groups.

Hilary was walking with Julia and Tony. The others had gone ahead, and Oliver had fallen back to adjust to Margery's slower pace, pausing to point out things she might find interesting *en route*, in his usual enthusiastic way.

'Nice bloke that,' said Tony. 'Decent of him to insist on getting our lunch – godsend, actually, in the circumstances.'

'Yes, *isn't* he a sweetie?' agreed Julia. 'So knowledgeable about everything – and so amusing! That story he told about the mad old farmer was priceless.'

'They do tend to be witty, of course…'

'Who do?' Hilary couldn't think what Tony meant.

'Homosexuals. I suppose it's a way of compensating socially.'

A cold hand clutched at Hilary's heart. For a moment she thought she was going to be sick… What was he saying – that Oliver was gay?

Her face must have reflected something, for Julia laughed and squeezed her arm. 'Oh darling, didn't you realise? Yes, he and that friend of theirs, Nigel – queer as coots, apparently. Isn't it a shame?'

Chapter Fourteen

'This is a nice car, isn't it, Daniel?' Shelley draped herself against Oliver's bonnet as if she was advertising it. 'Bet it's really comfy. Not like that old thing of Tony's.' She looked across disparagingly to where the Discovery was parked, not far away. Frances could see what was coming. 'Plenty of room in here, too. I'm still covered in all them bloody needles... Reckon the old guy would fit in another, if you asked him nicely?'

Whether or not Daniel would have asked Oliver nicely, Frances was not to discover, for he didn't have to bother. Hilary had just come up – looking rather pale, but then she had been walking rather fast. 'That's all right, Shelley, you can swap with me. I'll go with Tony and Julia.' She hurried away before anyone could argue.

Shelley shot a look of triumph at Frances, and scrambled into the back the moment Oliver unlocked the car. 'Come on, Dan – we'll let her ladyship have the front seat... Ooh, this is cosy – a real limo.'

'Where's Hilary gone?' Oliver stared after her.

'I don't know,' said Frances, equally puzzled. 'I mean, she said she was going in the other car, but I'm not sure why.'

How *could* she have been such a fool? The question pounded through Hilary's head with every twist of the road. Julia and Posy were chattering away beside her – she probably responded – but she couldn't have repeated a word of what was said... Of course Oliver was *gay*! How could she possibly not have seen it? His cultured, sensitive mind, the artistic eye with which he viewed buildings and the landscape, that talent for cooking, even his rather delicate good looks. It was all there, to anyone but the most naive.

Had Tony and Julia realised just how naive she had been? She glanced at Julia, hot at the sudden thought – but no, they would never have let it rest. If they'd had the slightest inkling that sensible, reserved Cousin Hilary had been tempted out of her grief, that for one moment she'd been crazy enough to imagine ... *oh God, what had she managed to convince herself*? That an attractive man – mysteriously unattached – was giving signals that could possibly be construed as romantic interest in her, an unexceptional middle-aged widow? Yes, right, Hilary!

And she might be safe from Julia and Tony's scorn, but it wasn't they who'd been given every opportunity to observe her in Oliver's company as they toured Cirencester this morning. How much had Daniel noticed? Or Frances, who had obviously been puzzled by her sudden decision to swap places with Shelley? Were they laughing at her even now in the other car – or worse, discussing her with sympathetic kindness? Hell, she wished she'd gone with them now, but she just couldn't face the thought of travelling back at Oliver's side, trying to recapture the cheerful, carefree atmosphere of the outward journey. The best she could hope was that they'd forgotten all about her, and were managing to do so on their own.

♣ ♣ ♣

It was a miserable ride back for Frances, sitting at the front with a taciturn Oliver, trying not to notice what was happening on the seat behind. She couldn't answer his occasional hurt and puzzled questions, and there was little to see outside in the already fading light. She'd have done better to go with the Shirburns.

After helping to put Tobias down for his nap, she sought sanctuary in the bedroom – but there she found Shelley lying in wait, avid to tell her what she didn't want to know.

'He's a one isn't he, that Daniel? Taking advantage of the way those twisty roads throw you on top of each other, naughty boy! Oh – perhaps you didn't have that problem. I expect he kept his hands to himself when he was sitting in the back with you.'

It was a huge relief when Julia put her head round the door. 'Having a lie down, Shelley? Good idea… Come and show us what you bought, Frances. We're longing to see.'

She picked up her parcels and followed gratefully across to their room. Tony looked up with a smile and patted the bed beside him.

'We were so glad to find that you'd made it to Cirencester after all. Rotten of that pair to try and leave you behind.'

'I expect it was Daniel's doing, wasn't it?' Julia sat on the other side of her.

'Well, his mother's really. She suggested I came in the car with them.'

'Ah, but who suggested it to her?' said Tony, tapping his nose.

'I'm not sure ...' It would be nice to believe what they were implying, but she'd no actual reason to believe that Daniel had put it into her head.

'Oh come on – he obviously likes you,' said Julia. 'And anyone can see the two of you get on like a house on fire.'

Frances blushed, and bent to put her parcels on the floor. They didn't seem all that interested in looking at her shopping.

'We did get to talk a bit while the others were in the church,' she admitted. 'It turns out we've got quite a lot in common.' Somehow she didn't want to go into detail about their fathers and his concern for Hilary, though. It seemed too private.

'Do you think he's told her all?' Tony glanced mischievously at Julia.

'Oh yes, he must have – come on, Frances, we've been dying to know the truth ...' Julia gave a little bounce of anticipation, reminding her of Posy. Frances quailed, ready to prevaricate if necessary.

'Was that climbing expedition of his really cancelled?' It was Tony who asked the question. 'Or was it just an excuse?'

'Oh no, I'm sure it wasn't.' Frances flushed with relief at not having to give anything important away. 'He was really disappointed... Anyway, why would he make it up?'

'We thought perhaps he'd heard about the get-together down here, and didn't want to miss out.'

'Daniel's very fond of his family,' explained Julia, when she still looked puzzled.

'Yes,' said Frances, remembering some of Daniel's dry comments about his cousins. She certainly hadn't got the impression that he was desperate to spend Christmas in their company.

'And of course we all adore him – especially my father. I'm sure Daddy feels much closer to Daniel than his real grandchildren …Oh don't worry, we don't mind,' she added, seeing Frances look uncomfortable. 'After all, given a choice between him and Tobias…'

'…The only four-year-old qualified to lecture on Roman Britain,' Tony chuckled.

'God, yes – fancy wanting to drag the poor little mite round a *museum*!' exclaimed Julia. 'Why can't those two just shop when they go to Cirencester, like normal people?'

'Oh, but they did go shopping,' said Frances. 'At least, they bought one thing – I saw them. Though I think it was supposed to be a secret.'

'Well?' said Tony, as she broke off. 'Don't keep us in suspense! What was it?'

'A bit odd, really. It was one of those forms you can get to make your own will. Do you think it was a present for somebody?'

William and Scratch had spent a mildly amusing morning terrorising Leo. First they led him to believe that he'd been left behind all on his own in the big empty house – then worse, that he *wasn't* alone, but accompanied by some invisible 'thing' that made strange little rustles and bumps, and mysteriously moved the curtains about and caused doors to creak open. Scratch blew that by pushing the kitchen door a little too far, to reveal William sitting at the table. He assured Leo that he'd been there all the time. They then had a pleasant little conversation about what lay in store for him this afternoon, the terrible behavioural problems suffered by poor Kath's boys, and how fortunate that Leo would be on hand, probably the only person with the ability to control such budding sociopaths. When William politely offered him lunch, Leo seemed to have lost his appetite, and kept making nervous dashes to the toilet.

In actual fact, William had assumed the children's parents would ensure that they spent long enough in Cirencester for Leo not to be put to the test, so he was surprised to hear them return so early.

'What did you want to skulk back here for, you silly old fart?' Margery dumped her parcels on the kitchen table and went to put the kettle on. 'Missed a decent lunch at the old Woolpack, though their coffee's rubbish … you must have been bored stiff.'

'Not at all. Leo stayed behind to keep me company,' said William, smiling sweetly at his nephew, who had just emerged from one of his trips to the WC.

'Huh.' Margery clearly thought this beyond her son's capabilities. 'Oh Christ, those brats of Kath Arncott's are due to invade this afternoon, aren't they?' she recalled suddenly, no doubt prompted by his pallid colour. 'We'd better make ourselves scarce. Don't want to hang around with that lot screaming about the place.'

William, now that it looked like coming about, had been thinking much the same thing.

'What do you fancy – a drive somewhere? Sudeley Castle's probably open…'

But William had a better idea. 'I'd like to go to Cheltenham.'

'Oh – righto! Some nice old buildings there. We could have tea…'

'It's the cinema I want,' explained William. 'They've got the new Bond film on.'

Hilary would have agreed to a trip to the moon, if it meant escaping Haseley, and leapt at Margery's suggestion that she might like to join them.

'A James Bond film? Yes, lovely. How soon do we need to leave?'

'It starts at three.' William knew.

'We'll have to get someone to drive us, of course,' said Margery. 'No, don't be silly, Leo! You're staying to look after the children… Oh, I'll ask Oliver! He won't want to stick around here with the place in mayhem. If he doesn't like James Bond, he can always look at the architecture.'

♣ ♣ ♣

'Does *nobody* have a number for that woman?' Lesley was frantic. 'Yes, Stephen, I *have* tried Directory Enquiries, since your father doesn't seem to have a telephone book in the house, but of course she isn't listed. Presumably she only has one of those exorbitant smartphone things – even though she does purport to live on the breadline! …Have you really no idea which her house is? You could go down and explain that it's not convenient…'

Tobias had woken from his nap and, egged on by Posy, was eagerly clamouring for the delight of playing with the Big Boys. Lesley, desperate to avert this disaster, was helpless when the only person with any means of contacting Kath had gone off to the cinema in Cheltenham. 'It's *so* inconsiderate!' she wailed, for the umpteenth time.

Stephen, with no more ideas to offer, vanished into the study with a briefcase full of books. Frances was next in the line of fire.

'If only you hadn't let Tobias get up so soon! I'm sure he could have slept a bit longer… Where's that wretched girl of Posy's? Doesn't she have any control of her?' Posy had just run shrieking past them, with Tobias in her wake. 'Oh dear, those awful boys will be here any minute, I suppose. What on earth are we going to do with them all?'

Frances couldn't help feeling a tiny bit sorry for Lesley, left to cope almost alone. Hilary and Oliver had gone to Cheltenham with William and Margery, and Tony had driven back to Cirencester, saying there was something important he'd forgotten to buy. Julia had shut herself away with the Christmas tree: 'No one must look! – it's going to be a lovely surprise.' Leo had obviously hoped to have hidden, but hadn't chosen the best place, as most people had discovered him when they went to hang up their coats.

Frances wished she could be as certain of the location of the remaining two adults. Shelley had disappeared from their room, and there'd been no sign of Daniel since they got home.

She forced her mind back to the problem in hand. 'We need to find something they can all join in that doesn't need too much brain power. What about a game of cards? Pontoon's quite simple, and they could use matches as chips...'

'I don't want Tobias learning to *gamble*, thank you!' Lesley automatically found a reason to veto any suggestion of Frances's. 'We'd better put them in the dining room, round the big table ... I think there's a box of old toys somewhere they can play with.'

♣ ♣ ♣

'We'll use the front door, seeing as we're visitors today... Leave that alone, Grime! It's somebody's house – not a stately home where you can just destroy stuff.'

If Kath could have persuaded her boys to wear suits and ties this afternoon, she would. As it was, they were dressed in their best tracksuits and trainers. This was an important occasion, as she had been stressing to them all the way along the lane and up the hill.

'You got to take your chances, if you want to get on. Can't just sit on the settee with your Xbox all your life, hoping it's going to fall in your lap. Who knows what it could lead to, getting to be friends with a girl like little Posy Britwell? Couple of years younger than you, Brine ... anything could happen!'

Grime sniggered, and dug his brother in the ribs. They were at that age.

'Stop scuffing them new shoes, Brine! They'll do for school when you go back.'

It wasn't just her boys that Kath had dreams for. She hadn't put on the skirt that was too tight to clean in and her expensive blouse in order to impress the children's parents. Yes, take your chance, and anything could happen, was Kath's motto. And she reckoned she *was* in with a chance there.

'Mr Watlington's going to be looking after you, remember. He's an expert on dealing with badly behaved kids, so it's no good trying to mess him about. A man like him won't put up with the sort of rubbish your dad does.'

'I still don't see why we couldn't bring the Xbox,' complained Brine. 'Old William likes that. He nearly beat me at Grand Prix.'

'They won't be doing that kind of stuff, I told you! Those kids'll play posh games.'

'What sort of games?' Grime asked dubiously.

'Oh, I don't know – Scrabble or something.'

'*Scrabble*?'

The children rushed into the hall when the bell rang. 'I'll go! I'll go!'

'No, Mrs Arncott doesn't use the front door … oh!'

Apparently Mrs Arncott did.

'Here we are, then! This is Grime, and that's Brine. Say hullo to Frances. You could shake hands, couldn't you, Grime – meeting a lady? Bet you thought we were never coming, Mrs Shirburn – time these two take to get ready!'

Grime was a lanky boy, with sandy hair cut badly so that it stuck up in odd tufts randomly over his head, and rather goofy teeth. Brine was more like his mother, a little podgy, with a heavily freckled nose, and small, sly eyes. Neither would have been snapped up by an advertising agency for their angel faces or cute charm, but it didn't stop Posy from simpering coyly, or Tobias gazing up at them as if they were Greek gods come to visit.

'And where's Mr Watlington gone to? He's the gentleman I told you about – the one you'd better watch your step with, Grime… Coo-ee, Mr Watlington! Where are you?'

'He's in there,' said Posy, pointing to the cloakroom helpfully. 'Come on, Brine, we'll play up in my room.'

'Oh no you won't!' Lesley grabbed her arm. 'And where do you and Daniel think you're going? Your job's here, young lady!'

Where had they come from? That was the question. Only the bedrooms lay up those stairs, and if Shelley hadn't been in hers…

Lesley shepherded people into the dining room and fussed about with chairs. Mrs Arncott and Daniel brought Leo in between them and sat him at the head of the table.

'Now, settle down everyone, and I'll show you the nice game I've found for you!'

'That's right, Brine, move up a bit closer to Posy,' ordered his mother. 'Nothing to snigger at, Grime! You sit on her other side … I'll come next to you, shall I, Mr Watlington?'

'Oh, there isn't room for all of us to play, I'm afraid,' said Lesley, producing a box and laying it on the table. 'No, Shelley, you stay and look after Posy. We'll be in the kitchen, if you need us.'

She dragged a reluctant Mrs Arncott away, leaving Grime to sum up their feelings.

'What the bleedin' hell do you think's in there?'

♣ ♣ ♣

So much for avoiding Oliver! But having heard that he was driving, it really would have looked pointed if Hilary had announced that she'd changed her mind about going to Cheltenham ... and after all, she'd got to face him some time. Even if she followed her first instinct and ran back home to London, there would be no escaping from Haseley till at least Boxing Day.

Anyway, it wasn't exactly a problem at the moment. Margery had been given the front seat, and was holding Oliver in a lively discussion about mutual friends that didn't include the passengers behind them. William remained silent, but Hilary could tell from the eager, upright way he sat that he was enjoying the ride and looking forward to his trip to the pictures. They should make sure he went out more often.

What a beautiful cultured voice Oliver had – too cultured, of course, she now realised – but deep-toned and sexy. Just the kind she found particularly attractive. It was probably Oliver's voice that had been her downfall, out in the darkness where they'd first met, even before she encountered the half shy, half mischievous smile that had so tugged at her heart – and long before she'd discovered how entertaining he could be, and the way his enthusiasm for everything made one feel that the world was an interesting place, and life worth living after all… Oh God, how was she going to manage?

Suddenly, for one ghastly moment, Hilary thought she was going to burst into tears.

♣ ♣ ♣

'What is it?' said Posy, staring, like the rest of them, at the battered old box.

'A board game, I think,' said Daniel. Something to do with space travel, as far as Frances could tell from the picture on the lid.

'A "bored" game? Oh yawn!' said Shelley, covering her mouth to make the point, with an arch glance at Daniel.

'Hold on,' said Leo, pulling the box towards him. 'I recognise this! It was Stephen and Julia's. We used to play it when we were children.'

'Dearie me!'

But no one was looking at Shelley. Leo had eased off the lid and began to unpack the contents with delighted recognition. 'It was a bloody good game, actually … you have one of these little spaceships, and you have to go off exploring and bringing stuff back to Cape Canaveral.'

'Where?'

'…and you get points, according to how valuable your cargo is… Come on, we each choose a colour.'

There were six of the little spaceships, and eight of them at the table – nine if you counted Scratch, who was sitting on Brine's lap, as eager to play as anyone.

'We'll have to join up a bit. I'll go with Tobias, and you can play with Posy,' Frances said to Shelley.

'Ooh, I can think of other people I'd rather play with!'

Grime sniggered, then looked nervously at Leo, but he was too immersed in setting out the game to bear out his reputation for discipline.

'I want the green one,' said Tobias.

'No, sorry,' said Leo. '*I* always have green.'

Hilary was aware of Oliver trying to get her attention on the short walk from the car park to the cinema. She took William's arm, ostensibly to support him along the busy street – and pinned him to her side for protection.

Oliver did manage 'Are you OK?' just as they were going into the foyer, and she said 'Yes, fine,' and privately congratulated herself on coming up with such a reasonable, well-collected answer.

With Oliver seated safely at the other end of the row, Hilary relaxed a little, and after a while the film began to grip her, despite herself. William was absolutely rapt. She caught Margery's eye as they glanced at him in mutual affection, enjoying his pleasure.

They came out of the cinema discussing the film, and for a moment, still in that other-worldly daze, Hilary forgot and turned to Oliver quite naturally to comment on some inconsistency of the plot. He replied, with a little lift of the brow suggesting his relief. She caught her breath at the reminder, but in the same instant determined to maintain the fiction, and carried on chattering brightly all the way back to the car … there! Easy. Normal service resumed. He would think he'd imagined the little blip in their relationship.

🌲 🌲 🌲

The board game wasn't going well. Tobias was too young for it, Shelley too stupid, and the older boys too unused to anything which didn't involve a joystick. Leo, on the other hand, was taking it with deadly seriousness, and increasingly failing to hide his fury at being beaten by Posy.

'It's all luck, of course,' he said, after a particularly inept move had lost him half his precious cargo.

'No it's not,' said Daniel unkindly. 'If you hadn't chosen to risk the Venture card, instead of throwing the dice…'

Scratch chose that strategic moment to give in to temptation, and see what a helpful paw might do for the course of Brine's little spaceship.

'Oh for *fuck's* sake, keep that cat off the board!'

There was a gasp of mingled horror and admiration. Frances just hoped that Tobias, staring open-mouthed at Leo, wasn't adding the word to his carefully prepared store of vocabulary.

Shelley tittered. Grime and Brine, sensing anarchy, began to kick each other under the table. Posy threw a six, and with a triumphant crow brought her piece to within one square of the mothership that represented Home.

'So how are you getting on?' Lesley came in with Mrs Arncott. 'Oh, Tobias darling, haven't you got any of your little thingies left… Look, Leo's got plenty. I'm sure he'll

212

let you have some of his, to make it more fair, as you're only small.'

'*Don't*!' said Leo through his teeth. Anyone could see he was restraining himself from slapping those predatory fingers.

'Who's winning?' said Mrs Arncott, as he made his move. 'Ooh, it looks as if you are, Mr Watlington!'

'Posy's just about to beat him,' said Daniel. 'You've come in at the death.'

'Well, she is a bit older than Tobias,' pleaded Lesley, reluctant to give her niece her due. 'I really think it would be fairer to start again, with some sort of handicap…'

But at that moment, Posy got the throw she needed.

She punched the air, leapt off her chair and did a triumphant dance in front of Leo, who turned as green as his spaceship. Grime whooped and for no obvious reason started to thump his brother. Scratch, not to be outdone, jumped onto the table, scattering all the pieces.

'No … look … you're all being very silly…' But Lesley was powerless to stop the mayhem.

'Well done, Posy,' said Frances, with a nod to show Tobias that this was correct conduct for the loser of a game, a role previously outside his experience. 'Let's play something different now, shall we? Something a bit more active that we can all join in.'

'I know – Sardines!' said Posy, still on a high. 'Have you played that, Brine? It's easy. Like hide-and-seek, but you all end up squashed together in the cupboard.' She looked at her new friends speculatively.

'No, I don't think that's a very good idea…'

But Lesley was outnumbered. She barely had time to declare the bedrooms out of bounds, before everyone bounded away with shrieks of delight.

🌲 🌲 🌲

'You have the front seat,' Margery suggested, holding open the car door.

Hilary hesitated. Was she ready for this? It was all very well being brightly normal for five minutes, but sitting beside Oliver in the dark on the long journey home…

'Er … why not let William go in front this time? We can gossip in the back.'

'Righty-ho.' Margery climbed in beside her. 'So – Christmas Day tomorrow,' she reminded them, as they set off. 'I trust you'll be dressing up in your red coat and beard to amuse the children, William!'

'Ha!'

Margery chuckled. 'Miserable old Scrooge! Bet you haven't bought them any presents, either.'

'Don't get a choice!' grumbled William. 'Bloody Julia's already had me putting my name to some parcel she's wrapped for Posy. And Ratso and Stephen seem to think I'm going to stump up for a bicycle for Tobias – as if he's old enough to ride one!'

'You bought Daniel his first bike,' said Hilary reminiscently. 'What a long time ago that seems!' She sometimes felt a little guilty at the generosity William had always shown Daniel, in contrast to his own grandchildren.

'I don't mind dressing up as Santa Claus, if you think the children would enjoy it,' said Oliver. 'Though I don't know what I'd do for a costume.'

'My red dressing gown!' said Margery at once, 'and cotton wool on your face. What's more, they've bought Posy one of those silly Christmas hats. I saw it on the peg.'

'He's going to look bloody ridiculous with that on his head!'

What a nice man Oliver was, Hilary thought, offering to make a fool of himself to entertain a couple of small children who are nothing to do with him. Just as he had driven them all this way so that William could see the film he wanted. Yes, Oliver Leafield was the sort of kind, amusing, interesting person that, in any other circumstances, one would be delighted to have for a friend... And why not? Lots of women had gay friendships, didn't they? Wouldn't that be the answer – a way of keeping this wonderful man in her life?

'Where is everybody?' said Margery, as they let themselves back into the house.

'I can't think.' Hilary, her mind still elsewhere, opened the cupboard to hang up her coat. 'Oh!'

'What?' said Margery at her shoulder. 'Oh my goodness!'

Buried among the coats in the darkness were Kath Arncott and Leo, closely intertwined in each other's arms.

Chapter Fifteen

'I thought only *one* person was supposed to hide!'

'Well yes, but when the others find them, they hide too…' There wasn't a lot of point in Frances trying to explain the principles of Sardines to Lesley, when the game had become a total free-for-all. The children were in and out of cupboards and behind doors, hiding and discovering each other with delighted screams, apparently at random. Inevitably Daniel and Shelley had vanished early in the proceedings – although Kath and Leo had just reappeared, looking respectively exultant and embarrassed.

'I really think we need to round everybody up now,' said Lesley. 'The others are back, and Mrs Arncott will want to take her boys home for their tea… Come here, Tobias… Posy, can't you stand still for a minute? Oh dear, where has her wretched nanny gone?'

'She went upstairs,' said her charge, 'to see if Daniel was hiding in one of the bedrooms.'

'Well of course not! I put them out of bounds.'

Before Frances could disillusion her, Julia emerged from the sitting room. 'Hello, darlings? Having a lovely time? I've finished the tree now, so you must all come and admire it after tea.'

'Did someone say "tea"?' Stephen appeared from the study. 'That sounds an excellent idea.'

'Oh no…' Lesley tried to lower her voice, 'we don't want to get involved in that – they're just about to leave.'

'Oh but you'll have to give them tea!' exclaimed Julia, raising an eyebrow at Tony, who was coming downstairs.

'Yes of course! Can't send a pack of kids home with empty stomachs – eh, Posy?'

'Tea! … Tea!'

♣ ♣ ♣

'Would you ever have thought it of Leo?' exclaimed Margery, as they went up to put their things away.

'I suspect Kath's more to blame than him. You know what a man-eater she is.'

'I dare say you're right.' Margery looked almost disappointed.

Hilary wasn't terribly interested in what Leo and Kath might have been up to in the coat cupboard – she was too preoccupied with the problems in her own emotional life. Would it be possible for her to remain 'just good friends' with Oliver Leafield? There was little doubt that he liked her as a person, and had been enjoying her companionship… Oh dear, what if he *had* noticed her avoiding him, and put it down to prejudice on discovering that he was gay? That would be terrible! The last thing she wanted to do was hurt him.

'Good heavens, girl, what are you doing in here?' Margery's exclamation came from across the landing.

'Oh, hi! Are you back? I was looking for Daniel.'

'Well you're not going to find him in my bedroom, are you?' Margery shook her head in bemusement as Shelley disappeared.

Hilary went into her own room and kicked her shoes off with a despairing sigh... If only she had known about Oliver from the beginning! They would have formed an amusing friendship in almost exactly the same way; he wouldn't have noticed any difference in how she treated him; and she would have been saved this awful, hollow sense of bereavement. The tragedy was that it was too late now. Having been stupid enough to fall in love with the man – and she might as well admit that's what had happened – she knew that trying to maintain a relationship on any different sort of basis would simply tear her apart!

🌲 🌲 🌲

It would have been a gross understatement to say that it was an uncomfortable tea party. They would have been better off in the less formal surroundings of the kitchen, but, assuming that everyone would want tea, Lesley had got Frances to help her clear the dining-room table and lay it with all the works. It was probably the first time in their lives that Grime and Brine had been faced with a linen cloth, bone china cups and a silver teapot, and they were suitably overawed.

In the event, Julia had bowed out, saying she would take the 'grown-ups' a cup in the sitting room, and Leo had made his escape with her, pleading an urgent need to talk to Hilary. Stephen, who hadn't been so lucky, sat at one end of the table, with Lesley at the other. Mrs Arncott alternated between sitting down, to confirm her role as guest, and standing up to carry the pot round, and made her children feel even more cowed by continually picking up on imagined breaches of polite behaviour: 'Not with your knife, Grime! Where do you think you are?'; 'Don't reach across, Brine! Say "Please would you kindly pass the jam?".'

Shelley eventually put in an appearance, but Daniel didn't. When Posy asked where he was, she raised her eyebrows and said 'I wonder!' in an arch way which suggested she knew perfectly well. He must have told her to cover for him.

Conversation was subdued and stilted, it being all too clear that everyone would much rather have been somewhere else. Even Scratch was conscious of the atmosphere of restraint as he nosed about under the table. No one had dropped any crumbs, and one glance at Lesley made him feel it would be unwise to jump on anybody's knee.

Julia popped her head in. 'Oh, don't you all look cosy in here? Mind if I borrow the sugar basin?'

Scratch decided to follow her back to the sitting room. So far Julia had managed to keep him and the tree apart, and unlike his master William, Scratch was very fond of Christmas trees.

🎄 🎄 🎄

Margery had been resolute in her refusal to come down for tea, saying that she needed to rest. Hilary wished she had the courage to do the same. Oliver would be there, and she still hadn't worked out a way of dealing with that. But Julia had seemed so keen for her to come and admire the tree she'd spent all afternoon decorating that she hadn't had the heart to insist on remaining upstairs.

The tree was lovely. One had to admit that Julia did that kind of thing supremely well. She'd resisted the temptation to add colour, or use the box of old decorations that had been in William's family from time immemorial, but she'd stuck to gold and silver, with real glass baubles, miniature candles, and a magnificent star at the top.

'Oh it's wonderful, Julia! I can never stop mine from trying to keel over, or having all the lights showing on one side. Someone ought to take a photograph.'

'Good idea! I'll get my camera after tea.' Oliver smiled at her. Unprepared, she felt a kind of whoosh and then a pain, as if he'd hurled a missile which had landed in her stomach. She made every effort to smile back, and failed.

'Yes, do! We must have lots of nice pictures of us all gathered round singing carols or something,' gushed Julia. 'Find a chair, Hilary … I'll be back in a tick. I forgot the sugar.'

'Come and sit here. I wanted a word…'

Oh no, she really didn't want to sit next to Leo … but then she didn't much want to share the sofa with Tony either – and as for Oliver, she daren't even look in his direction, for fear of that blow striking again.

William, bless him, must have noticed her hesitation. 'It would be nice if you kept an old man company for a change. There's a perfectly good seat here.'

She took it gratefully. For a moment it seemed that Leo was going to draw his chair nearer. Then he sat down, staring at the window.

'Have you ever thought this place might be haunted?' he asked no one in particular.

'Good lord, Leo, a rational man like you doesn't believe in ghosts?' exclaimed Tony, with an amused glance at the others.

'No, of course not – really.' Leo's gaze was still on the window. No one had drawn the curtains yet, making a pretty effect with the reflections from the tree. 'I had some rather strange experiences when I was alone here this morning, that's all ... and I could have sworn that curtain moved just now.'

'Well there's a howling draft from the window,' Tony reminded him. 'Needs double glazing.'

'My God, it's just too funny!' Julia giggled as she came back with the sugar. 'You should *see* the ghastly tea party they're having next door – all the best china, and Stephen and Lesley playing Lord and Lady of the Manor to the Tenantry, teaching those poor little boys to crook their little fingers and use a butter knife!'

'Practising for when they inherit Haseley House, I suppose – God help us!' chuckled Tony. 'There'll be no holding them then, will there? ...Sales of work for the Poor and Needy of the Parish, Open Days for the local yokels – with Lesley in a terrible hat and Stephen making one of his speeches.'

'Aren't we horrid?' said Julia cheerfully. 'But I can't think what possessed Lesley to make the Arncotts stay on for tea. I thought she was as keen to get shot of them as everyone else, and they really have had a fair whack. Poor little Posy's exhausted!'

'Personally I think Tobias will go to the bad,' Tony continued his speculations. 'He'll get some unsuitable village girl up the duff – an Arncott cousin, probably – and end up being forced to make her his Lady of the Manor... What do you reckon, Hilary?'

'Shotgun weddings aren't very fashionable nowadays,' she pointed out, uncomfortable at being drawn into this.

'Don't, Tony!' Julia shuddered. 'Just imagine if the whole cycle started again with another Lesley? It's quite unbearable.'

'Scratch,' said Oliver suddenly, 'what are you doing?'

Oh betrayer! And he'd been so close!

Scratch had crept in behind Julia, eager to see if this Christmas tree lived up to expectations – and discovered cat heaven! Strands of gold and silver lametta wafted provocatively to and fro in the draft; delicate balls of glass dangled just within reach; every branch held a tempting spiky candle that made one's paws itch to poke them. No one could have been more appreciative of Julia's efforts, and Scratch had been about to enjoy them to the full. Foiled in mid-spring, he sat back on his haunches and directed a look of deep reproach at his erstwhile friend.

'Oh no, *how* did he get in here? I'll swear I haven't let a soul past me all afternoon,' wailed Julia. 'Naughty cat! You mustn't jump on the Christmas tree,' she told him, with the effectualness shown in bringing up her child.

About to treat that command with the respect it deserved, Scratch was suddenly distracted. He stiffened, staring at the bottom of the curtain.

'There! The *cat*'s seen something now.' Leo pointed a triumphant, if slightly shaking finger.

'Probably a mouse,' said Tony, eyeing Hilary, but it was Julia who obliged with a little shriek.

'Funny colour then,' said Oliver. Risking a look, Hilary saw that he was laughing.

The curtain laughed back, then flung itself aside.

'Oh all right then, fair cop!' said Daniel. 'But admit you never would have found me yourselves.'

Frances felt another wave of homesickness as they bathed the children and put them to bed. Christmas Eve had always been such a magical time at home! Although it was several years since even Alex had believed in Father Christmas, they still kept up the fiction – everyone, including Frances, hanging their stockings up in delighted anticipation of the annual miracle that would see them bulging with little parcels in the morning. And the excitement of waking in the early hours and unwrapping them all had never quite died, even though no one expected more than novelty pencil sharpeners or chocolate teddies, with the regulation tangerine in the toe.

Posy and Tobias had been given stockings to hang up too, but the magic of the occasion was tainted by a subtly materialistic atmosphere which Frances found depressing.

'My stocking's bigger than yours, Tobias. That means I'll get more presents!'

'Nonsense, Posy! Do you think Father Christmas gives more to children with fatter legs?' Or to children whose mummies wore long sexy nylons, rather than thick woollen socks.

'And Santa only brings stuff to kids who've been *good* this year,' Shelley reminded her, with a playful clout.

'When we're at home I have a pillowcase as well,' went on the irrepressible Posy, 'else all my presents won't fit in.'

Having glimpsed the collection of 'stocking fillers' scattered over Julia's bed ready for packing, Frances could see the logic of this. She just hoped that some tactful compromise would be reached with the mother of a child who'd only been given a woolly sock to fill.

'Sounds as if the chimney won't be wide enough for all your presents,' she observed drily. 'Perhaps Father Christmas will have to save some for later.'

'Oh no, I don't like saving. I like to have everything now,' Posy informed them. 'Anyway...' she went on, with a sly look at Tobias, '...I *know* something about Father Christmas – something secret. Shall I tell you what it is?'

'No, Posy, you're not going to tell him *anything*!' Frances interrupted fiercely. 'If I hear one more word on the subject, believe me, it won't only be Tobias's Christmas that'll be spoilt!'

'Ooh ... oo!' crowed Shelley, in a tone that hovered between derision and respect at her vehemence.

Posy looked from one to the other, and opted to scramble into bed. 'When this is my house, I'm going to have the chimneys made *enormous*,' she stretched her arms to demonstrate. 'Then there'll be room to get all my presents down, and lots more extra.'

Tobias looked at her, puzzled. 'But *I*'m going to live in this house when I'm big – are you going to be there as well?'

'I'm not having *you* living with me!' Posy informed him with infinite scorn. 'I shall have a proper husband. He's going to be very rich and buy me presents all the time.'

'You tell him, Pose!' chuckled Shelley.

It occurred to Frances that Posy's rather dubious moral standards weren't likely to be raised by her nanny.

🎄 🎄 🎄

'We don't want much of a meal tonight, do we?' said Julia.

'Don't we?' said Margery, who hadn't had any tea.

'Not after that massive lunch – and turkey and plum pud tomorrow.'

As one who was quite sure she'd never be hungry again, Hilary had nothing against this.

'Oh dear,' Julia went on, 'I suppose somebody's going to have to get up early and cook it all. We can't really ask Kath Arncott to come in on Christmas Day…' She glanced at William, hoping he'd contradict her.

'That's OK, I'll do it,' said Oliver.

'What? Cook the whole of Christmas dinner?' Everyone stared at him.

'Yes, why not? Someone can help me with the veg.'

He didn't look in Hilary's direction – it would have caused her problems if he had, of course. She could hardly have refused to help him … but *she* was his co-chef, wasn't she? Why hadn't he turned to her?

'Daniel will give me a hand, I expect. We make a good team.' He smiled at Daniel, and Hilary felt her heart contract... Christ almighty! Surely she wasn't jealous of her own son?

♣ ♣ ♣

Lesley came to read the children their bedtime story, and Frances was sent off to clear up the bathroom. She wasn't as grateful as she might have been when Shelley offered to give her a hand. Apart from wanting some time alone to indulge in missing her family, she suspected that Shelley was itching for the chance to tell her exactly what she and Daniel had been up to this afternoon. He had turned up eventually, the story being that he'd found the perfect hiding place by creeping into the sitting room when Julia's back was turned, and taking advantage of the fact that she was keeping everyone else out to remain undiscovered till teatime ... yes, well. It would need a gullible jury not to pick holes in that as an alibi! And where was Shelley supposed to have been all that time?

But her first words on the subject took Frances by surprise.

'I reckon Daniel Watlington's gay.'

'I beg your pardon?' Frances paused in the act of folding a towel.

'Well it happens, doesn't it? Some blokes just aren't interested in women.'

'Yes, but I don't think Daniel's one of them.'

'Oh, right? And you've checked that out personally, I suppose? I don't think so!'

Frances was too relieved at the implication of what Shelley was saying to mind her sarcasm. 'So you didn't … um … I mean…?'

'Oh, shut up! …He's gay. I can always tell.' Shelley kicked Posy's top up off the floor and caught it glumly. 'I knew with that Mr Leafield the moment I saw him.'

'What? You mean *Oliver*'s gay?' Frances leant back against the bath and stared at her.

'For God's sake! How naive are you? Of course he's gay, dummy!' Shelley gave up any pretence of folding Posy's clothes, and pulled down the loo seat to sit on. 'Man of his age – no wife or girlfriend, poncing about taking pictures of everything?' She seemed to run out of evidence at that stage. 'Anyway, Julia told me … and you went all round Cirencester with him, and never noticed? Oh dear!'

'But I thought that he and Daniel's mother… I thought she liked him.' Frances gazed at the bathmat, trying to make sense of things. She'd been pretty certain that Hilary felt more than liking for Oliver Leafield, and up to now she would have said that he was quite keen on her as well. Surely Daniel had noticed it too? If it was possible for two people that old to be falling in love, Hilary and Oliver had shown all the signs.

'You mean Daniel's mum *fancies* him? Oh yuck!'

'Well he's sort of good-looking…'

'As in *gay*! They always are, aren't they? And they take care of themselves, those people,' said the knowledgeable Shelley. 'Anyway, he's got *wrinkles*!'

Shelley couldn't summon up the imagination to see how a man that age could possibly be attractive to anyone, but Frances had more breadth of vision. Oliver had a great deal of charm, he was good fun and interesting to talk to, and he had a nice, fine-featured face, to which a few lines merely added character. She could quite understand his appeal to a woman more of his own generation. She liked Hilary, but at first she'd found her somewhat withdrawn – more crushed by her widowhood perhaps than her own mother, with four lively children to drag her back to reality. But on this morning's expedition, in Oliver's company, Hilary had begun to come out of herself and show a girlish, fun side – more of the person she must have been before her husband's death... At least, that's how she had been until lunchtime – no, throughout lunch too. Frances had seen her laughing cheerfully at the other table. It was when they'd got back to the car, and Hilary had suddenly, mysteriously, decided not to go back with them – run away, almost, as if she could no longer bear to be in their company...

'Oh my God!' She must have just found out – on the way back to the car park. She'd been walking with Julia and Tony, hadn't she? They must have told her ... oh poor, *poor* Hilary! If the news had been a shock for Frances, what had Hilary felt on discovering that someone she had just begun to fall in love with was never going to feel the same way about her? No wonder she had looked so ghastly, and leapt at the excuse Shelley gave her to ride in the other car! Poor Oliver, too. He'd been awfully upset and had spent the whole journey wondering what he could possibly have said or done to offend her. Well, Frances could have answered his hurt questions now, but she had no intention of betraying Hilary's feelings – and anyway perhaps by this time he had worked it out for himself.

♣ ♣ ♣

'Fancy a walk, Daniel?'

'What, now?' He looked at Oliver in surprise. 'It's a bit dark.'

'We can take a torch. I just fancied a bit of fresh air.'

'Well, yeah – OK.'

'That's a good idea!' said Leo. 'Come on, Hilary.'

'Er … no, thanks. I don't want to wander outside in the cold.' Or play gooseberry to whatever was going on between those two.

Tony's beady eyes followed them as they left the room. He leant towards her and murmured slyly. 'Nothing for it, I'm afraid! The man's going to cook Christmas dinner for us, after all. Daniel's virtue has to be sacrificed to the greater good!'

At that moment, Hilary seriously could have killed him.

♣ ♣ ♣

Peace at last! William didn't even bother to put the TV on. It was so nice not to have people talking all round him for once. The children's parents had gone upstairs to resolve some problem with stockings – trouble brewing there, to judge by Lesley's face! Margery was making herself a sandwich in the kitchen, and Hilary had offered to do one for William, probably as an excuse to escape from Leo, who seemed determined to get something off his chest. He had gone off to the study now in a sulk.

Poor Hilary was looking tired this evening – unwell, actually. He must try and find out if anything was wrong.

She and Oliver seemed to be avoiding each other, after being such friends earlier, and now he'd gone for this mysterious walk with Daniel – hardly to seduce him, whatever Tony said.

It had been a good day. William had found several ways of entertaining himself, apart from that most enjoyable film. Even the Christmas tree was looking rather attractive with all its twinkling lights, and when Scratch saw his chance and made towards it, William took the trouble to pick him up and put him on his lap instead. They both settled down for a little snooze.

'Ah good, he's alone!'

William shut his eyes tighter and gave an inward groan.

'Are you awake, Father?'

No.

'We wanted to have a little word with you.'

'I'm asleep,' said William.

'It's so difficult to find a moment, with all these people in the house.'

He gave in and sat up slowly. Scratch did the same, glared at Stephen and Lesley, and climbed down onto the floor.

'If you're trying to persuade me to move into a home again…'

'No, no, it's something completely different,' said Stephen.

'Though I still think it would be far more sensible…'

'In that case,' said William, 'you must have come to find out what I want for Christmas.'

'No, Father,' she gave Stephen an 'oh dear' look, 'we've already got your present – we told you, remember?

It's that book we thought you ought to read...' Irony was quite lost on Lesley.

'It's nothing to do with Christmas,' Stephen interrupted. 'Rather a sombre subject, I'm afraid, but it's something we all have to think about.' He produced a piece of paper that one might almost say he'd been concealing behind his back. 'We want you to sign this.'

'What is it?' – as if he couldn't read what it said on the cover.

'Well actually, Dad, it's a will form.'

'You want me to make out my *will* – on Christmas Eve?'

Even Lesley wriggled a bit. 'It was the only time we could get you alone, Father – to talk discreetly, I mean.' She looked at Stephen for help.

He tried the firm approach. 'It's got to be done, Father. Everybody needs to make a will. Lesley and I went to a solicitor as soon as Tobias was born...'

'I don't think they let you give them back!' murmured William.

'...to make sure he'd get everything if we were in an accident or something. It's only common sense.'

'And you just want me to sign it. What about the rest?'

'Oh, we can fill it in later. You needn't worry about that now.'

William didn't intend to worry about it at all. He turned the document over and scanned every word of it with infinite slowness. Any moment Hilary would be back with his sandwich.

'As you say, it's a very serious subject...' He picked up the pen Stephen had handed him, and put it down again with a sigh. '…I really feel it deserves some more weighty consideration.'

'Yes, but not too much more, Father.' Lesley glanced at the door. 'After all, you are going to leave things to Stephen …' *Got her*! 'It's just a matter of signing your name, and we can sort out the details.'

'Well, yes, so it is,' said William, hearing Hilary and Margery coming down the hall, '…if that's what I *am* going to do… Oh thank you, Hilary! That looks delicious.'

Chapter Sixteen

Christmas Day! The sinking feeling was all too familiar. People might say that you don't know what you've got till it's gone, but Hilary had always known that those Christmases when Ben was alive and Daniel a youngster were precious. Even then she'd had the nervous underlying feeling that perhaps they weren't forever – in those days it was the mother's fear that something would happen to her child. So every Christmas morning since Ben had died, Hilary had woken with that awful thump of grief, in the realisation that they would never share it again. And this year, just when there might have been a glimmer of light in her long tunnel, it had been suddenly snuffed out, making the gloom even deeper than before... How she wished she'd never come down to Haseley! If only she'd had the strength of mind to refuse William's plea and spend it at home eating chocolate and watching TV on her own as she'd planned. The idea seemed positively blissful now.

'Mum?' There was a knock at the door.

'Yes, come in, darling.'

'Happy Christmas!' He gave her a bear-hug. Thank God for Daniel in her life!

'The children are already at each other's throats over their stockings,' he reported cheerfully. 'Leo wanted to know if you were up yet, so I said "no", and if you were, you certainly wouldn't want to waste Christmas morning listening to him yabbering…'

'Oh, Daniel, you didn't!'

'Well, perhaps not in so many words. And Oliver said to wish you "Happy Christmas".'

'That was nice of him.' A strange kind of message. What did it mean?

'Yes – well he's a nice man.' Daniel was giving her one of his close looks. She fiddled with her hairbrush to avoid it. 'You do *like* Oliver, don't you, Mum?'

'Of course I do. He's charming.' That sounded natural, didn't it?

'He hasn't offended you in some way – or said anything to upset you?'

'Good lord, no! Why would you think that?' Change the subject – quickly! 'We had a nice day yesterday, didn't we? How are you getting on with Frances?'

He made a face. 'I'm not sure … I mean, I like her a lot, and when you were in the church, she was really beginning to open up, and tell me all about her family and everything.'

'So?'

'Well, then she suddenly withdrew again, and I felt I couldn't get near her … it's partly to do with those bullies she works for! I think she's afraid that if Ratso sees her fraternising with the Young Master, she'll turn her off without a character.'

'Oh, Daniel!' Hilary was amused, but in a way she suspected he was right about Frances. She was a sensitive girl, and must cringe at the thought of her behaviour being compared to that of the dreadful Shelley.

'At least, I *hope* that's what it is, and she hasn't just gone off me,' he sighed. 'We don't want two broken hearts in the place.' Was that really what he'd said, or had she misheard? Did he *know*? But he wasn't looking at her.

'I'm sure she hasn't gone off you, darling. She's far too sensible!' And Hilary was far too sensible to add how much she herself liked Frances, and would love things to work out. No sense in killing the relationship off before it had begun!

🎄 🎄 🎄

'It's not *fa-air*! Posy's got more presents than me!'

'No she hasn't, darling. We counted them very ... I mean, it just *looks* more because Posy's stocking is more stretchy.' Lesley pulled at it to show him.

What was wrong with the child? Frances's brothers would have had that stocking dismantled and half the contents eaten by this time of the morning!

'Why don't you just open them, Tobias?' she suggested. 'Posy's started hers already.'

Tobias glanced at his cousin, and set to work, as if there might be a danger of her moving on to his, if he wasn't quick enough – perhaps he was right.

'While he's busy...' Lesley murmured, raising an eyebrow at Frances. She beckoned her across the landing into their room. 'Perhaps you could give us a hand in here.'

'Good heavens!'

Stephen sat on the bed, surrounded by Christmas paper and presents, obviously making an attempt to marry the two together. He looked up in relief. 'Ah, Nanny? Are you any good with this kind of thing?'

As it happened, parcel wrapping was one of Frances's talents. She sat down beside him and got stuck in. Lesley took on the task of labelling, and Stephen of finding things at her instruction. He wasn't very adept at that either.

'I know I brought down that vase we got for Julia! Is it still in the suitcase? Well, *look*, Stephen – it could be in the lining or something... Oh dear, where's Margery's soap gone? I had it a moment ago ... no, that's for Hilary – it's freesia. Margery's is the lavender one.'

Frances worked quietly, noting how every other gift to be wrapped was something 'a little extra' for Tobias, and musing on Lesley's complete lack of imagination when choosing presents for anybody else. They must have forgotten she was there after a while.

'I do hope your father's going to read this book! It was very expensive ... such a pity he was so stubborn last night.'

'Yes, it makes one wonder who he *is* planning to leave things to,' said Stephen, staring with a worried frown at the worm-eaten old wardrobe, though it probably wasn't quite what he had in mind.

'I'm sure he wouldn't do anything silly...' Lesley's expression suggested she wasn't all that sure. 'It's not as if Julia had a son to carry on the name.' She glanced affectionately in the direction of the room next door.

'Aunt Margery clearly thinks the options are still open,' Stephen pointed out grimly. 'She didn't ask Dad to the cinema yesterday because she's a fan of James Bond!'

'You mean she has hopes for Leo? Oh God save us!'

'Well, if Ben had lived… It's no secret how William dotes on Daniel,' said Stephen, by way of finishing his sentence. 'But Leo hasn't any children of his own, at least, so Daniel would be his natural next of kin.'

'And that's why Hilary's hanging round him, of course,' said Lesley, with the confidence of one who's fathomed out another's deepest motives, '…to make sure nothing goes astray, so to speak.'

'Yes, she won't want him marrying someone else and starting another family…'

Frances thought she'd been remarkably restrained not to jump up and throttle them both. As it was, she must have let out a choking noise. Whatever, it was enough to make them glance in her direction and then at each other.

'Yes, well,' Stephen coughed, 'perhaps we should talk about this another time… Is that Tony's you've wrapped there? I'll put it in the pile.'

Hilary decided she could do without breakfast – everyone being bright and Christmassy, and Oliver would be down there, starting on the dinner. It wasn't as if he needed her help – he'd made that quite clear – no doubt in reaction to her own apparent coolness, since she could no longer persuade herself he hadn't noticed anything wrong, after Daniel's unsubtle attempts at interrogation. She didn't feel up to the effort of trying to convince him that he was mistaken.

The weather didn't look too bad this morning. Perhaps she could slip out for a while? On occasions like this, one was grateful for the back stairs…

'There you are, Hilary! I've been looking for you.'

'Oh, Leo … right … I was just off for a little walk.'

'Good. I'll join you.' Not a suggestion of asking whether she minded. How wonderful to go through life with such self confidence!

'Er … if it's OK with you, Leo, I'd quite like to be alone.'

'No, that's fine,' said Leo obligingly. 'We won't tell anyone else we're going.'

He all but marched her out of the house and along the lane, turning uphill towards the windy field known as Haseley Common… Hilary had rather fancied going down to look at the village on Christmas morning.

'I've been wanting to have a word with you about yesterday afternoon,' he said, as soon as they could be considered out of earshot. 'You must have been wondering what was going on.'

No, she hadn't. For a moment she couldn't even think what he might be talking about… 'Oh – you and Kath, in the cupboard!'

'Yes, quite.' Leo reddened at the memory. 'I wouldn't want you to think… We were only playing Sardines.'

'Of course you were.'

'You needn't sound like that!'

Like what, for heaven's sake? The man's a walking touchpaper.

'The woman dragged me into the cupboard with her. It wasn't my fault! Good Lord, she's the last person I'd ever … I mean … ugh!'

Leo's expression was so full of distaste that Hilary was hard put to it not to giggle. She wondered how far to tease him, but it wasn't so much fun on her own.

'It's all right, I quite understand – Kath isn't really your type, is she?'

'No, my "type" is a different kind of woman altogether,' he said, with an arch look that made her hurry to change the subject.

'Did you find it difficult coping with her boys yesterday? I expect they gave you quite a hard time.'

Oh no – he had taken this as criticism! His face stiffened defensively. 'Anybody would have had problems keeping those children under control – they're completely out of hand! I did manage to exert my influence in the end, and encourage them to calm down.'

'How clever of you.' It was easier to play the game.

'So did you enjoy your trip to the cinema?' Leo went on, not wanting to know. 'Nice of William to invite you out, I thought.' His raised eyebrow suggested an agenda here.

'It was your mother's idea really.'

'A James Bond film?' His eyebrow couldn't get any higher.

'Well, not the film, obviously…'

'Yes, he might have chosen something a bit more suited to your taste, but it's the thought that counts, as they say – and you had the sense to indulge him.'

'It wasn't a matter of sense, or indulging him. I *like* William.'

Leo shook his head with that 'I know you better than you know yourself' look which made one want to stamp on his toes in spiked boots.

'And William's made it clear that he's very fond of you, Hilary – that's all I'm saying,' the odious man went on. 'Good news, I would have thought – for you, and for Daniel.'

🌲 🌲 🌲

'Hey, Frances! I don't seem to have wished you "Happy Christmas" yet,' said Tony. 'Where have you been hiding all morning?'

She told him about the parcel-wrapping session, and he laughed. 'Trust those two not to be able to get their act together without Super Nanny coming to the rescue! Do you think they realise how lucky they are yet? Tell you what, there's no one in the study, but there *is* quite a nice sherry with our name on it. How about a Christmas morning drink?'

'Well, they don't seem to need me at the moment.' In fact they'd virtually shooed her away, so why not have a drink with Tony? She jolly well deserved it.

'Interesting what you were telling us yesterday about their little purchase in Cirencester,' he said, when he'd filled their glasses, and found her a comfortable chair.

'Oh! I think I've found out a bit more about that.' Was it fair to tell him? Of course it was! 'They started talking when we were wrapping the presents – they must have forgotten I was there – and it sounds as if they tried to get your father-in-law to sign the will form, and he refused.'

'Oh bravo, Frances,' Tony exclaimed, as if it had been her own doing. 'I love the idea of you melting into the counterpane while they chattered away over your head! What else did they say?'

'Well, they've got this really stupid idea about Hilary.' It made her angry even to repeat it. 'They think she's aiming to hook up with Leo Watlington because they reckon his mother's plotting to get William to leave everything to him!'

'*Leo*? Good Lord!' Tony looked thoughtful.

'I know,' said Frances, appalled, as he must be, at the notion of any poor woman being saddled with Leo.

'That explains the attraction there, then.'

'Oh, I'm sure she's not attracted to him!' Frances hastened to correct him, but stopped short of telling him why she was absolutely sure. It was one thing to give away Stephen and Lesley's secrets.

'No, you wouldn't exactly want him for his body, would you?' Tony made a humorous face. 'Although Leo does have a very fine mind, he tells me – tells everyone, in fact, constantly.'

'You should have seen him trying to impress those children yesterday!' giggled Frances, and made him laugh with a description of the awful board game.

'Oh there you are, Hilary! Come on, we're going to do presents now in the sitting room,' Julia announced. 'Posy,

Tobias? Where are you? We've got a very special visitor this morning.'

Margery's head appeared over the banisters from the floor above. 'All ready? Get on with it, then, before everything falls off!'

The children were rounded up and everyone herded into the sitting room.

'Where are the presents?' began Posy in disappointment.

'Wait and see,' said Lesley, holding Tobias's hand and looking towards the door.

'Ta-ran-ta-ra!' Margery's version of a fanfare outside it.

Father Christmas came in, wearing a red dressing gown rather too short for his large frame, a pair of smart Hunter boots covering the gap, a moustache and beard that must have taken a whole packet of cotton wool and shivered perilously in the draft – was that Sellotape underneath? – and a child's Christmas hat clinging to the very top of his head.

Hilary let out an involuntary chuckle, then glanced guiltily to see if she'd spoiled it for the children, but Tobias was staring open-mouthed. Even Posy seemed lost for words.

'Don't forget your presents, Father Christmas,' ordered Margery.

'Oh yes, sorry.' He turned to collect two huge pillowcases from behind him and heaved them across the room towards the tree. 'Blimey, these are heavy!'

'You left out "ho, ho, ho",' said William naughtily.

'Ho, ho, ho,' responded Father Christmas, with an ungrateful look at his host.

'But … but is it *really* Santa? I thought he didn't…'
Posy was suspicious, but unable to penetrate the disguise.

'Of course it is, darling.' Julia patted her hand warningly. 'And what a lovely lot of presents he's brought for us!'

'Do I have to hand them all out?'

'Perhaps just the children's,' said Lesley. 'If you can find them. Oh dear, they may have been at the bottom.'

'Tip the whole sack out,' advised Daniel.

Frances stepped forward and helped him pick some she apparently recognised from the pile.

'Right … er … this one's for Tobias,' he read the label.

With a push from Lesley, Tobias ran up to receive it, delighted.

'And this is for Posy… Have you been a good little girl, this year?' Father Christmas remembered his duties.

'Of *course* I have!' The coy look suggested that she realised there was a man under there, at least.

His assistant elf found him a few more presents to give out, and then he declared that it was time for him to fly away. 'I've left the reindeer prancing on the roof.'

'Oh, can we go out and see them?'

'No, Posy, they're right at the top, hidden behind the chimney,' said Frances.

Father Christmas made his escape, grimacing at Hilary for laughing again as he nearly shut his beard in the door.

Julia and Tony took over, and soon everyone had a pile of presents in front of them. Oliver slipped back in quietly, bringing Scratch with him.

'OK, everybody! One – two – three – go!'

A moment where nothing could be heard except scrabbling and rustling. Scratch sat on his haunches, gazing from one to another, unable to decide where to pounce.

Hilary set to work on hers … soap. Thank you, Lesley. That could go with the mound in the cupboard … exotic candle from Julia – more fun, though how she was going to get it home intact was another matter … an amusing book from William, who swore he didn't do Christmas, but he'd known it would appeal to her … the earrings she'd told Daniel he really shouldn't buy, but was so glad he had … and, what was this? A CD of that choral piece she'd been discussing with Oliver when they were cooking supper together, a lifetime away. He must have got it in Cirencester — hell, she was going to cry!

He caught her eye. 'It's the arrangement I told you about … I think you'll like it.'

'Oh, *Oliver*!' All the mixed emotions of the past few days seemed to well up inside her and threaten to come bubbling out. She pressed her lips fiercely together to try and keep control. Oliver had bought her a present, and cared what she thought of it. He *did* care. Whatever her head had done to make her so miserable, her heart knew better. He was still holding her with a gaze unmistakable in its meaning, and she was responding in kind – an outpouring of coded message in that one long look between them.

Frances was touched to find her little parcel from Tobias. He'd even had a hand in wrapping it, by the look of things – or was that one of Stephen's attempts? There was one with 'Love from Posy' as well, scrawled in Julia's hand, with lots of kisses – and Hilary had got her that bag she'd been eyeing in the shop, bless her! ... And then there was another parcel – Shelley? Surely not. Too neatly wrapped, for one thing ... oh! 'It's that Saxon pendant from the museum!' she gasped aloud.

'I hope not, or we're in big trouble,' chuckled Oliver. He was looking more cheerful.

'It's only a replica,' said Daniel, 'but I thought you might like it.'

'Like it? It's *fabulous*!' And all the more so because Daniel had bought it for her. Thank goodness she had wrapped the T-shirt for him and slipped it into the pile at the last moment, hoping he wouldn't think she was being pushy.

Had he got Shelley something as well? Her pile of presents seemed very small, but then she didn't appear to have given many either... Oh – one glance at her face answered that question! Frances couldn't resist a tiny gloat.

'We'd better go and sort out dinner in a minute,' Oliver said to Daniel, with a nod in William's direction.

'Oh, yes ... now look, Uncle William,' Daniel went over to him, 'Oliver and I have got you a joint present, but it's a secret, and we're not going to give it to you yet.' He grinned to see that he had the attention of the room. 'You have to come for a little walk on the Common with us, when dinner's over, and you can have it then.'

'Well, I don't know!' William shook his head, but he was obviously pleased.

'Oh, can *we* come to see Grandpa's present?'

'Yes, I want to go to the Common too!'

'No, sorry kids,' Daniel was firm. 'This treat's just for Grandpa.'

William looked even more pleased. Lesley didn't.

'Oh dear, that's a bit of a shame! It would have been nice for Tobias to have a little walk after dinner. I'm sure Grandpa doesn't want his present all on his own.'

But Grandpa didn't rise to the hint, and Oliver and Daniel went off to dish up their meal, leaving Lesley still grumbling.

'That boy knows which side his bread is buttered,' Frances heard her mutter darkly to Stephen. 'Never mind, Tobias, *we'll* go for a walk after lunch as well – somewhere much nicer than the Common. Won't we, everyone?'

'Yes, of course, we will!' said Julia, after the silence had lasted just a little too long.

'After all that food? You must be bloody joking!' murmured Shelley.

🎄 🎄 🎄

Oliver and Daniel had managed to fit everyone in the dining room without much trouble by bringing an extra table in from the pantry. With a cloth over, one was hardly aware that it wasn't all one, though Lesley complained when the children were put there, in case Tobias might feel inferior at being an inch lower down. Julia had been politely kept away, and if the decorations weren't as spectacular as last night's, there was a simple elegance to the table which suggested Oliver's more subtle hand.

'Oh, it *does* look lovely!' Hilary exclaimed.

'Shame to eat off it,' Leo agreed.

'Come on, you two,' said Tony, indicating the chairs next to his. 'I know you'll want to sit together.'

'Well, not really.' What on earth had given him the idea that she and Leo…?

'Don't think we didn't see you!' Tony went on, with an arch little leer. 'Slipping out of the house for a private walk before dawn!'

Oliver and Daniel, carrying in the starters at that moment, both stopped in their tracks to stare at her.

'It wasn't exactly before dawn,' said Leo, as if that had any relevance to anything … why couldn't he just set them straight? Whatever she said now would only add fuel to Tony's irritating fire.

Instead, he took the chair Tony was offering, leaving Hilary no option but to sit between them. She avoided Oliver's eye as he put a plate in front of her. 'Just like a posh restaurant!' she said brightly.

It was rather. He had done something clever with mushrooms and cream, and that was followed up by the most wonderful Christmas dinner she had ever tasted. The credit was given to both cooks, but even a fond mother couldn't believe that Daniel had had much to do with those perfectly crisp roast potatoes, deliciously moist turkey and parsnips that melted in the mouth.

Tony had chosen a good wine, and was generous in dispensing it. 'Go on, Lesley, it's Christmas,' he urged her, when she protested that she didn't really drink.

'When can we pull the *crackers*?' demanded Posy, seizing one as she spoke, apparently about to rip it apart.

'After the pudding, usually,' said Stephen, just as his wife was saying 'all right, Tobias, pull yours now.'

Frances showed him and Posy how to pull crackers by crossing their arms, and made sure Tobias got the business end of his. Plastic toys shot all over the room in a satisfactory way, and soon even William was wearing a paper hat.

'To think someone earns money writing this stuff!' snorted Daniel, after reading a joke that Tobias was the only one to find remotely amusing.

'Bear in mind he's probably Chinese,' grinned Frances. 'I expect his material goes down a riot in Beijing!'

'This wine's rather nice,' said Lesley, fingering the stem of her glass affectionately before passing it across for a refill.

'You need a different kind for pudding,' Tony explained, 'stronger and sweeter.'

'Like you, Tony!' Good Lord, the woman had made a joke! She gazed up at him as he poured her a good measure of the new wine, eyes glowing and her cheeks a cheerful red ... was it possible that Tobias's mummy was a tiny bit tipsy?

'Talk amongst yourselves for a minute,' said Oliver. 'Oh Tony, I'll need the brandy.'

There was a cheer when he came back with a pudding covered in bouncing blue flames, and an even bigger one when the holly in the middle caught fire.

'Happy Christmas, everybody!' cried Julia, raising her glass and clinking it with Stephen's next to her.

'Cheers!' – 'Merry Christmas!' The call was taken up round the table.

'Happy Mismass,' Tobias echoed with the others.

'Happy Chr... oh, whoops!' exclaimed his mother, as her chair somehow slid sideways, nearly landing her on the floor. 'Tony, I do believe you've got me drunk. You are a *very* naughty boy!'

Chapter Seventeen

William wouldn't have said he was a great one for surprises, but he was enjoying this one. Daniel and Oliver walked him up the short distance to the Common, carrying an ungainly parcel between them. William privately decided it must be a kite.

When they got there and he was allowed to open it, however, it turned out to be better than that: they'd manage to find him a huge balsa-wood aeroplane.

'You put it together from a kit,' Daniel explained. 'We didn't know whether you'd have liked to do that bit, but it would have taken so long, and we did want to see it in action!'

'So do I!' said William.

It flew beautifully. Oliver, with his extra height, helped William launch it, and there was just enough breeze to carry it a satisfactory distance along the field. Daniel did the running about at the other end.

'You can see why we didn't want the kids along,' he panted, after retrieving it for the third time. 'They'd have taken over completely, and never given you a look in.'

'They'd have had to get it off me first!' said William, launching it again.

Meanwhile Lesley was trying to organise Tobias's walk. The trouble was, nobody else wanted to go. Most of those who weren't helping to clear up were already asleep, and Lesley herself kept yawning as she gave instructions to Frances.

'Don't take him far … oh dear! … just enough to get a bit of fresh air. I would have come with you, but … dearie me! … I think I'm going to have to have a little nap.'

Any sensible child would have wanted to play with his new toys on Christmas afternoon but, having been promised this 'treat', Tobias was grimly determined not to relinquish it, even if it did mean a dull trek up the lane with no one but his nanny for company.

Frances wouldn't have minded some exercise – they always had a walk after Christmas dinner at home – but Tobias's snail's pace could hardly be called that. She wished she could have gone with the others to the Common, wherever that was.

'You'll have to remember I'm a stranger round here,' she told Tobias, as they set off down the drive. 'Have you had a walk at Haseley before?'

'Um … don't know.'

'We'd better be careful not to get lost, then.'

There wasn't much danger of that at the moment. Once the lane met William's drive, it gave up all pretensions and became a rutted farm track. One could only really go the other way.

'There was a ruined house.'

'What?'

'When we came before – when I was little,' said four-year-old Tobias, 'we saw a ruined house.'

'Oh – right. That sounds interesting.' He must be talking about an abbey they'd visited or something.

She wondered what present Daniel and Oliver could be giving William that had to be used on the Common. A quad bike perhaps?

'What are you laughing at?'

'Nothing… Which way shall we go now?'

The lane had joined a bigger road, giving them a choice of uphill or down.

'The ruined house is this way,' Tobias pointed down.

'Really? Alright … oh, hang on a minute, I've just had a thought!' She pulled out her phone. The land was a bit higher here – *yes*!

'Hello Mum. Happy Christmas! … No, I couldn't get a signal before.'

'*I* want to talk on the phone,' said Tobias, after waiting quite patiently for a while.

'OK, then.'

Of course he didn't know what to say. After a little prompting to wish everyone Happy Christmas, he was glad to give her the phone back, but her mother was amused. 'He sounds rather sweet. Is he really such a horror?' Frances was hardly in a position to reply!

✸ ✸ ✸

Kath was a bit bored. All that the boys wanted to do, when they got back from the White Hart, was play with those stupid things Himself had bought them. And where had the money come from, she'd like to know? Those computer games cost a fortune – and if Himself was earning a fortune nowadays, it wasn't showing up in the child-support cheque, that was for sure!

No good phoning any of her mates on Christmas afternoon. No shops open … perhaps she'd better just take herself off for a walk on the Common and 'see what she could see', as her mother used to put it – might be someone else about.

What Kath saw, as she climbed the road from the village, was William, Oliver and Daniel, on their way down, carrying an aeroplane.

'Blimey! What you got there, then?' She waited for them at the junction of the lane. 'Somebody's Christmas present?'

'Mine,' said William proudly. 'We've been flying it on the Common. Goes pretty well.'

'And now you're off home for a nice cup of tea, I suppose?'

'That's right.'

'Well, I was just going back myself… Tell you what …' She scanned all of them, though she knew William wouldn't. 'Why not come and have a cuppa at my house? You were saying yesterday that you'd be interested in looking at my old cottage,' she reminded Oliver.

'Er … that's very kind…'

'Go on, Oliver,' urged Daniel. 'You don't want to miss a chance like that! I'll see Uncle William back with the plane.'

'Oh … um, right… OK then.'

Kath led him home with all the triumph of a hunter who has successfully bagged a plump deer for the pot.

🌲 🌲 🌲

'We'd better not be out too much longer,' Frances warned Tobias, after reluctantly making her phone call fairly short. 'It's getting a bit dark.'

'But I want to see the ruined *house*!'

'I think it might be too far away…'

'No, it's not. It's just down here.'

She let him lead her a hundred yards downhill to humour him – and there it was!

'Good heavens! You were right. How pretty!'

A derelict cottage lay a little back from the road, almost buried in its tangled garden. The roof had fallen in, showing the big old timbers that had once supported it outlined against the sky. All the windows were broken, and the door off its hinges. Nevertheless, there was something picturesque about the scene. Frances wondered if she might get a chance to come back with her sketchbook one morning.

'Let's 'splore.' Tobias squeezed past the dangling gate and ran up the path.

'I don't think we'd better. It doesn't look very safe.' But he was already out of earshot.

Inside, the house was almost pitch dark, and smelled strongly of decay. Even Tobias had hesitated in the hallway but, seeing her follow, ran boldly into one of the rooms.

'Tobias stop, for heaven's sake! This floor's all rotten. You'll fall through and hurt yourself.'

'No I won't!' He showed her how he could run across, dodging the holes in the floorboards, and shot her a look of gleeful challenge from the other side.

How could she put an end to this? The more she chased him, the further in he'd go. There was another doorway beyond. 'Well I'm going back now. But if you want to stay in this mouldy old place on your own…' She turned to go, stepping round a half-decayed plank, listening for what he would do behind her.

'I'm coming *too*!'

Thank God! She hurried as much as she dared on the perilous floor.

'Do watch this one. It's wobbly … agh!' She broke off, with a little scream of pain.

Avoiding the wobbly board, she had stepped on one that had gone right through. Her leg had disappeared into a void. She tried to pull it out, but the rest of the plank clung stubbornly to her ankle, refusing to release it.

She sat down gingerly, finding a stable board to rest on. This was ridiculous! Of course she could get her foot out, if she just kept calm, and breathed through the pain … *ouch*! No, she was never going to force it. Picking at the wood with her fingers wasn't any use either. Even the woodworms had had to give up on this one!

'Well this is silly, isn't it, Tobias?' She tried to sound cheerful. 'My foot doesn't seem to want to come out. What *are* we going to do?'

He glanced at her to see if she meant it, then came over. He, too, tried to pick at the board with his little hands … that nearly unmanned her! But it was no good crying.

Suddenly she had an idea.

'Of course – I've got my phone!' She didn't have a number for Haseley House, but perhaps her mother… 'Oh. No signal.' They must have already walked too far downhill.

'Are you crying?' said Tobias in fascination.

'Listen, Tobias,' said Frances, when she had got her voice back. 'Do you think you could find your way home on your own?'

He thought about it. 'I'd rather go with you,' he concluded.

'I know, but I can't move, and I think the only thing is for you to fetch help … even if you could get back to the road and flag a car down, it would be something.' Better not to think of what Lesley would say about Tobias accosting strange cars.

'I think I'll go home to Mummy.'

'But do you know the way…?'

Too late. Tobias, having made his decision, had already disappeared.

🌲 🌲 🌲

'I dare say you're wondering why I didn't give you a Christmas present, Hilary.'

She should never have said 'yes' when Leo had offered to help her put the china away in the dining-room cupboard. He wasn't actually doing anything, and it was obviously an excuse for one of those confidential talks she found so wearying.

'No, Leo, that's OK. I didn't get you one either.'

She tried and failed to recall Leo ever giving a present to anyone, even Daniel when he was little. In those days he had tried to ascribe it to some kind of Marxist ideology – everyone knew that, in fact, he was just too mean.

'The truth is, I didn't want to cause problems by leaving anyone out – you know what this family's like! And the old purse strings wouldn't run to presents for everybody, I'm afraid... Well, you're in the same position yourself.'

No, actually. She *had* made the effort to get something, however small ... oh, never mind! Best to stop listening and let him talk himself out. Then he might leave her in peace.

She wondered what present Daniel and Oliver had got for William. It was a secret even from her – a kite, perhaps, if they'd had to take it up to the Common... How she'd have loved to have gone with them! But she could see that if they relaxed the ban for one person, they'd have had no excuse to keep the children away, which had obviously been the idea – probably was a kite, in that case.

'It's a bloody nuisance, being poor all the time.' Leo was moaning again. 'Life would be so much easier, with a bit of cash around.'

'Yes, wouldn't it? Pass me that jug, will you. I think it goes up here.'

'Or even the prospect of having some in the future.'

'Absolutely! No, the big jug, not the gravy boat.'

'Well, *you'll* be all right on that score, Hilary. Not much doubt about that.'

'Will I?' Easier to climb down off the chair and fetch it herself.

'Why – what are you saying?'

God knew! Did Leo really think she was concentrating on whatever he was rabbiting on about? She was trying to get all this china into the cupboard without breaking anything – and if he wasn't so damn self-centred, he'd realise that and make more of an effort to help.

'You're afraid he might skip a generation? I suppose that's possible ... hmm. Food for thought, isn't it?'

'Definitely.' Perhaps he should go away and think about it then, and leave her to get on.

'So *this* is where you two are hiding yourselves!' said Julia, as if she hadn't sent her in here in the first place. 'The others are back now. I'll put the kettle on.'

Alone in the derelict house, Frances succumbed to a fit of shivering – reacting to the shock of her injury as much as the cold. Then she grew still as the cold took over, seeping into her body, freezing out the urge or ability to move ... at least it had numbed her foot a little. The sharp dagger pain had turned to an all pervasive throb, part of her whole being now, rather than just her leg.

She tried not to think how serious the situation was. If Tobias couldn't find his way home, or was knocked down by a car, or abducted ... well, no one would care what had become of her, for a start. And if he did make it back to Haselcy, would he be able to explain what had happened, and exactly where she was? Would he even bother to try?

How long was she destined to spend in this cold, empty ruin? Not all that empty either. She could hear little rustlings and creakings... God knew what might be creeping about under these floorboards, looking for its next meal, and tempted to sample anything stray it found in its path! Horrified by the thought, she made one more attempt to move her foot away, but it jarred unbearably.

Did anyone at Haseley House care enough about her to notice if she wasn't around? Daniel? Hilary? Nice Julia and Tony? Or would they carry on with their Christmas celebrations, assuming vaguely that she was somewhere else in that big mansion? It seemed more than likely. How long had it been before people realised that Stephen and Lesley were locked in the cellar? The best she could hope for was that her services would be needed badly enough at bath-time for Lesley to bother to investigate where Nanny Frances had disappeared to… God, how she'd love to be in that bathroom right now – deep in the huge old bath, sinking into warm, scented water.

William and Daniel were back, but Oliver had somehow been magically changed into a model aeroplane.

'What? Oh no. This was Uncle William's present. Isn't it mega?' exclaimed Daniel, putting it down on the hall table. 'There's a funny story about Oliver, though. I'll tell you in a minute … hey, Gran! Have you seen what we gave William?'

Hilary had to contain her impatience, while every antic of the plane was described both to her and to Margery, who was coming downstairs after her nap. William had obviously enjoyed himself as much as Daniel, and she couldn't help being pleased.

'But you were going to tell me what happened to Oliver,' she was able to get in at last.

'Oh God, yes! It was so funny.' They exchanged a glance of mischief. 'Poor guy, we shouldn't have done it really.'

'Done what?' She didn't trust their sense of humour. Had they left him up there, tied to a tree or something?

'Well , we were just on our way home, when we met Kath Arncott, out for a walk.'

'Out on the prowl,' corrected William. 'That woman doesn't do walks.'

'And she kindly invited us back to her house for a cup of tea.'

'It wasn't *me* she was inviting back to her lair!'

'Well anyway, old Oliver had once made the mistake of saying that he'd like to see round her cottage, and she was obviously desperate to have him – in every sense! So I'm afraid we … er … accepted on his behalf. To coin a phrase, the man may be gone some time! What do you reckon, Uncle William? I can't see her letting him out again much before Hogmanay!'

'Daniel, you're a very naughty boy,' his grandmother told him. 'And you're no better, William … poor Oliver! You know how polite he is! Once that vamp gets her claws into him, God knows when he'll ever get away.'

'If at all,' said the unrepentant Daniel. 'He might have to settle in and marry her, and have a few more Grimes and Brines!'

Hilary didn't find this nearly as funny as he and William seemed to. She was about to protest, when she realised there was a peculiar noise at the front door – not exactly a knock. More like a kick, low down.

'What on earth's that?' Margery heard it at the same time.

Daniel went and opened the door. 'Oh, hello, kid! Lock yourself out?'

'I couldn't get in,' said Tobias. 'The handle's too high… I want Mummy now.'

'What *have* you been doing, Tobias?' Hilary asked him, as Margery obligingly hallooed for Lesley. 'You're covered in cobwebs!'

''Sploring,' said Tobias.

'I thought you were going for a walk with Frances.'

'We went for a walk, and then we 'splored the ruined house,' he explained.

'Oh good heavens, Tobias, you're filthy!' exclaimed Lesley, hurrying down the stairs. 'How on earth did Nanny let you get into that state? Come on, we'd better run your bath.'

'But where's Frances, then?' said Daniel.

'In the ruined house.' Tobias was being hurried up the stairs.

'What ruined house? Why didn't she come back with you?'

'She can't. Her leg's stuck in the floor. She said I had to come back on my own.'

🌲 🌲 🌲

'Poor Frances – I do hope she's not badly hurt,' said Hilary, when Daniel had grabbed his mountain rescue kit and bolted out of the house. They could hear his car speeding off down the drive. 'Thank heavens Tobias found his way home!'

The hero of the hour, after a close debrief on the exact location of his ruined house, was now in the bath, no doubt being told how wonderful he was by Lesley. Whatever she said, Hilary found it hard to believe that Frances had irresponsibly led him into danger – much more likely to have been the other way round.

'She'll want to go straight up to bed, whatever the case,' she went on. 'It's a pity she has to share a room.'

'With that ghastly girl,' Margery was blunter, 'playing her pop music at all hours, no doubt, just when the child needs to rest! Well, there are plenty of others, aren't there?'

They found a perfectly good one across the landing, not as palatial as the bedroom Frances currently shared with Shelley, but it was fairly clean, and had a neat single bed which only needed sheets and blankets. Hilary fetched them from the airing cupboard and Margery helped her make it up.

'When I was young, this was all one,' she observed, pointing to the wall of Julia and Tony's room next door. 'They put that partition up so Nanny could sleep next to William – he was a fractious little boy!'

'I bet,' grinned Hilary.

'We all spoiled him dreadfully, of course,' his sister admitted. 'That's why he's such a selfish old cuss now ... still, he was never such a monster as that!' They could hear the familiar wail as Tobias was coaxed from the bath up to bed. 'They're going to miss that nanny of theirs if she's laid up for any length of time – likeable girl.'

'Yes, isn't she?' said Hilary. 'And Daniel definitely thinks so!'

'I could see that!' chuckled Margery. 'Dashing off to her rescue, like a medieval knight ... nice to see so much romance in the air!'

'What do you mean?' said Hilary, aware that her mother-in-law was regarding her quizzically across the bed. 'Oh no, not you as well, Margery! Why does everyone in the house think there's something going on between me and Leo?'

'You and *Leo*? Good God, you've not taken a fancy to that freak of nature, have you?' exclaimed his fond mother, momentarily appalled. 'No, you've far too much sense ... and anyway, it isn't Leo that makes your face light up whenever he's around.'

Hilary tried to meet her gaze, and failed.

'I don't know what's holding you back there,' Margery carried on as if she'd spoken. 'He's a charming man – well off, too, for what it's worth – and you've all kinds of things in common.'

'I ... er ... don't think Oliver's very interested in women,' she ventured. If Margery didn't realise how things stood, she hesitated to be the one to tell her.

'Oh, of course he is! He just needs a push, that's all. Men are diffident creatures at heart, always so terrified of rejection... To be honest, Hilary,' she patted her hand, 'we all feel that it's time you stopped mourning poor Ben, and moved on with your life – and men of Oliver Leafield's calibre don't turn up every day. It would be an absolute tragedy if he fell into the hands of a harpy like Mrs Arncott, just for the want of a bit of encouragement!'

♣ ♣ ♣

'Wake up! Frances, wake *up*!'

Thank goodness, it had all been a horrible dream … ouch! No, it hadn't. Her foot hurt as soon as she tried to move, and she was still sitting on the old wooden floor.

But Daniel had his arms round her – *that* must be a dream. He was stroking her hair, holding her against his warm body, close and safe.

'Oh, *Daniel*!' Suddenly the tears came, and she wept as if she would never stop. 'I'm sorry,' she gasped at last. 'It's just – I thought no one would ever come! I was afraid I'd have to spend all night like this … I didn't think anybody at Haseley would notice I wasn't there.'

He held her tighter, and said gruffly: 'You think *I* wouldn't notice if you weren't there?' His lips felt hot against her icy forehead. 'God, you're freezing!'

He began to kiss her, moving gently across the rest of her face, finally settling on her mouth … after a while Frances realised that she could happily spend the night here after all!

♣ ♣ ♣

For one glorious moment, Scratch found the sitting room empty. There it all was: discarded wrapping paper, some exciting looking presents, and that wonderful tree – unguarded, waiting for him to do what he liked with. It was too much. He didn't know which to go for first in this embarrassment of riches.

That moment of hesitation lost him his chance. Now there were voices behind him – people coming in with tea. He turned to wash himself instead – an innocent cat, busying itself with a troublesome tangle in its fur.

'Poor little Frances!' Julia was saying. 'I do hope she'll be all right.'

'Yes, dreadful thing to happen – Christmas Day, too,' agreed Tony, putting the tray he was carrying down on the table.

'And Stephen and Ratso are such callous pigs! Are you going to have some of this cake, Daddy? They would have happily left her there all night, once they knew Tobias was safe.'

'Just as well Daniel was around,' said Tony, 'to appreciate what was going on, and fly to her rescue!'

'Yes, well, one does wonder how necessary that was.' Leo chose the most comfortable chair and dropped into it before anybody else had a chance. 'If the situation was really so urgent, it might have been more sensible to call out the emergency services, instead of diving off on his own in that rather hot-headed way.'

'But far less romantic!' argued Julia, taking some cake herself and putting her feet up on the sofa. 'It would almost be worth having to sit in a haunted house for a while, to have a handsome hero come rushing to save you like that!'

'Well, I think most of us would consider it a trifle irresponsible,' said Leo, attempting to include William in a 'we know better' smile. 'But then a sense of responsibility has never been Daniel's strongest point.'

'Oh, come on, Leo! He's been wonderful with Hilary since – you know.'

'Yes, but one has to remember that since Ben died,' – Leo was less delicate than Julia – 'Hilary has been his only source of financial support. It would have been foolish to … er … bite the hand that fed him.'

'I thought you were saying that Daniel *was* foolish,' William pointed out, after the short silence that greeted this enormity.

Leo beamed at him like a schoolmaster whose pupil has been attending. 'Oh, I've nothing to say against his intelligence. I believe it's quite hard to get into medical school. All I'm suggesting is that Daniel tends to be a little rash and impulsive. I know it's been hard for him, losing his father, with the consequent … er … financial restrictions that has entailed … on the other hand…' He balanced his cup carefully on the arm of the chair. 'One might argue that it's been a blessing in disguise for someone of Daniel's rather unsteady temperament *not* to have a large amount of money at his disposal. When he's much older, perhaps, one would be very glad to see him comfortably off, but at his present stage of maturity, one can only be glad that hasn't happened.'

'You're trying to suggest it's a good thing that Ben died?' Tony stared at him.

'Oh no, of course not! And even if he hadn't, I don't think that printing business was ever likely to become a gold mine. Ben wasn't particularly good with money either, when it comes down to it … no, I'm just saying that if Daniel *were* to come into a fortune, theoretically speaking, it wouldn't be in the safest of hands!'

Seeing he had their attention, Leo risked going a little further. 'And while nobody appreciates that medical student humour more than I do,' his smile broadened in an attempt to endorse this blatant falsehood, 'one can't deny that Daniel's idea of fun verges on the eccentric at times … just a tiny bit of instability there, perhaps? – not on our side, obviously! But Hilary's relatives were always rather an unknown quantity, weren't they?'

William, Julia and Tony gaped at him, totally bereft of speech.

Scratch, following the direction of their gaze, beheld the irresistible combination of his favourite, Leo, and the best chair in the room.

'Ouch!' Leo leapt up furiously and swore. 'That blasted cat nearly had my tea over!' He snatched his cup, and a slice of Christmas cake from the plate. 'I think it would be safer to take this next door, if you'll excuse me.'

'Personally,' said William, when Leo had gone off to the study. 'I would have said Daniel was one of the *saner* members of this family – and by far the most trustworthy pair of hands for any fortune.'

🎄 🎄 🎄

'You can't call a doctor out on Christmas Day!'

'Not for a twisted ankle.'

How sweetly sympathetic the Shirburns were about their traumatised nanny!

'It's not just her ankle,' Hilary tried to keep her voice under control. 'I don't like the way she's so cold.'

'She'll soon warm up with that hot water bottle,' Lesley indicated the kettle Hilary had put on to boil.

'And a good night's sleep – obviously we won't expect her to resume her duties straight away,' said Stephen generously.

'She was half comatose when Daniel found her – I'm worrying about hypothermia.'

'Oh don't be ridiculous, Hilary! That's what Arctic explorers get, isn't it?'

'It was freezing cold in that place, you know. It didn't have proper windows or doors.'

'Well, Tobias was in there too, and he's OK,' Lesley argued.

'Tobias had a nice hot bath when he came in!' And Tobias's bath had taken all the hot water. Otherwise it would have been the first thing she would have given Frances.

'Oh, don't start all that again!'

No, she was wasting her time. The fact was the Shirburns daren't allow there to be much wrong with Frances, or they might be expected to take some responsibility for her accident.

She filled the hot water bottle and took it back up to Frances's new room. Daniel was still sitting on the bed, trying to get some warmth into her by chafing her hands.

'She still looks awfully pale.'

'I know, and she's half asleep the whole time. I'd be the last person to call some poor sod out if it wasn't necessary …'

Seeing that much concern on the face of her medical son was enough to make up Hilary's mind for her. 'I'll phone the doctor.'

Chapter Eighteen

Hilary supposed she should have been grateful that Kath was prepared to come in and help get breakfast on Boxing Day morning. Instead she found her cheerful humming and the bright way she said 'good morning' to everyone who entered the kitchen grating on her nerves. She had been busy with Frances when Oliver had come back last night, so she hadn't found out what had happened at Kath's cottage, but from the way the two of them were joking together, and teasing each other about the cooking – he was no longer 'Mr Leafield', she noticed – it was clear that they must have got on like a house on fire. Hilary tried to be glad that Oliver had enjoyed himself. Instead, she felt unaccountably jealous.

'How's poor little Frances doing this morning?'

Oh dear, it was mean of her to feel irritated by Julia's concerned enquiry too – especially as Stephen and Lesley had done nothing but complain about the inconvenience of having their nanny out of action.

'We're not sure yet. Daniel's up with her now.'

'It's so nice having her next door to us! She only has to call out, and we'll hear.' Yes, that would be more reassuring if one could be sure they'd do anything about it! There had been a lot of sympathy from that quarter, but not a great deal of practical help so far.

Hilary chastised herself again for being unkind … the fact was that she was really rather worried about Frances. She couldn't help putting herself in the place of her absent mother, and had spent a restless night wondering whether they should have phoned her straight away, or left her in blissful ignorance. It would be a shame to spoil her Christmas if it was just a minor accident. But if Frances turned out to be really ill…

'I'll go up and visit her in a minute,' Julia was saying.

'No, don't!' Hilary found herself crying out. 'I'd rather you didn't disturb her – we'll see how she is first. I've got to decide whether or not to tell her mother.' Oh why did the responsibility fall on her? It should have been Lesley and Stephen doing all this heart searching! But if they admitted to the problem, it would mean opening themselves to the possibility that they or their precious son was to blame for what had happened. Bugger them! And Julia for her specious sympathy – and Kath, who was teasing Oliver in an odiously arch way for frying up plum pudding with the bacon. Why couldn't she just leave him alone?

But suddenly he was at Hilary's side. 'Don't worry! Frances's mother will know you're doing everything you can. I can always drive over to Warwickshire and fetch her, if necessary – it's not that far. But I'm sure there won't be any need.'

Simple words, but it was as if a burden had been taken from her shoulders. She smiled back, almost tearful with gratitude for his understanding her concern, and knowing what to say to reassure her.

'Fetch her mother down? Of course that won't be necessary!' exclaimed Stephen. 'The girl's only twisted her ankle, for heaven's sake! She'll be right as rain in a day or two.'

'You'd better hope so!' Oliver told him, in an icy tone that Hilary had never heard him use before. 'Because if it's anything more serious, the least of your problems is going to be breaking the news to her mother.'

Someone was holding her hand – the doctor again? Frances had been vaguely aware of his visit last night, jarred back to consciousness by the jabbing pain as he examined her foot, and overheard the blessed words: 'Keep her warm, and let her sleep'. Now there was a sensible man!

'Hello – are you back with us now? How are you feeling?'

It was Daniel's voice – Daniel who was holding her hand. She smiled weakly at him. 'Better, thank you.'

'How's your foot?'

'Um – best not to move it,' she discovered.

'Well, there's nothing broken,' he informed her, 'but it's very badly sprained – and you're suffering from post-traumatic shock. The doctor says you're to stay in bed for the next few days.'

'What? No, I can't stay in bed!' Frances tried to sit up. 'Who's going to look after Tobias?'

'His bloody parents, why not? I don't know what those two have got to complain about!' Daniel went on impatiently. 'They should be grateful you don't *sue* them for what that child did to you, but instead of punishing him

272

for getting you into this mess, they're treating him like some kind of hero.'

'Well, he was rather brave in the end.' Frances gave a little shudder as she thought of what might have happened if Tobias *hadn't* found his way home. 'Oh dear, are they going up the wall?'

'Just a bit,' he grinned. 'You've obviously made yourself indispensable! They're trying to persuade that dim bird Shelley to take over, but she's useless enough at looking after Posy.' 'Dim' and 'useless' – what delightful words, when applied by Daniel to Shelley!

Hilary put her head round the door. Frances was surprised and touched to see how worried her face was. She relaxed a bit as soon as she saw that Frances was sitting up and chatting to Daniel.

'Well, you're a better colour than you were last night! How's the leg?'

'It hardly hurts now.'

'Except when she moves. I'm trying to get it into her stupid head that she mustn't get up.'

'No, of course you mustn't! The doctor said you had to rest ... and if Lesley and Stephen see you stir, they'll expect you to take charge of Tobias again – and probably Posy too, as I gather poor Shelley's feeling *tired* this morning.'

Frances grinned. There was no mistaking the sarcasm of Hilary's tone.

'Could you manage some breakfast?'

'A bit later, perhaps – though I'm sure I could fetch it myself.'

'For heaven's sake!' Hilary sounded quite impatient. 'It's such a relief to see you better. I was wondering what on earth we were going to say to your poor mother!'

'Oh … best not to worry her,' said Frances, after a moment's consideration. 'I did manage to speak to her yesterday, just before…'

'Well, that's what I thought,' said Hilary, tactfully ignoring her sudden reluctance to recall what had happened next. 'You can phone her yourself this evening… Come on, Daniel. The girl needs to rest.'

Frances lay back on her pillows, grateful for the excuse not to move. She found that she was feeling rather weak and trembly… What did that matter, though? What if she did feel headachy, and slightly sick this morning? Last night, Daniel had realised she was in danger and had come to rescue her! Daniel had *kissed* her, and told her that he was never going to let her go again, as he carried her back to the car – in fact, Daniel had made it clear, even to Frances's diffident soul, that he loved her! Frances would have sprained both ankles – and another, if she'd had one – if that was the price to pay for the secret happiness she was hugging to herself at this moment!

A brief knock woke her from a doze she hadn't realised she was having.

'Here we are. I've brought you some breakfast!' Julia triumphantly presented her with a plate laden with fried food, the mere smell of which made her feel queasy again. 'We can't have you missing out on Oliver's wonderful cooking, just because you're stuck up here in bed! Hilary said she didn't think you were well enough for visitors, so you must tell me to go away if you like…' Frances, of course, shook her head. 'There, I knew you'd want to see your special friends!' She rested the tray on the coverlet and settled down beside it. 'Tony sends tons of love, by the way.'

'That's kind.'

'Now, I want to hear everything about this terrible accident – and the way Daniel came flying to the rescue. It sounds so romantic!'

'Oh yes, it was!' Frances was sorely tempted to tell Julia just how romantic it had been. Some members of Daniel's family might not approve of their relationship – she was rather dreading what Hilary was going to say when she found out – but the sympathetic Julia would understand entirely.

However it wasn't for Frances alone to divulge their secret, so she gave an expurgated version of her dramatic rescue, longing though she was to confide every wonderful detail. She was surprised to find herself shaking, as she described her lonely wait, trapped in that cold, eerie place for what had seemed like hours. For some reason, her voice kept breaking, as if she was about to cry. She didn't really want to go through it all again, but Julia kept asking more eager questions. '…and then I must have passed out or something,' she finished at last, 'for suddenly Daniel was there – and he got me home.'

'So you were barely conscious by the time he carried you up to bed? What a fabulous story! I expect you're dying to tell Shelley, aren't you? – I *know* you are! Let me go and fetch her.' She had gone before Frances could think of a way of explaining that she couldn't have been more wrong!

♣ ♣ ♣

Hilary went back to her room, still not altogether happy about her patient. She'd heard that quaver in Frances's voice, and seen her hesitation when it came to talking about her ordeal. The doctor was right – the accident had obviously taken its toll, and the best thing was for her to get some peace and quiet. The main problem would be keeping the Shirburns off her back – if Oliver hadn't scared them into leaving her alone ... what a different side that easy-going man had showed to himself this morning! She had seen Lesley positively quail – and Hilary didn't blame her. Oliver was extremely impressive when he was angry.

At times like that it was hard to believe ... no, she mustn't kid herself. It was just that her conversation with Margery kept replaying itself in her mind. Margery seemed so sure that Oliver wasn't uninterested in women. And if she'd thought differently, she wouldn't have hesitated to say so – Margery wasn't prudish about such things. How come Julia and Tony who, like Hilary, had only met Oliver for the first time the other night, knew so much more about him than the friend who had brought him down to Haseley?

'Hilary, darling...' Speak of the devil. Julia knocked briefly before coming in. 'I've taken the poor little invalid some breakfast – she's very pale, isn't she? Still, it's not surprising, when you hear what she's been though. I made her tell me everything, and it was just too ghastly!'

'Julia,' Hilary tried to keep calm, 'Frances is supposed to be *resting*. She needs absolute quiet.'

276

'Oh, of course! I wouldn't dream of getting her to do a thing – even though it is a bit of a pain, having no one to keep Tobias under control. Stephen and Ratso should *never* have been allowed to have children! All they manage is to wind him up – and then Posy gets going, bless her...'

'Frances shouldn't even have visitors,' Hilary interrupted firmly. 'She's still very upset and shaken.'

'I know, poor little lamb. You could tell from her voice – I think she was about to cry, at one point! Never mind, we'll soon cheer her up, won't we?' Julia made herself comfortable on Hilary's bed. '... and something tells me your Daniel's going to be the one to do that.' She raised her brows in a question.

'Yes, they do seem to have fallen for each other,' Hilary answered it, still wondering how to prevent this impossible woman from finishing poor Frances off completely.

'Oh, how lovely! I guessed she must be smitten, from the way she was talking about him. I'm so glad he feels the same way ... the gods of love are certainly smiling on Haseley this Christmas, aren't they? Not only you and Leo,' she said, as Hilary pulled a face. 'I was thinking of Kath Arncott and Oliver ... who would have put money on her pulling that one off?'

'What do you mean?' said Hilary sharply. 'Oliver's gay, isn't he?'

'Well, I know – but it looks as if she must have turned him, doesn't it?'

'Oh don't be silly, Julia!' Hilary snapped. 'It's not something you simply change your mind about!'

How typical of Julia to alter the facts to make a better piece of gossip, she thought crossly, when she'd finally gone off downstairs, having persisted in concocting an elaborate scenario with Oliver and Kath as lovers ... for heaven's sake, the man was either gay or he wasn't – unless, God forbid, he was bisexual – but in any case, he was hardly likely to have let himself be seduced by Kath! Even if she was a notorious predator, and apparently, for some reason, had a magnetic attraction for men – and would no doubt be quite shameless about making it clear what was on offer ... of course it was ridiculous to think that a man like Oliver might be tempted to take what a sexually attractive woman was handing to him on a plate – with no emotional strings attached – wasn't it?

🌲 🌲 🌲

'Well, look at *you*,' said Shelley, when Julia had left them alone to 'have a nice gossip'.'Breakfast in bed like Lady Muck, while everyone else does your work!'

'Have this, if you want. I haven't touched it.'

Shelley obediently took the plate and started picking at the bacon.

'What is it that's supposed to be wrong with you? A sprained toe, or something? Oh dear – good idea to call the doctor out! Bet he had a right old laugh! ... I've got to hand it you, babe,' she went on, 'that was a very nice stroke you pulled! *Accidentally* getting yourself trapped, and making the kid run home and fetch *Daniel* to rescue you – like there was no one else around who could have done it.'

Frances was too weak to argue. Let her think what she liked.

'Who knows? I might even have come and pulled you out myself,' Shelley declared, with unabated sarcasm. 'Oh … but then *I'm* not in line to inherit a fortune, am I?'

'What do you mean?' Frances gazed at her.

'Oh, *right*! Of course, you're the only one who hasn't noticed how pally he and the old man have been getting lately – special presents, secret little expeditions together … they've been like *that* this Christmas.' Shelley crossed her fingers to show how close she meant.

'They're fond of each other, that's all.'

'Yeah – well it looks like paying off, in Daniel's case.'

'I don't know what you're talking about,' said Frances wearily.

'Seems the old boy's thinking of leaving him everything when he pops his clogs,' Shelley explained. 'All this house and stuff.' She waved her arm at the room.

'Oh come on, he'll leave it to Stephen, surely? Or Julia, I suppose. Daniel isn't even his grandson.'

'Yeah well, from what I heard, the old man practically told them it was all going to Daniel … so I tell you, babe, you've got more sense than I thought!'

♣ ♣ ♣

William was genuinely sorry that Frances wasn't well, but he couldn't help being amused by the chaos her absence was causing. Who would have guessed that her gentle influence was so essential when it came to keeping those children calmly under control? Already bored with a mound of toys that would have kept any normal youngster content for the next six months, Posy and Tobias were pestering the grown-ups for attention, and everyone was racking their brains for a way of entertaining them.

At Julia's hint that she might play with one of her Christmas presents, Posy had begun by plastering her young face in the make-up Shelley had seen fit to give her, and then she had adorned Tobias in a similar way. Lesley had screamed at the sight of her four-year-old boy in lipstick and eyeshadow, and for some reason laid this transformation at Oliver's door. William's idea, based on a Japanese game show he'd once watched, of seeing how many worms Posy could place on Tobias's bare stomach without him running off howling, wasn't very well received either.

'When I was young, we would all have been following the Hunt on Boxing Day morning!' declared Margery. 'Oh bugger it, what about Racing Demon? It's what we always used to play at Christmas… No, Lesley, it isn't gambling – not unless we bet on it… Come on, William, I know you've still got those old packs somewhere, even if some of the cards are missing… Yes, I know that isn't fair, Posy. You'll find *life* isn't fair, if you stick around as long as I have. The sooner you learn that, the better.'

'I should warn you – I'm good at this!' said Oliver, as they ranged themselves round the dining room table.

'You won't beat me,' said Margery. 'I'm older than you, and I've been playing since childhood… Come on, Tobias, spit spot! You don't want to keep everyone waiting, do you?'

William, who'd been quite a dab hand at Racing Demon himself, was about to join them, when Tony tapped him on the shoulder.

'J and I thought we might slip down to the White Hart,' he murmured. 'Come and join us.'

Julia was beckoning from the door. William glanced from her to the table... Oh well, he probably wouldn't have won anyway. Oliver had a grim determination about him, and Margery was almost as good as she thought.

'Very well,' he said, 'if you're buying.'

♣ ♣ ♣

'God, you're looking really ill again!' exclaimed Daniel. 'Didn't you manage to sleep?'

'I've had rather a lot of visitors!'

'What? But Mum told everyone you hadn't to be disturbed, and they'd got to keep away! We knew it would only make you worse if you had to talk to people.'

'Oh well – perhaps the message didn't get through.' Frances was unwilling to believe that Julia had deliberately ignored it. And of course it wouldn't have occurred to her that Shelley would only want to bitch. That girl hated not being the centre of attention, especially where men were concerned – which was why she'd made up that stupid story about Daniel, of course.

'Anyway,' she sighed, 'I'm awake now. Come and tell me what I missed yesterday. You never said what present you got for William.'

'Oh – a model aeroplane. It was ace!' He described the fun they'd had flying it on the Common, and how they'd met Kath on the way back, and cruelly abandoned poor Oliver to her clutches. 'And I don't know what time he got home – having more important things on my mind! – but it must have been pretty late. So we've yet to find out whether she had her wicked way with him, or if he escaped with his virtue intact.'

She chuckled. 'Well, I don't think Kath can really have got very far,' she pointed out. 'He *is* gay, after all.'

'*What*?' Daniel stared at her. 'Oliver's *gay*? Of course he isn't! What are you talking about?'

'I know! I was amazed too – but that's what Julia and Tony told Shelley.'

'There is no *way* that man's gay! Good Lord, we went for a walk together last night – talked about all kinds of stuff. There wasn't a hint of anything … at least…' He stopped suddenly.

'What? He didn't start coming on to you, did he?' said Frances, for some reason appalled.

'Oh no, nothing like that! It just explains some of the remarks people like Tony and Leo were making – oh and Lesley! She's obviously terrified he might corrupt Tobias.' Daniel paused, frowning, as he digested the news. 'But hang on, I thought he and Mum … they were getting on a bomb in Cirencester. I was beginning to size him up as stepdad material – until after lunch, anyway.'

'Yes,' said Frances, watching him make the connection. 'And after lunch, Hilary was talking to Julia and Tony.'

'You think they told her then? Oh my God!'

'Quite,' said Frances. 'And imagine how you'd feel if you were falling for someone, and then found out they could never love you back.'

They looked at each other. Daniel bent forward and kissed her softly.

'The funny thing is,' he frowned again, 'I could have sworn that Oliver *was* pretty keen on Mum. He was really upset when she seemed to go off him, you know. The only reason he asked me to go for a walk was to batter me with questions, trying to find out what was wrong.'

'Well, now you can tell him,' said Frances grimly.

🌲 🌲 🌲

William knew most of the people gathered in the White Hart for Boxing Day, and of course all the villagers knew him. He had a chat with old Blockley, who was sitting at the bar, while Tony got the drinks in.

'Daddy, you're so good at all this!' said Julia in admiring tones, as they took them across to a more secluded table.

'All what?'

'All this "lord of the manor" stuff.' She treated Blockley to one of her dazzling smiles. 'Don't you think so, Tony? Imagine Stephen and Ratso coming down here and talking to the gardener like that, as if he was an old friend!'

'Well, he is,' said William.

'I can't see Stephen fraternising with the *hoi polloi* in his local pub,' Tony agreed. 'And Lesley wouldn't want to risk betraying her origins, would she? Reckon they'll be safe down here, if those two ever inherit the house ... bit of a shame, though.'

'Oh dreadful! The family have always had a huge connection with Haseley village,' said Julia. 'It would be a terrible pity to break the tradition ... I'll tell you what,

Daddy, you were very sensible not to let them bully you into anything.'

'I'm always very sensible,' said William, 'and I never let myself be bullied. Which particular attempt did you have in mind?'

'A little bird told us they tried to get you to sign a will in their favour,' Tony admitted. 'Typically tactful, collaring you on Christmas Eve. I suppose they thought you wouldn't notice what you were doing after a glass or two of sherry.'

'They were wrong, then.'

'Of course they were! Dear, sensible, Daddy.' Julia patted his hand.

'Not that it isn't advisable to get things sorted out one way or another,' Tony went on, casually fiddling with the mat under his whisky. 'Morbid subject for Christmas, I know, but it might give you peace of mind to think your affairs were in order.'

William looked at him.

'It so happens that we've got one of these ourselves.' Tony suddenly pulled an envelope out of his inside pocket. 'Thought it would save you some hassle … I'm sure you can think of someone a bit more suitable to make things over to!' He smiled at William's daughter, as he handed him another blank will form.

'Someone more suitable than Stephen and Lesley.' William took the document, and the smart fountain pen Tony was offering. 'Oh – you mean *Hilary*? Yes, I'm very fond of Hilary, and she's had a bad deal in life. She could certainly do with a bit of help.' He uncapped the pen.

'*No* ... oh – yes, poor Hilary,' said Julia quickly. 'Dreadful about Ben and all that! Even though it was quite a long time ago now, and one does have to move on, doesn't one?'

'And apparently Hilary *has* moved on,' said Tony, exchanging a swift glance with Julia. 'Lord knows what she sees in that arsehole, but there you are!'

'You mean Oliver?'

'No, of course not – he's gay!' said Julia. 'Tony's talking about Hilary and Leo.'

'You're saying Hilary's in love with *Leo*?'

'Can't keep the two of them apart,' said Tony. 'Quite endearing, really. We caught them sneaking off for a walk yesterday, didn't we, Julia?'

'It's an awful shame, when darling Hilary's so nice,' Julia sighed, 'but I suppose you can't choose who you fall in love with, can you? She must be able to see his similarities with Ben – though nobody else can, that's for sure.'

'But obviously anything left to Hilary is in danger of ending up in Leo's hands,' Tony pointed out, 'and I really don't think any of us would like to have *him* installed at Haseley.'

'God no! Better to have Stephen and Ratso and that dreadful child,' said Julia, 'if there was no other choice, anyway.'

'Oh, there's plenty of choice,' said William cheerfully. 'Let me see…' He took a sip of his ginger wine. 'Daniel's a nice young man – if he can keep that tendency to madness under control.'

'Oh dear yes! Wasn't Leo horrible last night?' exclaimed Julia. 'After all, if there *is* anything wrong like that with Daniel, why should it come from Hilary's family, rather than Ben and Leo's? Uncle Denis was quite off the wall, I seem to remember.'

'Have to be – married to Margery,' William pointed out.

'Anyway, Daniel's going to have enough problems, by the sound of it,' Julia went on. 'Have you two heard the latest?'

'Come on, you old gossip,' Tony grinned, 'What have you heard?'

'*Well*,' Julia leaned forward confidentially, 'it seems that little nanny Frances has been a bit clever! No, I think the accident was genuine enough. We went through all the details ... but she certainly used the situation to her advantage. She put her heart into playing the old damsel in distress, and by the time Daniel had got her free, she'd got *him* pretty well trapped! If you believe Hilary, they're now desperately in love.'

'Demure little Frances – who would have thought it?' chuckled Tony. 'Still, you can't blame her, can you? Family's pretty badly off, I gather – widowed mother and scores of children. And he'll be earning a packet as a doctor – not to mention what Margery leaves him ... I suppose she *might* even have got the idea that he was in with a chance of Haseley.'

'Oh surely not! ... God, do you think so?' exclaimed Julia. 'My dear, just imagine! That poor little thing – overrun with kids, no doubt – trying to manage that huge house, and wondering what hat to wear, and which fork to use at dinner parties! Hard on poor Hilary, though,' she sighed. 'She's being very brave about it, but let's face it, Daniel could have had anybody – the last thing she'll have wanted was for him to fall into the clutches of another gold-digger, using him to claw her way up the social scale… Why *is* this family so prone to them?'

Chapter Nineteen

'There we are, duck! Mrs Watlington thought you might be able to manage a bit of soup for your lunch.'

'Oh, thank you.' Hilary was kind! It was just what Frances felt like.

'And there's a turkey sandwich to go with it, if you want,' Kath relayed the rest of the message.

'No, this is fine.'

'Well, you seem to have had a right old do yesterday!' Kath sat down, ready to chat. 'That old ruin should have been pulled down years ago – full of dry rot, so it's never going to sell. Better to start again with a nice bungalow.'

Frances could see that she was going to be made to go through the details of her accident again in a minute, and quickly changed the subject. 'I hear you had Mr Leafield round yesterday. Did you have a good time?'

'Oh, yes thanks – couldn't have been better!' Kath exclaimed happily. 'He's a lovely bloke, isn't he? Not at all snobby! Ever so good with the children, too. The boys liked him a lot. He loved my old cottage – well, I knew he would. *Very* excited about one of the beams in the bedroom … yes, I'm afraid we did end up in the bedroom,' she giggled. 'No, it's OK. Oliver's a perfect gentleman, shame to say – though it was pretty obvious he would have liked to take things a bit further.'

'*Really*?' Frances couldn't help expressing her surprise.

'Oh yes,' said Kath, with the confidence of one sure of her own powers. 'There's no mistaking that look in a man's eye, is there? Still, you've got to hold back a bit on the first date. We did have a *very* cosy little chat though,' she hastened to tell her, 'on the bed, sitting as close as I am to you. I've got a gift for drawing people out, as a matter of fact,' – Frances knew from experience that this meant asking a lot of nosy questions – 'and Oliver really poured his heart out to me, once I got him going. He lives all on his own, in one of those posh flats in Kensington, near William's sister – worth a mint, I imagine. Can't earn all that writing articles, can he? I think there's some family money around. Anyway,' she leant forward eagerly, 'I bet you're asking yourself how a great catch like him has managed to stay single all these years!'

'Um, no…' Frances didn't like to state the obvious conclusion.

'Well,' Kath went on regardless, 'it seems that when he was young, poor old Oliver had a disappointment.' Like discovering he was gay? 'He fell in love with someone who let him down really badly. It broke his heart, and by all accounts he's never found anyone else to match up to her – until now, that is. He did say 'until now',' Kath stressed, with a gleam in her eye.

'Are you sure he said '*her*'?' said Frances gently.

'Of course … oh, did you think he was gay?' Kath chuckled, as if this was the funniest joke in the world. 'No, I can put you right on that score! Oliver Leafield is definitely all man – even if I didn't go all the way to proving it, if you get what I mean.' She winked at Frances.

'I did tell him how I find older men so much more attractive than younger blokes, especially nicely spoken, upper-class types – and a bit of substance behind them doesn't go amiss either. He got the message! He said he'd probably be popping down to Haseley again to finish off his article, and I don't think it's just old William he'll be coming to see … shall I take that, if you've finished?'

'Oh … er … thank you.' Frances came back to earth as she handed Kath her empty bowl. It wasn't just food she'd brought her – but food for a great deal of thought!

♣ ♣ ♣

'It really isn't fair – poor little Tobias had never played before! The children should have been given a start.'

'They should have been given a handicap, if you ask me! Quite unfair to pit their nimble little fingers against these stiff old hands.'

God, were they still arguing about that game?

'Oh come on, Gran, you very nearly won, from what I heard! If Oliver hadn't got that last minute King…'

'Yes, and that King of Clubs was mine,' Margery glared at the offender, who was heedlessly stirring the pan of soup. 'I had it only three cards further down! … Mind you,' she went on generously, 'if William had been here he would have beaten the lot of us. I don't know what possessed those three to sneak off like that!'

Hilary too had been a bit surprised that Julia and Tony had seen fit to disappear, just as everyone was about to start a game.

'Yes, we all might have liked to go to the pub, if we'd been invited!' complained Stephen, who had never been known to set foot in the White Hart. She saw his point though. If it was suddenly so essential to go for this drink, why take William along, and not the rest of them? What, in short, were those two up to?

'I don't know whether we should wait for the others, or go ahead and have lunch,' she said doubtfully. The children had been fed some time ago, and persuaded to play in the garden under Shelley's reluctant guardianship. The rest of them were rather hungrily contemplating a plate piled high with crusty bread and slices of turkey.

'It is only sandwiches,' said Lesley, disregarding the exotic soup that Oliver had of course conjured up out of nothing.

'And this'll stay hot,' he said, without rancour.

'I suppose we'd better wait a bit longer then,' sighed Hilary, pretending not to see Leo's face fall.

Kath came back with Frances's bowl. 'Well, that went down a treat, Oliver love!' So he was 'love' now, was he? 'Just what the doctor ordered, you clever old chef, you!' She went up and gave him a squeeze as he stood by the stove.

'Thank you, Kath. I'm sure you'll be wanting to get off home now,' said Hilary. Not that Kath showed the slightest sign of wanting to leave, but Hilary felt that she'd had about as much as she could take of her company for the moment! At least, to be fair, it was Oliver in Kath's company she found so trying – the constant innuendoes and little jokes suggesting that whatever happened between them last night had made them the most intimate of

291

friends – lovers even, the way Kath was behaving – and Oliver seemed to be encouraging, rather than doing anything to dispel this impression.

'Oh! I thought Frances might fancy a cup of tea.'

'I'll make it. We really mustn't keep you hanging around any longer… No, that's fine. We'll do our own washing up.'

Kath had finally departed, with a lingering look, but not quite kissing Oliver goodbye, when they heard Julia's voice in the hall.

'Hello, what are you all doing in the kitchen? I thought you were playing a game.'

'We finished that ages ago,' Margery told her.

'Really? Who won? … Oh, well done, Oliver darling! Daddy'll be ever so jealous. He loves Racing Demon.'

'If we'd known something else was being planned, we could have postponed it for another time,' said Lesley pointedly.

'Oh – you didn't want to come with us, did you? We only popped down for a quick one before lunch.'

'Well it's ready now,' said Hilary. 'Where's William? He must be hungry. You know how early he eats as a rule.'

'That's OK,' said Julia. 'He's had his – we all have. They do such nice meals at the pub, that we thought we might as well eat there… Oh dear, I hope you weren't waiting for us!'

There was a pained silence. Margery rolled her eyes, and began to hand bowls out. Hilary did the same with the plates. Daniel grinned, and helped himself to one of the sandwiches. 'I'll take this up and have it with Frances. Is that her tea?'

'How sweet! They can't be parted for a minute, can they?' cooed Julia, as he disappeared upstairs.

'What do you mean?' Lesley paused in the act of spooning soup.

'Oh, darling, didn't you know?' Julia glanced round mischievously, as if they all shared a secret. 'Daniel and Frances have got a thing going!'

'You mean – they're romantically involved?' Only Stephen could put it like that.

'It seems so.'

'Isn't that nice?' said Hilary, knowing the Shirburns wouldn't agree.

'Darling Hilary's being very understanding.' Julia treated her to a sympathetic little smile, which set her teeth on edge.

'Rubbish! I've a lot of time for Frances.'

'Oh, of course – she's a sweet girl.' A 'but' hung in the air.

'Daniel's having a relationship with our *nanny*?' Stephen struggled to take it in. 'Oh dear, I'm afraid that won't do.' He turned to Lesley for confirmation.

'No,' she came back to life, 'no, I'm afraid it would be most unsuitable … one has to think of Tobias, after all. He's at a most impressionable age.'

'Why? Are you afraid it might corrupt his morals?' Oliver couldn't help enquiring.

Aware of his amusement, Lesley glared nastily at him. 'Yes, well – you'd know!'

Oh God – stupid woman! So *that* was why she and Stephen had always seemed so anxious to keep him at arm's length from their precious son. It was nothing to do with the damp patch in the pantry.

Oliver glanced round the table for enlightenment as to this unprovoked attack, but Margery could only give a mystified shrug, and Stephen dropped his gaze. Julia tittered and, failing to catch Hilary's eye, tried Leo – but he, with his usual self-concern, was the only one of them carrying blithely on with his lunch. Hilary wanted to scream at Lesley that she was way behind the times. All the signs were that Oliver Leafield wasn't gay at all, even if he did have a very strange taste in women.

'Don't be ridiculous!' She felt she must say something. 'Tobias won't care who his nanny is seeing – and you can hardly tell her who she can or can't fall in love with!'

'But it'll make things so *awkward* …'

Yes, if Frances was attached to a member of the family, the Shirburns might have to start thinking of her as a human being instead of a servant. Most inconvenient for them!

'Can't you have a word with Daniel?'

'No of course I can't! Good heavens, do you think anything I said would put him off? Even if I did want to discourage the relationship, that would be the very worst way of going about it!'

'But you're his mother…'

'Precisely.'

'We men are very perverse,' explained Oliver.

He could say that again! What could he possibly see in a woman who was such a contrast to him in every way, someone with absolutely no pretensions to culture or refinement, someone as plump, and brassy, and blatantly sexual as Kath Arncott? If that was his type, he might as *well* be gay as far as Hilary was concerned, because she herself certainly had no chance!

♣ ♣ ♣

'So what are we going to do?'

'I don't know.' Daniel stared out of the window at where the children were playing in the garden.

Frances sipped her tea, relieved to be sharing the burden of her news. 'At least Oliver's not gay – but I *can't* believe he'd rather have her than your mother! I mean, Kath's very nice, but she's actually quite fat, and I wouldn't have called her pretty exactly, would you?'

'Well, I don't fancy her,' Daniel reassured her, 'but then I go for slender, mousy little women, without much to say for themselves.' He pinched her knee. 'A retiring sort of guy like Oliver *might* be attracted by that in-your-face approach, I suppose. You know what they say about opposites.'

Frances wrinkled her nose. Were men really that unpredictable when it came to sex? Perhaps they were.

'No,' Daniel went on suddenly, 'he's keen on Mum, I know he is. We've just got to find a way of sorting things out and getting them back together.'

'Couldn't you have a little chat with him – explain what happened?'

'You must be joking!' A look of horror came over Daniel's face. 'What am I supposed to do – take that poor guy aside, and tell him that everyone thought he was gay? I'm sorry, but no *way*!'

♣ ♣ ♣

'We've been playing Desert Islands,' Tobias told his mother.

'That sounds fun, darling.'

'I was the castaway and Posy was the person who owned the island. She gave me special berries to eat.'

'*What*?'

'I wasn't sick,' Tobias assured her.

'But what did she give you? Where's that girl, Shelley? Why didn't she stop her? ... Stephen, come here at once! We must call a doctor!'

'Don't panic, Lesley,' Hilary tried to calm her. 'He doesn't look at all ill. I'm sure he would be if he'd eaten anything poisonous.' Daniel was coming down the stairs. Thank heavens!

'OK, mate, how many of these things did you eat? Come and show me where you picked them, Posy.' He took charge, and led them into the garden.

He came back a short while later, grinning and mopping his brow. 'Rose hips. That won't do him any harm. No, it's all right, Lesley – full of Vitamin C.'

She would have been less reassured, however, if she'd heard what Daniel confided to Hilary when the children had been swept upstairs for a rest.

'That wretched girl really was trying to poison him, you know! She said that she hoped Tobias would die, because then she could live here all on her own when she's grown-up!'

♣ ♣ ♣

'Well, Nanny, how are you getting on?' None the better for a visit from Lesley. 'Stephen and I are very sorry to see you laid up. And Tobias is missing you badly – there was a most unfortunate incident in the garden just now! ... I wonder how long it will be before you're back on your feet?'

OK, she got the message! The Shirburns loved her so much, they were desperate to enjoy the pleasure of her company again. She told her what the doctor had said, and watched Lesley contort her face in a 'harrumph' of irritation. After that there wasn't much to talk about, since she obviously hadn't come to cheer her up with any little items of news or gossip, and Frances lay silent, waiting for her to go.

But, instead, Lesley drummed her fingers, sighed and gazed out of the window. Eventually, just as Frances was plucking up courage to say that she really needed to sleep now, she spoke.

'I do hope you're not going to get involved in any silly distractions while you're here, Nanny.'

Frances stared at her perplexed. What did she have in mind – wild games of Scrabble? An over-stimulating crossword puzzle?

'Stephen and I have always thought you were such a sensible girl – quite unlike Tobias's last nanny! And it's Tobias that has to be considered here.'

No, she still couldn't put the clues together.

'Children need to know exactly where the boundaries are, don't they, in their little lives? We adults are more adaptable, but it's very confusing for a child if his perception of where those lines are drawn should be disturbed. Poor Tobias has already had enough to upset him recently, what with his adventure yesterday, and the incident this morning…'

Frances shook her head, still utterly mystified. What could she possibly have done, lying here in bed, to upset Tobias? He hadn't even visited her since her accident.

Lesley saw that she'd have to make herself clearer. At last she came out with it.

'I understand that you've embarked on some kind of romantic liaison with Daniel Watlington… Whether or not his family look kindly on such a relationship, Stephen and I thought you should know that it really won't be acceptable to us, as your employers.'

Frances drew in a sharp breath of disbelief.

'We're only thinking of the effect it will have on Tobias – he's very fond of his cousin… As I said, you're a sensible girl,' Lesley went on, when Frances could find no reply to this *non sequitur*. 'I'm sure you wouldn't want to cause any embarrassment, especially to young Daniel.' She patted the bedclothes in a would-be friendly manner. 'We can't always follow our own desires, when there are other people to consider, can we?'

'Are we going to have Grime and Brine round again?' asked Posy, fresh from a 'nap' in which Hilary suspected little sleeping had been done.

'No, darling, not today.'

'Can we go round to their house?'

'No,' Lesley backed Julia up. 'Grime and Brine are busy this afternoon.'

'But Mrs Arncott said they'd like to "return our hostipality",' Posy reminded her aunt with a sceptical look, 'and they got *Roadkill V* for Christmas.'

'There are *much* nicer things we could play here,' said Lesley quickly, seeing her son about to express a heartfelt longing for *Roadkill V*.

'Oh yes – that islands game!' His eagerness suggested he bore no ill will for its dietary contingencies.

'No, *not* that,' said Lesley, glaring at the insouciant Shelley who, having done her duty of bringing the children down, was lounging in one of the sitting-room chairs.

'Let's find something we can *all* do,' said Julia. 'Gosh, there are lots of us, aren't there?'

'What about a quiz?' said Stephen.

'That's no good – we haven't any questions,' said Lesley. 'Oh dear, we should have brought Trivial Pursuit.'

'Good heavens, anyone can set a quiz!' exclaimed Leo. 'It doesn't take many brain cells to look up a few reference books.'

'Good man, Leo,' Stephen took this as an offer. 'There are plenty of dictionaries and things in the study.'

'Oh … well, all right then. I won't be long. You could be finding pencils and paper.'

'Or what about charades?' said Julia, when he'd gone. 'That's huge fun, and the children always love dressing up.'

'We've got enough for three teams…' Tony began to divide them up. 'Four Shirburns with William. Three

Britwells plus Shelley … yes of course you are, Shell, you'll love it!'

'…and me, Mum and Gran, with Oliver,' Daniel finished for him. 'You can be an honorary Watlington.'

'Many thanks.' Oliver came and sat beside Hilary.

'We'd better get the rules straight, first of all,' said Margery, with an eye on Lesley. One of the grudges the family had against her was that she had been taught the miming version. 'We're not doing it that silly American way! …Oliver, do you know how to play this?'

'You take a word, and act out each syllable?'

'No, you've got to *introduce* the syllable into each scene, with the whole word in the last one.' Margery was a strict upholder of the version played in the Shirburn household for the past few decades.

'You're supposed to slip them casually into the conversation,' Hilary explained to him. 'But it's quite difficult to find something normal-sounding. Otherwise it sticks out like a sore thumb and everyone spots it immediately.'

'We mustn't have things that are too hard for the children to guess…'

'Yes, Lesley, we're not going to ruin the game, just so Tobias can win!' Margery told her. 'Come on, get into your teams and think up your words – no more than three syllables, or it takes for ever. You can stay here, Lesley – we'll never get William out of that chair. Julia's lot can have the hall.'

'Isn't this fun? Just like when we were little! I wonder where the old dressing-up box got to…'

'Only a quarter of an hour to plan in!' Margery gave a final order, as she led her own team towards the kitchen. 'If we let them start messing about with costumes, they'll be all day!' she added, before the door was quite closed.

Oliver thought of a word at once. 'Sentiment,' he suggested, Julia's last remark obviously echoing in his ears.

'Oh yes. "Sent", "tea", "meant" – that's good!' Daniel nodded.

'Hmm, cheating really, using the consonant twice,' said the Authority. 'But I bet they do!'

'OK,' said Oliver, 'what if you and Hilary are a mother and daughter, and we've been *sent* to tell you some bad news...'

With each of them contributing to the increasingly unlikely plot, they ended up with a melodrama, in which Oliver arrived to tell Daniel's mother and sister that he'd shot him in a duel. Despite the offender's breach of good taste in bringing the body along behind him, they still felt compelled to offer him a cup of *tea*, and he was then to assure them he'd never *meant* to do it, with a final scene in which the mother was to declare herself overcome with *sentiment*.

'No, that's too obvious.' Daniel waved an objecting hand. 'We need to make it more complicated, or they'll get it at once. Suppose this guy and the daughter fall in love?'

'...Though they "never meant this to happen"!' Oliver and he laughed as they chorused the words together. 'And then the son, who turns out not to be quite dead after all, objects, and he's got a gun...'

'What a load of rubbish!' Margery chuckled at the finished result. 'Now, where are we going to get our props from?'

Her quarter of an hour had been exceeded by about times three, when at last everyone was back in the sitting room, ready to perform. The Shirburns went first with a classical theme.

'The Founding of Rome', with Tobias as Romulus cuddling *near* to his mother under a fur rug as the she-wolf, led to some giggles from the audience. William played the eponymous hero in 'The Death of Caesar', letting out a series of passionate 'oh's, as he was stabbed with the poker by his treacherous consul, Stephen. Tobias then returned in a towel for a toga, and waved his hands rather ambiguously about in the air – a mystery solved when, in reply to the question: 'What are you doing, Nero?' he explained that he was fiddling while Rome burned.

'Good God, you can't use obscure proper names!' exclaimed Margery in horror, even though no one had had much difficulty in guessing the word. Julia's team had inevitably spent more time on their costumes than their script, which featured a fairy with the unlikely name of Chris, who kept begging her nanny not to 'muss' her hair up. Hilary was amazed to see a show-off like Shelley freeze into wooden immobility, when called upon to deliver a line she might have uttered every day in normal life.

'You needn't bother to do the third scene!' said William rudely, but Tony went ahead and re-enacted Oliver's role as Father Christmas, using enough of the original costume to produce outraged accusations of theft of intellectual property from those who had helped devise it.

'Right, it's our turn!' said Margery, with the air of someone who was going to show others how things should be done. 'Where are those shawls?'

She and Hilary sat by the fire, telling each other how cold it was – a red herring suggested by Daniel. There was a knock on the sitting-room door, and Oliver announced that he'd been sent – by whom, wasn't clear – to tell them the bad news that their 'son-stroke-brother' was dead. 'In fact,' he admitted, 'I'm afraid I killed your son-stroke-brother in a duel, in a rather sneaky way.' He twirled imaginary moustaches at the audience, who booed obligingly.

When he opened the door to reveal the corpse, even Hilary gave a little scream. That wretched boy must have run off and found William's ketchup bottle, for he was now smeared in horribly realistic gore! Margery's polite offer of a cup of tea at that point nearly brought the house down.

She left the stage and, apparently uninhibited by the presence of the corpse, the daughter and the villain declared the passion for each other that they'd 'never meant to happen'.

So far according to the script. What Hilary hadn't bargained for, was that Oliver then took her in his arms and kissed her. Totally taken by surprise, uncertain what to do, she kissed him back. Thoughts fluttered through her head. Surely he couldn't be acting this? How should she respond? Dear God, she didn't appear to have any choice in the matter! It was a kiss that demanded a response from her whole body. And everyone was watching. What would they think? After a moment or two, she didn't care. This was where she should be, the right thing to be doing.

It seemed an age before Daniel the Corpse came back to life, told the offender to take his dastardly hands off her in an uncomfortably apposite way, and produced an imaginary gun and 'rid the world of a despicable scoundrel'. Oliver had the presence of mind to clutch his chest and die at artistic length. Hilary's reaction of dazed shock was luckily appropriate, and Margery returned to speak her line.

The audience cheered as if they'd never stop. Was it the spectacle she and Oliver had just given them? All Hilary's self-consciousness returned, and she found she couldn't look at them, or him, or her son.

They were having surprising difficulty in guessing the word. Eventually William got it, to renewed cheers.

'You're awfully noisy in here!' Leo came in, bearing a huge wad of paper. 'It took a bit longer than I said, but I've finished the quiz now.'

Chapter Twenty

Frances drifted into an uncomfortable sleep at last, and woke to hear Lesley still arguing... No, not Lesley – that was Julia's voice. What a relief! She was talking to Tony in their room next door. It was comforting to think of them so nearby.

'Well, we've got to do *something*!' she heard Tony saying. 'There'll be another set of those bloody bills waiting when we get home. I can't stall the bank for ever.'

'If only you hadn't invested in that stupid website thing!'

'Yes, well, they seemed like perfectly sound blokes, and one of them *was* in IT...'

Had Julia and Tony got financial problems then? She'd assumed they were pretty well off ... she was trying not to listen, but the wall was so thin, they might have been sitting beside her.

'It would be an awful shame to have to sell the house.' There was a creak that suggested Julia had flopped onto the bed.

'Wouldn't do any good if we did. It's all owed to the mortgage company.'

'I suppose Posy could drop ballet, but she's doing so well.'

'It'll take more than the odd ballet class, I'm afraid!'

'If you're suggesting we should send her to that ghastly little state school …' The bed creaked again, angrily.

'All I'm saying is that it's a bloody shame your father has to mess everybody about. He's sitting on a gold mine here, but it's no use to anyone at the moment.'

'I'm sure we'll be getting it all eventually. He can't still mean Stephen to inherit Haseley, after everything we've done to show him what a bad idea that would be!'

'*Eventually*'s no use. We need that money now. It's no good seeing off all the other contenders, if we can't get him to put pen to bloody paper!'

'But even then, we'd have to wait till he dies,' Julia pointed out. 'Or are you suggesting we murder the poor old thing?' She gave heartless little giggle that made Frances's blood run cold.

She couldn't be hearing this! She must be still asleep, having one of those awful nightmares where one's nicest of friends turn into monsters.

'Once he's signed that will, we can get Power of Attorney,' Tony was explaining. 'And then if he still refuses to move out, it shouldn't be too difficult to get him sectioned. Everyone knows how eccentric he is – and Stephen might co-operate, if he gets a bit of a sweetener. There'll be plenty for all, once the house is sold.'

Frances slipped her legs out from under the covers, and gingerly tried her ankle on the floor. She didn't know what she was going to do, but she couldn't just lie there.

'Well let's give it another try now, before supper. Where did you put that form?' Frances heard the bed creak again. Julia was getting up, about to go downstairs and make poor William sign his life away…

'*No!*'

'Frances! Aren't you supposed to be in bed? Good lord, you look as if you've seen a ghost.'

'Her room's right next door,' Tony gave a rueful grimace.

'Oh – did you overhear some of what we were saying? I'm sure you must have misunderstood.'

Frances shook her head. There had been no possibility of misunderstanding. She wished there had. If only she could have convinced herself that it *was* a nightmare, or the two cruel strangers with Julia and Tony's voices had turned out not to be them after all!

'Now, Frances, come and sit down.' How often had Tony beguiled her with that sympathetic tone? She leant against the wardrobe to take the weight off her foot, rather than rest it with him beside her. 'You must know that we only want what's best for William. He'd be far better off in care.' This from the man who'd been banging on about the evils of retirement homes!

'Of course he would! Much better than living all alone in this horrid great house.' Seeing her face, Julia tried a different tack... 'Look here, darling, let's not beat about the bush. We all want this money. You were hoping Daniel would get it, weren't you? Well, you're wasting your time there. I'm afraid Daddy and Margery are the most awful snobs, and neither of them would think of leaving him anything if he marries a nanny – I'm sorry, but there it is.'

Frances stared at her in disbelief... What had Shelley been saying? Had she poisoned their minds with her ridiculous accusation – or was it they who had put it into Shelley's head? Surely Julia and Tony couldn't possibly believe she was so mercenary… Oh, she didn't know what to think any more!

'You're not going to say anything silly to Daddy, are you?' said Julia, as Frances turned away in despair. 'I'm sure we could come to some arrangement if you're really hard up.'

'She can't get down the stairs, remember? You go back to bed, Frances, and rest that ankle of yours.'

It was true that her foot was hurting, and all she wanted to do was to go and bury her head under the covers. Frances hobbled out of the room and shut the door behind her.

🌲 🌲 🌲

No one was really in the mood for a quiz, but they felt rather guilty that Leo had got left out of the charades, particularly in the knowledge that they'd had much more fun without him. Shelley took the children upstairs when it was clear they hadn't a hope of joining in, and Julia and Tony had soon given up and gone off as well, leaving the rest of them to struggle with a set of questions which would have given *University Challenge* a run for its money.

'Come on, Hilary, you must know this!' Leo was beginning to show signs of irritation at her ignorance, but it was difficult to bend her mind to obscure events in Emily Brontë's life, when it was so preoccupied with recent events in her own. She was still reeling from Oliver's kiss. One thing was for sure – that man wasn't gay! He had meant it when he kissed her. The touch of those strong lips had been sensuous and demanding, and she was shocked at the uncontrolled passion it had awoken in her. Wasn't she supposed to be beyond such heights, at her age?

She passed on her question, causing Leo to tut disappointedly, and stole a glance at the man who had caused a respectable middle-aged widow to act so shamelessly. He met her eye, and she immediately dropped her gaze, blushing like a schoolgirl. Heavens, she mustn't behave like this – everyone would wonder what was going on! They probably already did. She'd been alarmed to see Daniel take Oliver aside just after they'd finished the charades. What was it he wanted to say to the man who had just kissed his mother?

'Now, William, here's an easy one for you. Who wrote *Decline and Fall*?' Leo's quiz had a distinctly literary bias.

Hilary could see from the gleam in his eye that William didn't appreciate being patronised. '…Gibbon, wasn't it?'

'No, that was *The Decline and Fall of the Roman Empire*!'

'Isn't that what you meant? You should have been more specific.'

'It's *perfectly* specific.'

'Evelyn Waugh, then… Come on, Leo, get on with it.'

'No, it was *William*'s turn,' He glared at Margery for answering for her brother. 'Now I'll have to find him another question!'

The door opened rather suddenly. Frances stood there, looking deathly pale.

Daniel shot to his feet at once. 'What are you doing here? You shouldn't be up!'

'I … took the back stairs,' she gasped, as if this was explanation. She was searching the room for someone.

'William …' She tried to get to him, but everyone was sitting in the way. 'Julia and Tony are coming!'

'But why…? What…?'

Frances shook her head, brushing aside their puzzled enquiries. '*Don't* sign anything!' she called across the room. 'Whatever you do, don't let them…'

The door opened again, sure enough to reveal Julia and Tony.

'Don't let them *what*?' Daniel was saying, but Frances was no longer conscious.

'You mean she rushed all the way down those stairs, on her bad ankle? No wonder she passed out!' Hilary exclaimed. Only this morning had Daniel really got the full story from Frances, and they'd learned why she had been so desperate to reach the sitting room, when she should have been resting in bed.

'I think that was the shock, more than anything,' said Daniel grimly. 'After overhearing what those two were plotting, she realised she simply had to get to William before they did.'

'Poor Frances! It must have been a real eye-opener for her, seeing Julia and Tony in their true colours,' Hilary reflected. 'Aren't they just beyond belief? The number of times I've heard Julia say she's not interested in money and she doesn't care who William leaves his estate to!'

'Yes, and making snide remarks about Stephen and Lesley, as if *they* were the mercenary ones,' Daniel agreed bitterly. 'Do you think Uncle William signed that thing of theirs?'

'I don't know.' Hilary gave a miserable shrug. They'd been too busy getting Frances back upstairs to find out whether or not her mission had been successful. 'I hope not, but it's too late now, if he has. Anyway, it was extremely brave of Frances to try and warn him.'

'Yes, she's a heroine,' said Daniel, playing thoughtfully with the brush on the dressing table. 'I could be very serious about a girl like that.'

'Are you there, Hilary?' Margery burst in with barely a knock. 'Now listen! I want to know who's responsible for telling you this ridiculous tale about poor Oliver.'

'Oh!' said Hilary, too startled to prevaricate. 'Julia and Tony said he was gay…'

'Right. I shall have a word.' Margery was gone as quickly as she had come.

'Good heavens! I wonder who on earth…'

But to her surprise, her son was grinning guiltily. 'I'm afraid it's my fault for telling Oliver the rumours about him. I wasn't going to say anything — well, you can hardly let on to a mate that everyone thinks he's gay, when he isn't! – but he kept wondering why people were making weird comments, or treating him strangely.' Had she imagined that he'd given her rather a close look? 'So in the end I told him the truth. He was a bit taken aback at first, poor sod, but then I got him to see the funny side. I don't think it's the first time, actually – being a bachelor, and some of the people he goes round with. Anyway, he must have said something to Gran, and now she's gunning for whoever started the story,' he chuckled.

Hilary tried to smile too, as one appreciative of an amusing misunderstanding.

'He *isn't* gay, of course.'

'Of course not!' said Hilary, as if she'd never thought he was. 'In fact,' she went on with all the airiness she could muster, 'I thought he might have something going with Kath Arncott.'

'Oh no, not at all!' her wonderful son assured her. 'I teased him about that, but he isn't the slightest bit interested.' Daniel sounded almost relieved. 'In fact, from some hints she dropped about liking older men, Oliver thinks that Kath might have her sights set on Uncle William!'

'*What*?'

'I know! Bit of a turn up for the books if he ended up marrying his housekeeper,' Daniel speculated delightedly. 'How do you think they'd all feel if Grime and Brine inherited Haseley House?'

♣ ♣ ♣

William and Scratch looked up balefully when Margery charged into their room. Neither was pleased at being disturbed this early in the morning.

'Never mind that!' she interrupted, as William started to point this out. 'What do you mean by going round telling everyone that Oliver Leafield is a homosexual?'

'Did I? I don't remember.'

'Well I've already spoken to Tony, and he says it came from you.'

'In that case, I suppose I just assumed he was,' said William, thinking back. 'You said you'd met him at Nigel Rofford's, didn't you? He's queer as a coot.'

'Yes,' said Margery crossly, '*Nigel* is. Oliver isn't!'

'Oh, fair enough.' said William. 'Does it matter?'

'Of course it does!' exclaimed Margery. 'Poor Hilary's head-over-heels in love with him. How do you think she felt?'

'I don't know,' said William, with a twinge of conscience. It wasn't as if he hadn't noticed how Hilary reacted to Oliver's presence – but then the man was so obviously smitten with her, he'd completely forgotten that he wasn't supposed to like women. 'Perhaps I should say something.'

'No, best not to interfere,' said Margery, causing a wry smile from her brother. She picked up the cat and sat down on his bedroom chair, her eyes piercing with another enquiry. 'Tell me what happened last night, after that poor girl collapsed – I saw those two taking you off to the study with them.'

'Oh yes,' William recalled. 'They wanted to revive a conversation we'd been having in the pub earlier, about the importance of leaving a will … in fact, they'd been kind enough to make one out already – to save me the trouble, they said. All I had to do was sign it.'

'And did you?' Margery was anxious to discover, as he paused.

'Well,' said William, 'I *might* have done, but then I pointed out that we'd need to have a witness to my signature – and not one of them, either, since they appeared to be the beneficiaries.'

'And what did they answer to that?' urged Margery, agonised by his slowness.

'They said I was being unnecessarily particular, and that Kath or someone could easily add her name to it later … most irregular!' William shook his head. He caught Margery's eye, and daren't spin the tale out any longer. 'So then I suggested that we asked Frances to do it. I said that I thought she was a girl who appeared to have my interests at heart, and I'd really like to take her advice before I put my name to anything.'

'Ha!' said Margery. 'So you're not completely stupid.'

'No,' said William. 'I don't know why everybody thinks I am.'

'They've got a point, though,' Margery surprised him by adding. 'You really should make a will out to *somebody*. Otherwise it makes things so awkward for everybody when you die.'

'Doesn't bother me!' said William.

Daniel had been wonderful this morning – full of praise for Frances's courage and concern for the ill effects she might be suffering. She loved him so much, it was almost unbearable!

In fact, from a physical point of view, Frances had got off fairly lightly. Although her ankle had swollen up again, she found that she could put some weight on it, with care. But emotionally – that was a different matter… Frances hadn't been able to disclose to Daniel the full extent of the mental torment she was undergoing as a result of last night's revelations. It wasn't only the shock of discovering that, beneath that veneer of charm, lay two utterly unscrupulous people who would stop at nothing to get their hands on William's estate – although that was bad enough. It wasn't even the way Julia and Tony had betrayed her, and the realisation that their sympathetic friendship had been nothing but a ruse to worm information out of her about the other candidates for William's fortune... No, what was really gnawing at Frances's heart, and what she couldn't reveal to Daniel, were the cruel things they had to say about her relationship with him, and its likely effect on his future. She had been devastated to hear Julia repeat Shelley's malicious suggestion that her interest in Daniel was purely for mercenary reasons. Would the rest of the family come to the same conclusion? And even if they didn't, and accepted that she genuinely loved him, was it true that his involvement with her would mean Daniel being cut off from his rightful inheritance?

That's what Lesley had been talking about – she realised now. She'd been warning her that their romance was likely to cause him harm. And of course the last thing in the world Frances wanted was to hurt Daniel... So there was only one thing to do – wasn't there?

Hilary was half expecting to find that the Britwells had slunk off home during the night. How were they possibly going to be able to face everyone this morning, after what they'd done? But when she and Daniel came down into the kitchen, there they were happily making breakfast, and greeting them with cheerful unconcern. It was Hilary who found it difficult to look them in the eye.

Daniel had no such qualms. 'No thanks, and I hope it bloody chokes you!' he responded, with his grandmother's bluntness, to Tony's offer of scrambled egg. 'What the hell do you think you were playing at last night, trying to pull that stunt on Uncle William?'

'I know, poor Daddy – aren't we horrid beasts?' agreed Julia, without a trace of *gêne*. 'But it was the only thing we could think of to rake in some money. We're desperately hard up at the moment – isn't it a bore? You wouldn't believe how expensive that child is!'

'…Bit of bad luck with an investment,' Tony explained, as if that excused everything. 'Hilary, you'll have some of this, won't you?'

'…And it's not as if we got anywhere,' argued Julia, as Hilary struggled with the moral dilemma of whether to accept food at Tony's hand. 'Daddy never did sign that will, you know.'

'Yes, old Frances must have succeeded in warning him off,' said Tony, in the tone of a sportsman admiring good play on the part of the other team.

'Oh yes – who would have thought of her taking the back stairs? I do hope she didn't hurt her leg too much!'

Daniel drew a sharp breath, only to let it out again in a frustrated snort as they heard the back door open – Kath arriving for work.

'Hello!' she said in surprise. 'What are you lot doing up so early?'

'We're off back to London today,' Julia divulged. 'I don't think there's much reason for us to hang around now, is there? Poor Shelley's busy packing all Posy's presents.'

'Oh, that's a shame,' said Kath, her face falling. 'Pity to break up the party, when everyone was having such a lovely time! What did you all get up to yesterday, after I'd gone? Hope I didn't miss anything exciting!'

Hilary thought back over the events of the afternoon – Posy's attempt to murder Tobias, her and Oliver's X-rated performance in the charades, Julia and Tony's plot to double-cross William. She could see from Daniel's amused expression that he was doing the same.

Both of them shook their heads. 'No, Kath, nothing at all!'

🎄 🎄 🎄

'So how are you this morning, Frances?'

'Ah, standing on the leg, I see!'

Both Shirburns – and calling her by her name! What had she done to deserve this honour?

'Stephen and I feel that it's time we took Tobias home – rather enough excitement for one small boy this Christmas! We were wondering whether you think you'd be well enough to travel back to Oxford today.'

Good heavens! They appeared to be consulting her feelings.

'Yes, I'm sure I will.' She'd have to be, because there was certainly no way she'd be wanting to stay at Haseley now.

'I do hope your … er … little sortie last night hasn't caused any lasting damage,' Stephen continued, almost as if he cared. 'We … um…' He looked at his wife. 'I believe we owe you a debt of gratitude.'

She stared at him. 'I understand that your timely warning prevented my father from making what would have been a terrible mistake.'

'Oh, I see.' Thank God! He hadn't signed it, then.

'So … um … we're grateful.' *Poor Stephen*! She could tell how much this hurt him. He made an awkward little gesture that might have been an attempt to shake her hand. A hug would have been too much to expect, of course.

'Clearly you felt you had a duty to the family, now that you're involved with one of its members in a *romantic* way,' Lesley explained to herself. It would be nice if they could have believed she would have done it in any case, that her relationship with Daniel had nothing to do with her struggling down the stairs to keep William out of danger.

'Yes – *Frances*.' Stephen had obviously been practising. 'I suppose we mustn't think of you as 'nanny' now, must we? Poor Tobias will find it very confusing at first.'

'I *was* wondering whether you might help us with his packing,' Lesley went on, her voice preparing to rise in grievance. 'But I dare say you'll be otherwise occupied this morning – saying goodbye to your sweetheart.'

'And perhaps, in view of your … er … change in circumstances, we can't expect you to care for Tobias any longer?' suggested Stephen uncomfortably.

'Oh yes – of course Frances may consider the role beneath her now!' Lesley tried to smile at what was barely a joke.

It was time to put them out of their misery.

'I've decided not to carry on seeing Daniel. We … er … turn out not to be suited after all.'

'Oh – what a shame!' Lesley failed to turn her gasp of delight into a convincing expression of dismay.

'Yes, indeed.' Stephen made an even worse job of hiding his relief – a kinder person would have taken pleasure in making two people so happy.

'But I do think you're very wise,' Lesley positively beamed at her. 'These things are never a great success, are they, when the couple are of such *very* different backgrounds? I know you wouldn't have wanted to distance Daniel from his family in any way, and I'm sure you'll find a more suitable young man quite soon, if you start mixing with your own type more.'

'We might even be prepared to relax some of our rules about male company, when we get back home,' Stephen conceded generously.

'Well then, Nanny, it really would be appreciated if you could help Tobias get ready. Our plan is to be off before lunchtime if possible.'

Lesley bustled off, pushing Stephen in front of her. All was now right with their world!

♣ ♣ ♣

'Oh, is everyone else up already? I thought I'd be the first.' Leo looked most disappointed when he came into the kitchen.

'What's the problem?' Daniel asked him. 'We weren't giving out prizes, mate!'

'No, well, I just thought I might get a head start on breakfast for once,' Leo admitted sheepishly. 'I suppose everyone's eaten all the mushrooms again ...'

'Oh Leo, *darling*!' laughed Julia. 'Sit down and we'll cook some, specially for you.' She pushed him into a chair and spread a table napkin in front of him with a flourish. 'What would Christmas at Haseley have been without Cousin Leo!' she went on. 'Don't you think so, Hilary? No, it's OK, darling!' She chuckled at what she saw in Hilary's face. 'That was all a bit of a horrid tease. We know you didn't invite him – in fact, I'm afraid we might have let it slip out ourselves,' she admitted, grinning at Tony.

'You rang me up, and told me everyone was coming down here for Christmas,' Leo reminded her.

'So I did – but I'm sure I never suggested you should come too.'

'No, you knew he'd invite himself!' said Daniel. 'You probably realised he'd inflict himself on Mum as well.'

'No, that was just – unfortunate.'

'I don't know what you're all talking about!' said Leo peevishly. 'I offered Hilary a lift out of the kindness of my heart.'

Lesley and Stephen came in then, looking a little smug, it seemed to Hilary.

'Well, we've just been in to see Nanny, and she appears to be on the mend.' Somehow she doubted that this accounted for Stephen's looking so pleased.

'Where is she? Is she coming down for some breakfast?' Daniel half rose in his chair.

'She's helping Tobias get dressed and do his packing,' Lesley repressed him.

'That's very kind of her,' said Daniel pointedly. It did seem incredible that the Shirburns could still only see

Frances as 'nanny', after what she'd done for the family last night.

'She thinks she'll be well enough to travel, so we'll try and get off this morning.'

'What – you're leaving? But ... oh, I must go up and see her!'

'She's busy now, Daniel. She'll be down in a minute.' Lesley looked faintly surprised. Hadn't she expected them to want to bid each other a fond farewell?

'We'd better tell Mrs Arncott we're going,' said Stephen. 'She'll want to clean out the rooms.'

'Of course she will!' said Daniel raising a sarcastic eyebrow. 'Each to their role in life... On the other hand, Kath's might just be about to change.'

'What do you mean?'

'Oh – hadn't you heard?' He couldn't resist the opportunity. 'She and William are becoming *very* close... I think a wedding might just be on the cards!'

🌲 🌲 🌲

After his interview with Margery, and another with Oliver, William felt that he deserved his breakfast – though, in fact, Oliver had taken the misunderstanding in very good part. He'd waved away what from William passed for an apology, and said that he was merely relieved to have an explanation for people's behaviour, and to find it wasn't because of some terrible *faux pas* he'd unwittingly made.

But William knew that his misinformation had done more damage than that.

'Would you like me to have a word with Hilary?'

Oliver looked at him closely. 'No,' he didn't bother dissembling, 'I'll sort things out with Hilary … and better sooner than later.'

Which was why, when Hilary passed him on her way out of the kitchen, he murmured, 'Don't let that man down.'

Beyond the door was a hubbub of voices – which stopped as soon as he came in. William pretended not to notice, or to have seen the anxiety with which they all regarded him – except for Daniel, whose eyes were brewing mischief.

'Well, Daddy, you'll be relieved to hear you're getting rid of us all today!' said Julia, a little too brightly, after a second too long.

'Yes,' said Lesley, as if she too had tried and failed to find a way of broaching a different subject, 'everyone seems to be going home now.'

William pulled out his secret store of bacon and began to fry himself some, in a proper amount of fat. None of them commented – things must be bad! Behind him, he heard Stephen clear his throat, but not come out with whatever it was he'd been going to say.

'Bet Kath Arncott's a good cook, isn't she, Uncle William?' said Daniel, helping them out.

'Atrocious! Those children of hers live on beefburgers.'

'Oh! Then why would you want to…?' – this from Leo. Want to what?

'Well, it's certainly not for her cleaning skills!' exclaimed Lesley. 'Those rooms upstairs are disgusting.'

'A woman can have more talents than housekeeping,' Tony reminded her.

'Oh, darling – not Kath!'

'Well, she's not unattractive, in a blowsy sort of way.'

It was almost as if they thought … *good grief*!

William decided it was time he contributed to the conversation. 'A very fine woman, Kath Arncott,' he said, carrying his plate across to the table. 'Warm, friendly soul, always ready for a chat – delightful children.' Had he gone too far?

Apparently not. '*Delightful*? Those terrible little boys? And to think of them running about at Haseley, cutting down all the hedges and driving their motorbikes round the garden…'

William glanced at Daniel. Was this a product of his imaginative invention, or some nightmare Lesley had created for herself?

'I really think it would be a *very* unwise move,' declared Stephen, as if William was now supposed to know what move this was.

'Marrying Kath Arncott? Very unwise indeed.' Leo dispelled any doubts.

'Do you really think so?' said William, frowning thoughtfully as he popped some bacon into his mouth.

'Unless you made quite sure she didn't end up with your money!' said the unsubtle Leo.

'My money? Yes, that would be a consideration, wouldn't it?'

Daniel's mouth twisted, as he tried not to grin.

'Yes, well,' said Lesley, perhaps a little suspicious. 'At least one member of the family won't be making that kind of mistake now.'

'What do you mean?' Daniel realised she was looking at him.

323

'I gather that Frances has decided to do the sensible thing concerning your relationship... Oh, didn't you know? She told me and Stephen that she didn't think you'd suit her after all!'

Chapter Twenty One

Hilary had gone back to her room, puzzling over William's words. Who was he asking her not to let down? Someone he'd just been talking to, and since everyone else was downstairs having breakfast, that could only mean Oliver. He must have been talking to Oliver – about her. What had been said? William, as ever cryptic, hadn't looked disapproving – one might say he'd been encouraging. Was she reading too much into those few words? But Hilary's spirits, contrary to their cautious, despondent nature, were lifting despite herself. Oliver wasn't gay. He wasn't interested in Kath. In fact there was no longer any reason to think that he hadn't meant every bit of that kiss!

She jumped to hear a knock at the door – but only because she knew who it was.

'Hello.'

'Hello.'

And suddenly there was no need to say more. They were in each other's arms again. And no, she hadn't imagined that kiss! But this time, she didn't have to make any pretence of not wanting to return it.

When they'd finished kissing, he continued to hold her tightly. 'Thank God!' he whispered.

After that there was some explaining to do. Even though Daniel and William had paved the way, Hilary needed to make clear on her own account why she had suddenly appeared to take against him, that day in Cirencester.

'You mean, you wouldn't still have loved me if you'd thought I was gay?' he teased her.

'I *would* – did! That was the problem…'

'Bloody Nigel Rofford! I can see I'm going to have to drop the guy — pity, though. He's good fun.'

'Don't you dare! If he hadn't introduced you to Margery at that dinner party…' She didn't need to say more.

'Look,' he took her hands in his, 'I know you're still grieving for Ben, and you'll say it's a bit soon to get too deeply involved in another relationship, but I do hope you'll feel it's OK to keep on seeing each other when we get back to London.'

'Well, of course!' said Hilary, startled by his diffidence. 'I've got to meet this Nigel Rofford who's caused so much trouble, for one thing.'

'I'll introduce you,' he promised. 'And now perhaps I'd better get some breakfast.'

'If Leo hasn't eaten it all.'

They parted outside her door with another brief kiss, and at that moment Daniel came charging downstairs from the attic.

'Darling…' she was about to tell him their good news, but he didn't even let her get started.

'*Don't* speak to me, Mum!' he snapped, with a ferocious glare. God, she'd never seen him look so angry!

Frances had a feeling of miserable *déjà vu* as she and Shelley brought the children down to breakfast. Her employers had been quick to reimpose her duties with renewed earnestness, as if to obliterate the unfortunate interlude when she had been in danger of becoming something more to the family than Tobias's nanny. If it weren't for the lingering stiffness in her ankle, Frances might have thought that the events of the past couple of days had been nothing but a vivid dream, from which she had just awoken.

Everyone glanced up. She had the impression that for a moment they were all staring at her in particular, rather than the others. Daniel immediately dropped his gaze, as if he couldn't bear to look at such a despicable person.

They had had a brief, unsatisfactory exchange upstairs. Lesley clearly hadn't done her any favours by coming out bluntly with what Frances had meant to think of a tactful way of breaking to him herself. Daniel had come charging up for an explanation, only to find her busy getting the children dressed with Shelley, and in the presence of those eager ears, her stumbling attempts to justify herself merely made her sound mercenary. Daniel had stormed off again, saying he was going to 'get the truth' out of Lesley, and it was no surprise that whatever she had said obviously hadn't done anything to mend matters.

Shelley had barely been able to conceal her delight. 'Never mind, babe! So what if Daniel wasn't as rich as you thought?' she'd chosen to misinterpret her reasoning. 'Plenty of other guys around – even for you, I dare say.' Now, of course, she was moving straight in. 'Hi there, Daniel! Are you going to make us some breakfast?'

And Daniel wasn't the only person Frances would have preferred not to encounter this morning. What was that look on Julia's face? Shame? Embarrassment? A hint of compunction, maybe? … No, it was sympathy. Oh lord, so they all *knew* what had happened between her and Daniel – and Julia, whose fault the whole thing was, had the nerve to be regarding her with pity!

'At last!' said Lesley, glancing at her watch and then at Frances, her meaning clear. 'You must be hungry, Tobias darling… No, not that cereal, Nanny! Posy can have that if she likes, but Tobias has this one, doesn't he?'

Daniel, who an hour ago might have come to her defence with some sarcastic comment, was returning Shelley's advances with interest – probably only a show put on for her benefit, but Frances felt a lump rise to her throat as she fetched Tobias's muesli… Being pushed around by the Shirburns, watching Shelley flirt with Daniel. It was as if she had been transported back a couple of days in time.

William had noticed the shock on Daniel's face, and the triumph on Lesley's, when she'd told him that his inconvenient romance with their nanny was at an end. He'd seen him bolt off to question her, only to return far too soon for them to have sorted anything out. They'd all heard him demand to know exactly what had been said, and witnessed Lesley's use of words which made Frances sound materialistic and self-centred … and now Daniel was madly pretending to flirt with that other awful nanny, leaving the nice one in tears. It wouldn't do! Whatever the reason William's friend and counsellor, Frances, had decided to end her relationship with his wretched nephew, it wasn't because she didn't love him. William caught Oliver and Margery's eyes. They were thinking the same thing.

'Frances, come next door a moment, will you? We need to have a little talk.'

🌲 🌲 🌲

When Oliver had gone, Hilary sat down on her bed, pondering about what had just happened. Daniel had been fine when she'd left him in the kitchen, mischievously throwing the cat among the pigeons with that ridiculous idea about Kath marrying William. She hadn't stopped to listen to the resultant outcry, wanting to come up and pack, and think about Oliver. And then Oliver had come in, and kissed her again, and made everything wonderful! ...But it wasn't, was it? Hilary's ever mercurial spirits sank at the foreboding storm. There could only be one reason for the sudden cloud on Daniel's thunderous brow. He had seen them together, embracing outside her door.

Recently she had begun to think that Daniel wouldn't mind her beginning a relationship with Oliver. He clearly liked him, and wanted her to like him – he'd been upset when they'd seemed to quarrel. But being on friendly terms with a nice person was one thing. Falling in love with someone who wasn't Daniel's father was to cross altogether a different boundary. Even Oliver had intimated that it might be too soon, that she would still be grieving for Ben. Well – was she? Of course. She would never stop loving Ben or feeling his loss, but somehow that no longer stopped her from loving another, quite different, person too.

All Hilary's old feelings of guilt overwhelmed her. Of course Daniel would see this as a betrayal – after everything they'd been through together! Perhaps grief and suffering was the only bond that attached them so closely. If she was beginning to find the strength to release herself, would she lose Daniel in the process? Should she really have to choose, of course it would be her son over a man she had met less than a week ago... Perhaps she ought to tell Oliver that she couldn't see him again after all.

🎄 🎄 🎄

Frances looked up in alarm. She knew the significance of a 'little talk' in William's family ... and Oliver and Margery were getting up too! She heard Lesley utter a protest, as her nanny was marched away under close arrest.

They sat her down in the drawing room, and drew up chairs to face her.

'Now,' said William, 'what's all this nonsense about?'

It did no good to pretend her ignorance.

'Why on earth have you given Daniel the heave-ho?' Margery accused her. 'The poor boy's heartbroken!'

'According to Lesley, it was for "financial considerations". Wasn't he rich enough for you?'

'Oh, for God's sake, Oliver!' exclaimed Margery, as this salt in the wound proved too much for Frances's fragile self-control. The poor man looked aghast at the effect of what had obviously been intended as a joke.

After that, she had to try and explain how she'd done what she thought was best for Daniel – breaking off in confusion when it meant expanding upon the snobbishness of his relatives. 'It was something Julia said…'

'Good heavens, haven't you learnt to ignore anything those two say by now?' snorted Margery.

But William was more persistent. 'What *did* Julia say?'

She told them. It didn't go down well.

Margery visibly blew up, her cheeks expanding, half-rising in her chair like a balloon about to hit the roof.

'Who the *devil* is Julia to tell people what I'm going to do with my money? As if I'd *dream* of trying to influence Daniel's choice – well, unless it was someone like Lesley, I suppose, or that creature he's flirting with in the kitchen at the moment. I never interfere – everyone knows that!'

'Frances, I'm sure you needn't worry about Hilary.' Oliver took her hands in his. 'She was almost as upset as Daniel when you had your accident. Anyone can see she's really fond of you.'

'Don't look at me!' said William crossly, as his sister clearly expected him to take his turn at reassurance. 'If you want to find out who I'm leaving my property to, you can read my will after I'm gone – if I bother to make one… But I'd certainly want to be sure it didn't fall into the hands of a miserable little creature like this!' he indicated Frances disdainfully. 'If it had been the nice, cheerful girl who kept everyone in order, and looked after my interests – now that would be a different matter … That's better,' he said, as Frances gave a watery smile. 'That's more the sort of person I'd consider a fit companion for Daniel… Now, let's go and sort this mess out, shall we?'

'Hilary, you're wanted downstairs … hey! What's wrong?'

It didn't help her resolve when he put his arms round her.

'Oliver, I'm sorry, but I don't think we can see each other in London after all,' she managed to tell him, in between gulps of distress.

'For God's sake! Why not?'

It was terrible to do this to him, after all the ups and downs of their short relationship.

'It's Daniel … he must have seen us earlier. He was looking *so* angry! I can't … I just *can't*!' Oliver was a hero if he could make sense of this disjointed description of her feelings.

But apparently he could. 'Are you trying to say you think Daniel's upset about us getting together?'

She nodded against his shoulder. How could she let go of this wonderful man?

'Darling, your son isn't the slightest bit interested in what you and I are up to at the moment! He's just had a stupid quarrel with Frances. That's why he's looking daggers at everyone.'

'What? Oh no, what happened?' She daren't acknowledge her relief.

'Your cousins spreading a little of their poison, I gather.'

'Not *my* cousins, thank you!' No good, her heart was lifting by the minute.

'Anyway, William's got every intention of sorting it out. That's why he wants you downstairs – I think it's a kind of family meeting.'

♣ ♣ ♣

'Surely you don't need the children here?'

'Why not? They're part of the family.' There was no reason at all, except to add to Lesley's obvious paranoia. William wondered what she thought he was about to do – line them up for a mass execution? Well, he did have something like that in mind.

'Right, then.' His eyes travelled round them all sternly. What a lot of them there were, every chair and stool taken, the children sitting on knees, Daniel and Oliver perched on the kitchen table. Only Kath missing, who didn't count as family, whatever they seemed to think – and one other. 'Now, I didn't invite any of you for Christmas,' Hilary, perhaps, but she would forgive him, in the interests of the point he had to make, 'and as I'm sure you know, Scratch and I would much rather have spent it on our own.' Where was Scratch? At the heart of the action, of course, sniffing for discarded Coco Pops under everybody's feet. He picked him up and set him in the middle of the table – witness for the prosecution. 'I won't say that having you here has done anything to change my mind. You've been a thorough nuisance, the lot of you!' Even poor Oliver seemed to be taking this meekly. 'I gather you're all going home today, and it can't be soon enough for me. *However*,' he raked them with his gaze – a headmaster with reprimands to dole out before the end of term – 'you can't be allowed to disappear with your lives in such appalling confusion, so let's get a few things straight before you go.' Who was going to stir? No, even the children quiet as mice. Oh dear, this was rather too much fun!

'Frances,' – mean to pick on her, but he had to start somewhere. 'What on earth possessed you to lend any credence to the stupid remarks of two people who'd already given you every reason to distrust them?' He glared in the direction of his scheming daughter and her husband. 'Daniel, the same goes for you! Surely you have more faith in the girl you're supposed to love than to think she'd suddenly turn into a gold-digger? Why believe Lesley's version of events, when you must know that family would go to any devious lengths to keep her as their nanny, even at the expense of your happiness and hers?' It was the Shirburns' turn to quail under his accusing frown. 'Hilary,' – yes, her too – 'it's high time you stopped punishing yourself for losing Ben. Nobody's going to blame you for moving on with your life… Oliver, if this woman still thinks you're a homosexual, I despair of you! … Tobias,' who had begun to wriggle now, 'contrary to what you've been led to think, you are *not* the most important thing on the planet, and the sooner you realise that, the less of an unpleasant shock it will be when you do find out. Posy, my advice to you is to leave off playing at a teenager until you have all the equipment – much more fun! Margery, I don't want the builders in. Stephen, I've no intention of moving into a home. Who else, is there? Oh dear, left out of things again! Never mind. There wouldn't have been any point in asking him to stop being a bore. I believe he's the only one of you who is actually incorrigible!'

'Where *is* Leo?' wondered Hilary, when William, with a satisfied nod and an enjoinment not to bother saying goodbye, had departed, and everyone dared move once more.

'Oh, Mum!' Her son, now content, with his Frances under his arm, gave her a look of amused compassion. 'I'm afraid your ex-admirer has deserted you for another – Kath's missing as well, you realise?'

'He's deserted me for Kath? I'm heartbroken! But why?'

'Because,' said Daniel happily, 'he now thinks that she's more likely to inherit Uncle William's money than you are!'

'Time we were off. Would you mind bringing Tobias's luggage down to the car, please, Nanny?'

'No, sorry, Lesley,' Daniel intervened, before Frances could say a word. 'She's not going to be working for you any longer.'

'What? But she can't…'

'She's coming back to London with me.' The information was new to Frances, but she hadn't the slightest desire to argue. 'She can live with us, and get a much better job – one where she won't be exploited. Nannies get something like the respect they deserve up there.'

'Oh yes, darling, come and work for us!' Could she believe her ears? 'Posy would simply love it.'

'But what about Shelley?' Just one of a few factors that Julia seemed to have forgotten.

'Oh, she's dreadful! I know quite well she's sleeping with Tony – and it's not as if she's even good at her job.'

Tobias, who had been listening eagerly, piped up with a suggestion. 'I'd like to have Shelley for *my* nanny.'

'There you are, Lesley,' Daniel grinned, 'problem solved!'

'Did you know you were getting a lodger?' Oliver murmured to Hilary.

'No,' she chuckled, 'but Daniel's Margery's grandson, isn't he? And actually, I love the idea of having Frances in the house. Stop me being too lonely!' He rose to the bait admirably. Hilary could be pretty sure she would never be lonely again.

'For God's sake, you two!' came the voice of her disgusted son. 'Better make Gran drive, if you're going to do that all the way home.'

'Well, it *has* been an exciting Christmas!' Julia declared, as they headed for their car, after affectionate kisses all round. 'Not quite in the way we intended, but still... Oh yes, I'm afraid we did mean to stir things up a bit,' she confessed. 'You see, we thought by getting you all down to Haseley and inundating poor Daddy with relatives, it wouldn't be very difficult to set him against each one of you in turn, and make him see how absolutely dreadful everybody was, except us. Aren't we beastly pigs? ... Never mind, we'll have a proper family Christmas next year.'

Back in the sitting room, William heard the last car depart down the drive, with a sigh of relief. Scratch jumped up and settled on his knee, suggesting he felt the same. Scratch wasn't averse to a bit of excitement, but this was where he liked to be best.

William reached for the remote control – no, a bit early. Still the blasted Christmas schedule, messing everything up!

What was that on the table? Oh yes, one of those blank will forms people had been so anxious to thrust under this nose. He supposed he'd be tripping over the things for months. Well, this one could go in the bin ... or ... wait a moment. Margery had said he ought to make a will out to somebody, hadn't she? Right then! William grinned as he picked up a pen. 'Sorry to disturb you, Scratch, but I need the table... No, you needn't sulk at having to move your fat bum – it is in your own interest, after all!'

END

Acknowledgements

My mother Barbara was a writer, and brought us up to think it was a good thing to be. My sister Katie got there first, but always encouraged me to follow. Peggy Garland, old Mr Cooper, my father, Edwin's father, and Yapple the cat, all now passed on, unwittingly formed some of the models for this book. I'm immensely grateful to Hazel Cushion and her colleagues at Accent Press, and to my friends in the Oxford Writers' Group and the Romantic Novelists Association for their constant support and encouragement. And Edwin continues to live through every up and down with me, in his role as soulmate. It's almost his book as much as mine now.

About the Author

Jane was brought up in Wimbledon, but spent most of her adult life in Oxford, and she and her husband now live in Minchinhampton in the Cotswolds, near her sister, the author Katie Fforde.